CROWN OF CROWNS

CLARA LOVEMAN

PRAISE FOR CROWN OF CROWNS

"Crown of Crowns is a sweeping, epic, futuristic YA novel that is so engrossing. The plot is well-paced and so well written, and the characters feel so real. A great read."
Kelly McFarland, TBHonest

"The mix of YA, sci-fi, fantasy and romance is a breath of fresh air, and when you add the unpredicted twists and turns in the mix, it's a combination resulting in a really good read."
NetGalley Reviewer

"The author succeeds in telling a story of a young woman's path to free her people from their shackles."
The US Review of Books

"Phenomenal ... Clara Loveman is a creative genius."
CovetedBooks, Book Reviewer & Blogger

First published in 2020

ISBN: 978 1838 06233 0
First Edition: August 2020

This is a work of fiction. Any references to historical events, real
people, or real places are used fictitiously. Other names, characters,
places, and events are products of the author's imagination, and any
resemblance to actual events or places or actual people, living or dead,
is entirely coincidental.

ClaraLoveman.com

For the wild, the unsung and the nameless

CHAPTER 1

ill they punish me for being here?
 I was far from where I was supposed
to be, far from NordHaven, my home. I must have
looked strange to the commoners. They were casual in
lightweight clothing, while I walked among them
wrapped head to toe in heavy blue garb. Gaard's brutal
sun had me stopping to wipe sweat from my brow, the
sound of my heartbeat thrashing in my ears.

"No time to stop," Roki said, looking back at me. "I
have so much to show you."

I smiled at his eagerness. "I'm coming."

Of course, I would have followed Roki anywhere. I
had already followed him from the safety of my home
and into the rabble of the city. I would have followed
Roki to the Surrvul Desert and beyond. This boy was
something new, something exciting that I'd never
expected to find.

"Just up ahead," he called back. "We're almost in the
square."

I paused another second to adjust my headscarf. I had it wrapped around my neck but also covering my nose and mouth. I looked like one of the Ava-Surrvul, the desert people who lived in sand huts. As I adjusted the scarf, someone bumped into me, and my sunglasses slipped off. "Oof," I said. I looked back and saw my four Protectors appear out of nowhere and surge into action like rabid machines out for blood.

Their mechanical hulls were shaped like human chests. Their legs were clunky metal limbs, and their arms were fully plated in bulletproof steel. They strode forward as a group, intent on the poor man who had bumped into me. Exactly what did they plan on doing with him? I held my breath.

"I'm sorry," the man said. He spoke with a commoner's accent. He was disheveled, wearing loose rags and a pair of weathered sandals.

The mechanized Protectors were almost upon him. I wanted to scream, "Leave the man alone!" But I had frozen, rooted to the spot.

Thankfully, Roki whisked ahead of me and stuck out his hand. "No," he said, and to my disbelief, the Protectors stopped, reversing back into the crowd and fixing their lifeless machine eyes on me.

"How did you do that?" I asked, gaping at Roki.

He shrugged. "Protectors may be controlling, the steel arm of justice and authority for all of Geniverd, but don't forget, Kaelyn, they are still machines. They're just robots. We made them, not the other way around. And because they are machines, they are programmable."

I blinked up at him, letting my head fall back, and crossed my arms. I was in ever-increasing awe of the man who had swept me off my feet. Roki was witty, charismatic, mysterious. "You fascinate me," I said.

He had a grin that conveyed secret knowledge. "You haven't seen anything yet." Roki took me by my hand. "Come, I want to show you more. More, Kaelyn. There's so much more!"

I let him guide me through the throngs of commoners in the historic district of the city. It was all so foreign to me, even though these were *my* people, the Ava-Gaard. I was fifteen years old, and yet I had never been among them. Not like this. Never had I struggled through crowds while sweat burned my eyes and so many shouting voices threatened to deafen me. I could feel my heart thudding in my chest, could hear blood rushing through my ears. This was the thrill I had been waiting for my whole life. It felt like everything I'd ever known—my dull existence inside the halls of Nord-Haven, my family, my friends—was all a monotonous blur up until this moment.

Still, I was quivery, my mind racing. What would Mama and Papa do if they knew where I was?

He must have sensed my trepidation. "I know you're nervous," he said, still leading me by my hand. "You've never pushed through a swarm of Ava-Gaard while they breathe in your face and step on your nice leather boots. This is a change for you."

I glanced awkwardly at my boots as if I'd just seen them for the first time. How much was there that I didn't know? Roki had only agreed to take me here after I'd begged him for days and promised to wear a disguise. He'd said my parents would never allow any of this, but because I'd been stubborn about it, he let me join him for part of the morning. I was thrilled to pieces to be among the people I might be honored to serve one day. But now ... even my disguise wasn't right. I was the only person in the market with polished leather boots— with boots that weren't scuffed or dirty or covered in muck.

Roki loved it here. He was like a kid let loose in one of Gaard's annual carnivals, and I stumbled behind him, giggling. His energy was contagious. I was bubbling over with excitement as we navigated through narrow streets packed with people, their skin tanned by the sun, their black hair somewhat lightened from long hours outside. No one paid me any attention. No one knew who I was. Only Roki knew what was in my blood, and he didn't care. I was sure he liked me for who I was.

"Here," he said. "Isn't it marvelous?"

We had stopped in a crowded square. Everywhere I looked, people were selling fruit and vegetables from makeshift stalls that had been erected in front of the regular businesses—chic cafés, modern restaurants, and stores that sold expensive clothing and futuristic home decor.

"What are they doing?" I asked Roki. "Why are they selling fruit? Look, there's a wooden stall with a man selling fish. Are those live fish? What is this place?"

Roki laughed as if I had asked him the dumbest question in the world. "It's a market," he said. "You really don't know what a market is?"

I shook my head, feeling stupid. "No," I told him, pressing my lips together tightly. "It looks old fashioned."

"It is!" said Roki, so unabashedly happy that he

grabbed a peach from the nearest stall and tossed it to me. "Look."

I caught it and gasped. "What is this?" The peach was cold and hard in my hands and had none of the fuzz the fruit is known for. "It's fake," I said, baffled. "Why are people buying fake fruit?"

Roki let out a deep, satisfying sigh, his countenance glowing. His chest was out, chin high, and even though he was right next to me, he seemed to take up all the space, like he owned the ground we walked on. Something cocky about him. Was he trying to prove something to me? That was just another thing that drew me to him. Roki's unpredictability and charm had kept me coming back to him for the past two weeks. I couldn't get enough. I didn't think I ever would.

"It's Market Reenactment Day." He spoke boisterously. "I can't believe you've never heard of it. Your parents are the ones who permit—I might add, *rarely* permit—the common folk in Gaard to hold this event. It's the same story everywhere in the world. You see, hundreds of years ago, people all across Geniverd set up markets to sell goods: fruit from the lush forests of Shondur, fish caught by the brave fishermen of Nurlie Island, herbal cactus extracts from the Surrvul Desert. They sold it all!"

I was surprised to hear of my parents' role, as they'd never talked about market reenactment. Were they hiding something from me, or was I too protected?

I peered up at Roki, sucking in a quick breath. "But not anymore," I stuttered, putting the fake peach back into its basket.

Roki hung his head. "No," he said, "not anymore. Markets existed before the great plague that wiped out nearly half the population, before the rise of technology. It was a simpler time. A warring time, perhaps, but simpler. Now, monthly food rations are delivered by Protectors. The food is healthy, don't get me wrong. It's just that we've lost the way."

I was stunned. How did I not know so much about my people, yet in a few years, I might be expected to govern them? Why was I being shielded from them?

Roki sighed and shook his head, looking nostalgic. "Life used to be hard," he told me. "Hard but simple. Things used to matter. Now, instead of a hardworking population of farmers, businesspeople, bankers, construction workers, fruit sellers, all we have is robots. Human beings used to work for something, Kaelyn; we used to do something. Now big, clunky Protectors do all the hard work that we should be doing. The machines toil in the fields, deliver our meals, take care of our infrastructure, build our hospitals. They even work in our hospitals, doing medical jobs that humans used to do."

I stared at Roki for a second. I had always thought him to be wise beyond his years, but now he was talking as if he had been around so many years ago to see these markets, as he called them. He spoke of the technological rise as though he had lived through it. There was such experience in his soft eyes, such knowledge. He was only sixteen years old!

"This market," Roki continued, "is a picture of the old life. In truth, I think people love this day so much because it makes them feel like they have a purpose. I think that people want it to go back to the way it was, before they got lazy and complacent and jobless, shuffling through poverty while clans of rich people lord

over the entire planet with inherited empires of—"
Roki stopped and looked at me. "Sorry," he said. "I
didn't mean ..."

"I know." I gave him a smile. "Don't worry about it. I
like it here. I like seeing all this old stuff. It gives me a
sense of our heritage. Maybe you're right, Roki. Maybe
the world is too easy."

I had to agree with Roki. What he was saying made
sense. I knew more about wealth and boredom than I
cared to admit, and now that Roki had brought me to
the market, I saw the world opening before my eyes.
Somewhere along the way, something had gone wrong,
and this was the result. Less than one percent of the
population had everything they could ever want and
were still bored out of their minds, while the rest were
just as bored, only they didn't have the money or means
to do anything about it.

"I'm glad you like it here," he said. "I was skeptical
about bringing you. I know it's rare for you to leave
your gilded cage, as I like to call it. I'm glad to share
your first outside experience with you."

I told him, "I wouldn't want to share it with anyone
else."

We smiled at each other then, a hint of something
dangerous in the air between us. I thought he wanted to
reach out and touch my cheek, maybe kiss me. My body
heated at the thought of it. Instead, Roki bit down on
his lip.

"Come," he said, quickly dismissing the sudden
tension. He took me by my hand and led me deeper
into the market. "We have to hurry. We only have a few
minutes before the Protectors take you back. There's
one more thing I want to show you."

It was a park, but inside the park were women with round bellies and small strollers, pushing the strollers with one hand while they held their tummies and laughed with their friends.

"What is this?" I asked Roki. I didn't understand.

"They're pretending to be pregnant," he said. "It reminds people of how we used to only have natural births, back before the clan leaders imposed strict regulations on how women are allowed to bring life into the world. This display reminds us of a happier time, when people were free and the world was natural."

I gave Roki a weird look. I wondered what more freedom would mean for the world order. I'd never appreciated these ancient things or considered them as an alternative. What would it be like to actually be pregnant? But Roki was also talking about these things again like he knew them firsthand. I thought, *That's just how mature he is. Roki knows his history better than me. He is more sophisticated than some grown men I know! Of course I'm attracted to him.*

Then again, I had been attracted to Roki since the night we first met, since the very first time I laid eyes on him, at a ball thrown by an Ava-Nurlie noblewoman in honor of my parents' successful leadership. Roki had bought his way in somehow. He had introduced himself, telling me, "You have the saddest yet most stunning eyes I have ever seen. They portray a longing that can never be fulfilled. I feel drawn to you. Perhaps because your eyes say what I feel about our world."

Yeah, that had unnerved me. He had seen me for who I was. Just me, plain and simple. Not an heiress, not a potential queen, not a rung on some political

8

ladder, just Kaelyn. I had been obsessed with Roki ever since.

"... and that was the reasoning behind artificial births," Roki was saying.

"Huh?" I realized I had been daydreaming and missed most of what he had said. I felt heat radiating from my face. While he was talking, I had been fantasizing about our previous dates, the cute things he had said to me the night we met, and how he had lifted me high and spun me in the air outside the noblewoman's mansion. I couldn't help it. Roki had been so romantic!

"I was explaining how Decens-Lenitas, our mighty moral code, put an end to natural births in favor of lab babies. Our rulers say that it's avoiding natural births that enables the gene editing that has eliminated cancer, allergies, and all but infectious diseases. Still, it's one of the things I wish hadn't changed, because pregnancy used to be a pleasant experience for many people." He narrowed his eyes at me and smirked. "Wait a minute. You were daydreaming!"

I was still blushing. "A little," I said. "I still can't believe you're with me. There are so many other girls to choose from. Can ... can I ask you why?"

He smiled and said, "There are no other girls. That's why. There's only you, Kaelyn. When we met, I saw a rebellious young girl with a sullen spirit in need of some much-needed happiness. I saw your soul, and I wanted to be a part of it."

I had to turn from Roki before my emotions boiled over and I started to cry. My cheeks were so hot they could have been sunburned. For so long I had lived in a bubble of bland nothingness, and now here was Roki, making me feel so alive, so overwhelmed with emotion!

"We should get you back to NordHaven," he said. "I don't want your parents to be upset with you before the big ceremony for your brother."

"You're right," I said. "Thank you for bringing me here. It was a relief after all the time I've been imprisoned at home. I hope we can come here again. I've never been happier than I am right now with you. To be honest, Roki, I don't think I can go back to the way things used to be."

"I feel the same," he said with a smile. "Don't worry, Kaelyn. We have all the time in the universe to be together."

* * *

I WAS HAVING separation anxiety even before I got home. I wanted to be with Roki so much. I missed him fiercely. Pushing open my front door, I could have sworn I smelled him in the foyer of our house. Could I have been so obsessed with Roki that I was now smelling him when he wasn't around? Then again, I had lingered during our parting hug in the square, with my face nuzzled against him. Perhaps his scent still clung to my clothes: earthy, herbal fresh, slightly smoky, faintly toffee sweet. I'd have to put off having them laundered for a few days.

Mama was descending the grand staircase into the foyer with a judgmental look on her face. Even when she was displeased with me, I held my mother in high regard. I venerated the long hours she put in chairing Gaard's council meetings. I admired her statuesque figure, now emphasized by her long olive-green velvet gown, and mirroring the shapely vases of roses flanking the heavy oak doors of NordHaven.

"Enjoy your morning?" she asked.

"It was nice," I said. I didn't want to lie, but I also didn't want to admit that I had spent the morning frolicking with the man of my dreams. Even if she suspected I'd been with Roki, I doubted she knew exactly where we'd been, considering Roki's control over the Protectors.

I tried to shift the conversation. "Where's Papa?"

"Getting our things into the flyrarc." Then Mama gave me that unimpressed motherly stare. "Where's your boyfriend?"

There was a touch of sarcasm in her voice that I didn't like. Mama irked me when it came to Roki. She had forbidden me from seeing him at first, accusing me of bringing shame to our family. Then she had restricted our time together. I had invited him over for dinner, hoping Mama and Papa would get to know Roki and like him as much as I did, but that wasn't what had happened. My parents had stepped out of the room during the meal, and I had overheard Papa telling her, "Don't worry, dear. Kaelyn will come to her senses soon enough, and we'll be rid of the lowborn scoundrel." The worst part was that Roki had heard it too.

Enough was enough. I said to Mama, "And so what if he is my boyfriend? Would it be so bad for me to date an ordinary boy from Nurlie?"

"Oh, honey," Mama said, shaking her head sadly. "You are the daughter of Gaard-Ma and Gaard-Elder. Have you forgotten that? As the highest-ranking family of Gaard, we are bound to the moral code of Decens-Lenitas. We are role models. We must marry people who are like us. I'm sorry, Kaelyn, but you simply cannot be with someone who doesn't share our moral code. Why not someone of royal blood from another clan? What about Jaken or his brother, Zawne?"

I was frustrated and angry at having this conversation over and over.

"I don't want to be with Jaken or Zawne," I said. "I want to be with Roki." I stomped my foot, not caring how childish I must have looked. "I don't care where he's from or if he doesn't agree with Decens-Lenitas. What does it mean, anyway, our moral code? Roki has a love for all things living. So what if he doesn't belong to a royal line? I know he would put his family first. And who cares if he doesn't believe in lab babies and if he prefers natural births?"

Mama gasped at this. "Family? I had no idea you two were getting so serious." She stood up straight and said in a domineering tone, "You are not to see him anymore. He believes in natural births? Is he mad?"

"He's perfect," I said. My composure was flaking apart. I was so angry with Mama. I spoke without thinking and didn't care if it got me into trouble. "Roki has my feelings in mind. He took me into the heart of the city today, to the Historical District, where I saw the market reenactment. He did it so I could escape this stuffy place and all your stuffy rules. I don't want this to be my life!"

Mama's eyes were wide. She looked mortified.

I kept on in anger. "You've never done that for me, taken me out into the city. Not with a chance of your face being on the news." I made quotation marks in the air and said, "Headline: 'Gaard-Ma seen with civilians.'" And I scoffed, "No, not with your precious reputation to uphold. You'd never go to where I went today, walking in the street with the people. We are supposed to adhere to the moral code, but why does the moral code need to make us so ... so lofty! We should be able to love who we want, go where we want, and do what we want. I hate being trapped in this system!"

A thousand emotions were passing across Mama's face. As she stood before me, frozen, I wondered what she was thinking, what she was feeling. I hadn't meant to denounce Decens-Lenitas. I believed wholly in its teachings. The moral code encompassed many things. For example, love for all living things, strength of mind, recognition of the class system and the monarchy, obedience to the Protectors, and outlawry of pregnancies in favor of lab-conceived and lab-grown babies. I just didn't understand why virtue meant being a snob.

"Kaelyn," Mama said. She appeared to have composed herself, though I could see a ferocious heat burning underneath her pinched smile. "In time you will come to understand that life is not easy. We must make sacrifices for the greater good, for the good of Gaard and for all of Geniverd. We clan leaders must maintain appearances and marry into other clans with hopes of ascending the throne. The more virtuous in the laws of Decens-Lenitas you are, the higher your chance of being promoted to king or queen. It's why Raad, now that he has completed his Aska training, is much closer to reaching the throne."

I couldn't have cared less about the throne. I was proud of my brother, Raad, and I loved him. Askas were considered to be highly skilled at Decens-Lenitas and at fighting, and so were highly esteemed. A few of them who weren't heirs were allowed to become engineers after their training, to oversee design blueprints for Protectors. Raad was brave and strong and wise for completing the brutal training, yet I didn't see what it had to do with Roki. I asked, "Are you upset with me because I haven't lived up to Raad? I'm not as virtuous or as brave as him. Is that why you torture me like this?"

"Honey ..." She shook her head. "Of course, no. I love you both very much. I just don't want you to waste your life. Look at what happens to those who don't follow our moral code. They become Gurnots. Have you not heard the reports about terrorism, about the anarchist Gurnots lashing out across the territories, lighting fires from here to Lodden in an attempt to sabotage the monarchy? I've even heard they are stealing dangerous weapons from the Protectors! These people are treacherous, Kaelyn. I don't want your angst to become something volatile."

"Angst!" I was in a huff all over again. "I have no angst. There are six clans on six continents, Mama. There are eighteen blood-born heirs and heiresses, plus their spouses. That's thirty-six choices for the crown. Let one of them have it. Let Raad have it. We all know my brother deserves to rule over Geniverd. Why can't you just let me live my life and be with Roki? Not all ordinary people turn into Gurnots. Look at Lordin. She's an ordinary girl from Gaard, and she's world famous for being one of the most wholesome, kind-hearted, moral people in the world."

"Lordin is an exception," Mama said. "She got very lucky. And we're not talking about Lordin; we are talking about you. The coronation ceremony will be upon us in just over three years, and either you and

14

your husband, or Raad and his wife, will replace us as Gaard's clan leaders. One of you might be chosen as king or queen. I just want you to make the right decision for your future."

She slid her fingers into silky leather gloves, signaling she was ready to leave. "Now hurry up and change. We need to head to the capital for your brother's ceremony."

"I can look after my own future," I said. "And I'm not going to Raad's homecoming ceremony."

I felt silly and selfish as I said this. Raad was my brother. He had just spent the last two years in the most dangerous conditions in Geniverd for his Aska training. Trekking through the Surrvul wasteland, brutal physical training in Lodden, swimming with sharks and fighting leopards. I wanted to see him, to celebrate his triumph and his transformation now that he was a skilled Aska warrior, yet I wanted to see Roki more. I wanted to gaze into the flecks of gold and brown in his dazzling silver-gray eyes, which complemented his skin. I wanted him to hold me.

"Does that mean you're firm in your decision?" Mama had her arms crossed, that bleak look on her face.

"Yes. I want to stay home. I can see Raad tomorrow when he gets home. I don't need to be flaunted before Jaken and Zawne just so you can try to sell me like fruit at the market."

Talking about the market again had Mama shaking her head. "Okay. Cool down, Kaelyn. We can discuss this when your father and I get back from the ceremony tomorrow. You're disappointing your brother by not being there. Think about that while you're with your boyfriend. I hope he's more important than your family." And with that, Mama flounced past me and out the front door.

At that moment, I desperately wanted to launch the towering vases of roses at the awaiting flyrarc, but instead, I stormed off to my sleeping quarters, getting there just in time to see the vehicle zipping past the window, rising high into the sky.

CHAPTER 2

*R*ight after Mama and Papa had left, I called Roki and invited him over. Sometime later my visin beeped in my ear for the tenth time. I tapped the top of my wrist, and the device produced a projection in front of me, a translucent screen in the air. It was Mama calling again. I tapped my wrist and the projection died. "I'm busy," I said sulkily, as if she could hear me.

I checked the time. It was nearly four. I had been brooding in my bed for over two hours! Roki was supposed to be at NordHaven any minute.

I launched myself out of bed and ran to my dressing room, where I fumbled with gown after gown until there was a pile of fabric in the middle of the floor. I finally chose a summery viridian dress and combed my hair quickly in the mirror. I smiled remembering the time Roki had said my extended eyeliner and long carbon-black lashes complemented my upturned eyes. My visin beeped again, and Roki's voice was in my ear.

"Hey. I'm out front."

"Coming!" I shouted by accident. I was so nervous I could hardly control my voice. This was our first chance to be alone, completely alone, without Mama or Papa around to spy on us. I had butterflies in my stomach. I had already forgotten about the argument in the foyer. I smoothed my dress and ran to greet Roki.

He was outside, leaning against the marble balustrade, handsome as always, in a casual jacket, his hair wild. "Wow," he said. "I never get tired of seeing your amber eyes. They're so beautiful."

Ten seconds in, and I was already blushing. "You're too sweet," I said. "Really, too sweet."

Roki extended his hand to me. "Take a walk?"

I took his hand, and Roki led me around our impressive estate and into the garden. Bees hovered above the flower beds, and butterflies fluttered merrily beside the cobblestone path. It was peaceful here, and I was happy in Roki's presence. The garden smelled sweet, like honeysuckle after a morning rain. I couldn't tell if it was naturally coming from the flowers or if it was the day's smell generated by the atmospheric bubble around NordHaven.

As we walked, Roki asked me, "Do you feel guilty about not going to your brother's homecoming ceremony?"

"A little," I said, feeling a sudden shame in my heart, "but there was no way I could have sat in the flyrarc with Mama for two hours after our argument. Raad will survive a day without seeing me. After all, he is an Aska now. He's supposed to have hardened his mind, soul, and body. He can survive one more day without his sister."

"True," Roki said. "Askas are the fiercest warriors in all of Geniverd." He hesitated, looking into a bed of roses. "But what happened with Gaard-Ma? I hope it wasn't an argument about me."

"It was and it wasn't," I said. It was a little embarrassing to tell Roki I had screamed at my mother, "He's perfect!" Instead, I said, "It was more of the same, the same argument we've been having a lot lately. You know, about the expectations my parents have for me to become clan leader, even to become queen. I'm just so tired of it, Roki. People think I'm set for life because of who I am. Mama tells me I should be excited about all the prospects I have, about all the potential suitors. All I want to do is hide under my bed. There must be more to life. There must be more than ceremonies and extravagant balls and fancy retreats all over Geniverd."

I knew by Roki's gentle expression that he understood what I was saying. Roki always got me. It was like he was tuned in to my frequency. He raised his bushy eyebrows and let me go on ranting.

"Mama's just mad because I'm not as good as Raad," I said. "She's also scared that if Gaard doesn't produce a king or queen soon, our family will be deposed, demoted to simple folk. Oh gosh, the horror! Mama always talks about how our lineage is cursed. It's a ridiculous thought. We aren't cursed just because I reject the path I'm supposed to follow."

"Why do you think that is?" Roki asked, back to admiring the roses. "Why do you reject what's expected of the First Daughter of Gaard?"

"Maybe I don't want to be the First Daughter of Gaard." I hung my head. Roki was trying to be sweet by asking me how I felt about everything, about my life,

19

but it was just making me depressed. "I hate how Mama wants to sell me off to the Shondur Clan like I'm a tool for trading. She wants me to marry Jaken or Zawne so that I'm in a better position to be chosen at the coronation in three years."

"Of course she'd want you to marry a prince." Roki raised his eyebrow. "It's been nearly forty years since the last coronation. Wow."

"Yes," I said. "A little over three years until the Crown of Crowns swoops down from the sky and lands on the head of the chosen one. Papa told me stories about the last coronation. He said it had been amazing to watch. He said that the bird had soared from the sky, seemingly from no place at all, and landed on the heirs of Shondur. They were made queen and king instantly. That was thirty-seven years ago."

A quirky smile came to Roki's lips. "I do wonder where that bird comes from. It's a real mystery," he said. Then he plucked a rose from the flower bed and gave it to me. "Here, a beautiful rose for a beautiful girl."

I smiled, twirled the rose in my fingers, and said, "I prefer to be with you. I don't want to marry Jaken or Zawne."

"I don't want you to either."

"And who knows?" I said with a sudden burst of energy. "Maybe if you divulge your intentions to Mama and Papa, and we are officially together when the time of the ceremony comes, the Crown of Crowns will land on your head. Can you imagine it, Roki, you and me as king and queen? We could make the kingdom a better place. We could make Geniverd better for the common man, try to loosen the stranglehold the upper class has over society, and make

Decens-Lenitas more accessible for everyone. Think about it, Roki."

Roki laughed somewhat sadly. "If only that could be. Let's try not to think about it. Gaard-Ma and Gaard-Elder would never allow our official union."

"In that case," I said, giving Roki a playful look, "I'll marry another clan head and take you for my secret lover."

"Your lover!"

"Sure. Why not? Mama told me a story once about a woman who was promised to marry an heir—I can't remember which one. Anyway, the promise was revoked at the last minute, and the woman felt horribly scorned. Then the heir became king. He took the woman as his one and only mistress, loving her more fiercely than he loved his own wife, the queen. Then, um ... Shoot, I forget the rest."

I stopped and scratched my eyebrow. It was hard to remember all the details. Mama had told me the story so long ago. In my brief confusion, Roki watched me with a smile. He was always so courteous.

"Oh," I said, "that's right. What happened was the Gaard-Ma at the time needed the mistress's help. See, the mistress had a huge influence over the king, more so than the queen did. Gaard-Ma beseeched the mistress to sway the king's mind over some land acquisitions he was trying to make near Cara. He wanted to steamroller farmlands and absorb them into Cara. He wanted to make the world's capital even bigger while displacing hundreds of Gaard farmers.

"The mistress refused Gaard-Ma's request. She claimed the king needed that land and there was nothing anyone could do about it. Well, Gaard-Ma was known for her vengeance. All Gaard-Mas are. She started a rumor among the upper class. She denounced the mistress as a harlot and a thief, a traitor to the king and a schemer against all the people of Geniverd. After the rumor spread throughout the kingdom, the king had no choice but to banish his beloved mistress. She was forced to live in the bitter highlands in the north of Gaard. Her climb to the top ended in misery."

Roki gave me a puzzled look. "Are you saying you want to have me as your lover just so you can banish me?"

"No!" I latched onto him, bucking against his chest. "I just thought the story related to our talk. I could never banish you, Roki! Not from my life, not from my heart."

He stroked my head as I hugged him fiercely. I liked the feeling of his fingers in my hair and his warm chest against my body. I could smell his sweet aroma; it was more powerful than the honeysuckle scent that permeated the air around us in the garden. I never wanted the scent of him to go away.

"That's a good fantasy you have for us," Roki said, "but let's focus on today. Okay? Let's enjoy our time together." We stood, and he took me by the hand. "Let's walk some more."

* * *

WE STROLLED through the gardens of NordHaven for what felt like years, trailing alongside the artificial creek with the backs of our hands touching as if we both wanted to hold hands but were too shy. We walked beneath the artificial apple trees and laughed together, strolled below the canopy of fake leaves and vines, and across the wooden lovers' bridge. The scents changed as we walked. I realized for the first time how much of my home was fake: the leaves, the low-hanging apples, the shifting scents wafting down from the atmospheric bubble. It was sunny and warm inside the grounds. I wondered if it was raining outside, if people were huddled under awnings in the city and shivering from the cold.

Roki and I walked until our legs got sore. Then we sat on the edge of the big marble pool Papa had built nearly forty years ago, when he had become clan leader of Gaard. There were fish in the pool, little blue ones swimming in circles and big yellow ones with bulging eyes, sucking the film off the bottom.

"So much simpler to be a fish," I said. "There are no fish heirs, no king or queen ruling over all the other fish, no Aska training or moral code to uphold. Yes, I think I would like to be a fish."

"Me too," Roki said. "It never ceases to amaze me how much in sync we are. It's like we share the same mind."

"Isn't that a scary thought!" I told him. "Can you imagine sharing your mind with someone else, someone living inside your brain, inside your skin? I can't. I prefer you just the way you are, our thoughts intertwined, and our fingers too."

He squeezed my hand and I squeezed back. It was so nice in the sun, the fish darting around our feet in the water. The Protectors were out of sight. There was no one around.

Still, my thoughts drifted. "Maybe I would be better off training with the Grucken than getting married off to a stranger," I said. "He is the guardian of Decens-Lenitas, after all, the most respected person aside from the king and queen. Oh, and aside from Lordin. She might be the most respected person in the world. And she trained with the Grucken!"

"The Grucken only accepts one intern per year," Roki said. "But I know he would select you. I've heard all he does is look in an applicant's eyes. He knows just from their eyes if they are the one to be trained. I'm sure he would take one look at your pretty amber eyes and know immediately. You'd be the next Lordin."

"I wish," I said. "She's not even an heir. I wonder who she'll marry. Surely someone important. Surely one of the clan heirs will take her for themselves to gain a better position for the seat of power, to be king. Her moral code is higher than anyone's. Plus she is loved by everyone in Geniverd. They watch every move she makes on their visins. She's the most popular person on this planet."

"I know," he said dryly. "I've seen it. They look at the girl like she's a goddess. But is she really? Be careful who you idolize, Kaelyn. People are different in their souls."

I frowned at him. "Now you sound like Mama. Soon you're going to be warning me about the dangers of natural birth, how I need to freeze my eggs at the clinic, how I need to prepare what genes I want edited in my baby, and insisting I get all my vaccines so I don't die of a superbug. Or worse, soon you'll be warning me of the dangers of the Gurnots!"

"I'd never," he said, so seriously I furrowed my brows at him.

"You don't side with those ... those Gurnots, do you?" I asked.

"Eh." Roki shrugged. "They aren't that bad."

"They're terrorists!" I almost shouted. "They're fire starters! Haven't you seen the news reports? They burned down another seaside estate this week. It was lucky the estate had just emptied for the season, or people could have died."

"Maybe," Roki said, his tone a little too relaxed for the topic of death. "Or maybe it was intentionally like that. They may seem like terrorists to you, Kaelyn, but to others, they represent change. Change for the people of Geniverd. I know the Nurlie Islanders support them. A lot of people do. Much of the world views Decens-Lenitas as an oppressive moral standard. They want to be rid of it. They are tired of this lopsided rule, these rich families who inherit power and then pass the power along. Nobody even knows where their power and wealth came from anymore!"

"What about the wars?" I asked. I could hardly believe what Roki was saying. "Aside from the Gurnots stirring up trouble, there haven't been major conflicts in two hundred years, because of our moral standards. Would you see people die?"

"No way." Roki looked at me, his eyes powerful in a way I hadn't noticed before. I thought they could make me do anything. He seemed so serious. "Gurnots are against classism, which is promoted by Decens-Lenitas. I hate the idea of hurting people. That's why I think we need change, so people don't get hurt. Maybe you'll be the one to do it once you're queen."

I sighed. "Sure, with you as my mistress."

We laughed. We held hands. We kicked our feet in the pool, and soon the sun was getting low.

I said to Roki, "We should go inside and dry our feet."

He smiled. "Whatever you say, Kaelyn."

* * *

I LED him past the sitting rooms, the kitchen, down the long hallway and up the back stairwell to the second floor.

"I've never been up here," Roki said as we walked. "We've always stayed downstairs, in the dining room or in the parlor, where your parents could keep their eyes on us. Where are we going?"

"You'll see," I said. My heart was hammering in my chest. I was more nervous than ever as we neared my room. It seemed like the right thing to do and the right time to do it. Me and Roki, alone in my bedroom. I'd never known a boy I felt so strongly about. For that matter, I'd never had a boy in my room. Everything felt so ... fated.

I pulled him through the threshold and stopped, turned to look into his eyes.

Roki made a loud gulp as he looked around. "We're in your bedroom."

"I'll get some towels to dry our feet," I told him, only half aware our feet were already dry.

I went into the adjoining washroom and came back with two fluffy white towels. Roki was seated on the edge of my bed. He looked out of place. Everything in my room was colorful, blue sheets and blue drapes, cute outfits hanging on hooks in the smaller closet, and makeup scattered on my vanity. I wondered how long it had been since Roki last ventured into a girl's room. I wondered if he ever had. It seemed unlikely to me that such a handsome character hadn't, even if he was still so young.

"Here." I passed him a towel.

"Thanks," he said with a laugh, "but my feet are already dry."

I looked at mine and burst out laughing, mostly from awkwardness. "Mine too," I said.

And that was when something happened, something powerful and indescribable. We both stopped laughing and regarded one another. The air thickened. Heat rose from an unknown place and overtook me. He parted his lips to speak, then stopped. Magnetism was drawing me to him, my hand to the flaxen scruff on his chin. It was soft, inviting. I said, "Roki ..." and he shushed me with his finger to my lips.

Now his hand was at my cheek, caressing my skin. I thought, *This is it. It's what I've been waiting—no, yearning for!*

"Can you feel it?" Roki said, his voice low and deep.

I nodded, swallowed dryly. "Yes."

He was leaning toward me. I could hear his shallow breaths. I touched his chest through his shirt, felt the hard contours of his pecs, ran my fingers down his sculpted abs. I was in awe of his perfect body. His eyes pierced mine and then glanced at my lips, as my fingers slowly rolled over the stubble on his chin and jawline. His lips were getting closer. Electricity prickled through me, and I leaned in to meet him—

"Kaelyn! Kaelyn, where are you?"

I jolted in surprise, pulled away from Roki just as my lips brushed against his. "Is that my brother?"

Raad's voice sounded again, booming through my open doorway. "Kaelyn, are you here?" His footsteps thundered and shook the house as he searched for me.

I looked at Roki. "He shouldn't be here until tomorrow. I … I …"

But our moment had passed. Roki's panic was clear on his face. He looked scared, like he had been caught doing something he shouldn't have been doing.

I touched his knee. "Don't worry. Raad's my brother. It's okay if he sees us together. We've done nothing wrong."

Before I could say more, Raad exploded into my room. "Kaelyn," he said, short of breath and totally wild. He looked different than I remembered. He was grown, burly, menacing. The Aska training had turned my brother into a fierce man.

"Yes, brother. I'm here. What is it? Why do you look so panicked? Shouldn't you be at the—?"

"It's Mama," he said, and the blood drained from my face. "Something terrible has happened."

Instinct maybe, or maybe the strip of mourning sackcloth wrapped around Raad's left bicep—either way, I knew what he was going to say. I could feel it, could see the devastation in my brother's tanned face. Already tears were welling in my eyes. I fumbled for Roki's hand but couldn't find it.

Raad took ten huge steps into the room and knelt in front of me. The tragedy was clear in his eyes, and I didn't want to see it. I gawked around the room but couldn't find Roki. He had vanished. But to where? And how?

Raad took my hands in his. I thought he was crying, but how could that be possible for an Aska warrior? Only something truly horrific could make an Aska cry.

"Kaelyn ..." Raad was sobbing into my hands. "Mama's dead."

That was when I fainted.

CHAPTER 3

I was alone in the darkness of my apartment, a stack of unread books and tea beside my sofa. The visin embedded in my wrist was emitting a projection, a square holographic screen in front of me. I was crying softly. It was the hundredth, maybe two hundredth time I had watched the video in the past year. It always made me cry. There was something so final about seeing the mausoleum Raad had helped construct, the polished white stone seeming to swallow her casket as the funeral procession carried Mama's remains into the structure.

Then there were the faces I recognized in the news footage. I was there, veiled in black and crying. Always crying. And there was Papa, hardly able to keep his composure. Raad was inside the mausoleum with Mama's casket. The other clan leaders were outside, dressed in their own ritualistic funeral attire. Ava-Shondur in leather, Ava-Surrvul in dark green fur, Ava-

Krug in white garments, Ava-Nurlie in full-length purple and gold silk, and Ava-Lodden in elaborate sisal.

The only person missing was Roki. It made me mad when I remembered he hadn't come. He had avoided Mama's funeral just as he had avoided me. The night of her death, Roki had sent me a message on my visin: *Sorry for disappearing so quickly. Everything okay? I miss you.*

I had typed a handful of responses, but none felt appropriate. I had just lost my mother. I was in shock, broken, wounded, and grief-stricken beyond belief. And I was angry because in my time of need, when I had fainted and then sobbed heavily in Raad's arms, Roki hadn't been there to console me. Poof, gone like a ghost. And he had never come back.

I turned off the video of Mama's funeral and flicked through the news channels on my visin. There were reports about a new species of fish found off the Nurlie coast. Another volcanic eruption had devastated Lodden, and three Aska trainees had perished trying to save the residents of a small village there. Gurnots had ambushed a tanker and stolen nearly sixty gallons of high-grade flyarc fuel, yet the Protectors couldn't find where they had stashed it. Three more fires in one of Surrvul's wealthiest neighborhoods, huge properties burned to the ground—the authorities were beginning to suspect a single individual, perhaps one specialized team of Gurnots. And Lordin and Zawne's wedding had just been announced.

I stopped on the channel showing Lordin and Zawne, took a sip of tea, and turned up the volume. They were quite the match. Lordin was highly esteemed and adored by all the people of Geniverd. Zawne was a prince.

The newscaster's voice came loud in my ear: "The dashing couple, after dating publicly for the past eight months, have finally announced their engagement. These lovebirds have been spotted flaunting their affection on all six continents, and now finally they are to be wed. What could this mean for the upcoming coronation? Could Lordin and Zawne be the next king and queen?"

I hoped so. They were the ideal couple. Lordin did enough volunteer work to put anyone to shame, and Zawne was the son of the current king and queen. They were all anyone had talked about lately—Lordin this and Zawne that.

"Have you seen the footage of them together on the beach in Surrvul?"

"Have you heard what Lordin did for the orphans in Gaard?"

"Have you seen the way they look at each other?"

"Have you seen the secret footage of their first date? They made a song together and sang so beautifully. They're truly in love!"

I adored them like the rest of the world, especially Lordin, a lowborn girl from Gaard who now had a shot at the throne. Lordin gave the people hope, real hope. She promised them a better future by potentially rising to queendom. I agreed with a lot of her reform ideas. I particularly liked Lordin's idea about giving some of the Protectors' jobs back to the people, reducing how much we rely on machines, if not just to give thousands of people some sense of purpose in their lives.

However, this line of thought reminded me of Roki, and I tried to ignore it.

The only thing that irked me was how quickly the news of Mama's death had gone away and been replaced by the unconventional lovers. Mama had been poisoned, and they had never found her killer. She had writhed in horrible pain and died before Raad's home-coming ceremony could be concluded, right there on the floor in front of all those clan leaders and nobles. The fact that it had been swept under the rug so quickly upset me.

I endlessly replayed the events of that day in my head. What had Mama wanted to say when she called me? Why hadn't I picked up? Why had I reacted so defiantly? Had she been right about Roki? If I'd been with her, could I have saved her? At the very least, if I'd swallowed my pride and resisted my craving for Roki, I'd have gone to the homecoming and been on better terms with her before her sudden death. I had thought we'd have more time together. Time to compromise. Time to mend our differences. Time for her to attend my wedding if I was to get married one day. And so her death didn't seem real. Every time someone visited NordHaven, my heart reflex-ively jumped at the thought it was Mama coming home.

It was only after the ritualistic one-month mourning period that I truly grieved. The heartache got worse as the visits, flowers, and cards from all over Geniverd diminished. How could she be gone, forever and ever?

I turned off my visin and stared into the darkness. It was going to be one of those introspective nights, I could tell. I was already dwelling on the past. I was wondering why Roki hadn't reached out to me after that initial message the night of Gaard-Ma's death. Sure, I had ignored him that one time, but I had been grieving! I had been angry with myself! My last conversation with Mama had been a fight, a silly rebellion. I had chosen Roki over my family, and I could never take it back. I hated myself for it and couldn't stand to talk to him right away. I had thought, *If I don't have Mama anymore, I don't deserve to have Roki either.* I had gambled with family and love, and I had lost both.

Then time had moved forward, and Roki had never tried to reach me again. I had hoped to hear from him once my emotions had cooled off a bit, but he never contacted me. I lost faith in him. I had been so sure he was the one for me. I still felt sometimes like he was, still smelled his scent on my clothes or when I walked into a room. I had been willing to profess my undying feelings for Roki and risk my family's obsession with public image to be with him, and he had never contacted me again.

Eventually, I didn't want him to. His silence justified my contempt. But I never stopped thinking about Roki. Obviously, I was still thinking about him a year later as I sat alone in my apartment, drinking fine tea by myself.

* * *

THE NEXT MORNING, I showed up to the office with a slight headache. It was nice to go to work. I had purpose here. It was my foundation, GMAF, Gaard-Ma Foundation, the organization I had set up in the capital city to keep Mama's memory alive. We were doing good work with orphans, wildlife preservation, women's shelters, education in rural areas, and other sensitive social issues. We were trying to regain some semblance of social purpose with the "normal" people, who happened to make up most of the world's population. They needed work, better lives, and some way to feel like they belonged. With so many Protectors buzzing around and not enough work for everyone, it was no wonder there was so much social divergence going on.

"Good morning, Kaelyn," Tissa said as I entered the space we rented in the bustling downtown. She was sitting at the table with paperwork splayed across it and a half-eaten granola bar in her hand.

"Morning," I said. "Is that your breakfast?"

"You know how I am," Tissa said. "Too busy to stop and eat. I can't help it. We've been getting so much work these past few weeks. Just this morning we received an aid request from Lodden. Apparently, they need more than just the Askas to assist after the vicious volcano two days ago. I'm going over the bankroll to see if we can move some funds around and pay for extra aid workers. I'm wondering if we should pause the construction of the new school in the secluded Butri province of Krug. That way, the construction workers can relocate to Lodden."

"No," I said, sitting down at the table with Tissa. "If money is a problem, I can ask Papa for more funding. I don't want to, but I can. We can also make some emergency calls for money if we need to. But that school is important. We should pay trained aid workers to go to Lodden and leave the construction workers in Krug."

"All right," Tissa said. "That sounds good to me. We sure are lucky to have Gaard-Elder to help support us.

He's been so generous since you started this foundation. I'm proud to be working here with you. I know Nnati is too."

I smiled—both at Tissa's kindness and at the thought of my father. "I think Papa needed to be a part of this as much as I did," I told Tissa. "We were both so distraught after Mama's passing. Papa was worse off than I was. It was like he had died, like his soul was empty without her around." I sighed, pushed some loose papers around distractedly. "I can't blame him for it. Times were tough. We were all depressed. It was GMAF that pulled us out of the slump. When I told Papa about my idea to start this foundation, he perked up for the first time since Mama's funeral."

I paused to chuckle, thinking back on the day. His reaction was priceless. "It could be good," Papa had said to me. "You can pursue a charitable career in advocacy while at the same time keeping your mama's memory alive. Not to mention that what you're talking about—a foundation for helping the lower-class citizens, using Decens-Lenitas—can help advance your own status as a well-versed woman of the moral code. It brings you closer to the throne. Perhaps we can involve the Grucken somehow, get it publicized. Any funding you need, I'll provide. I'll help you move to the capital city. I'll help you with all my business connections. Anything you need for this endeavor, daughter, I will help with."

Tissa must have known I needed a friend-to-friend therapy session. She listened attentively as I said, "I remember the sparkle in his eyes. It was exactly what Papa needed. He helped me with the research, with finding this space for our office, with hiring you and Nnati, and with getting us noticed by the public. At the same time, he made sure I had private tutors to help me finish my studies. And now look at us, Tissa. We have daily requests coming in for our assistance!"

She gave me a coy smile as she produced a letter from her pile of papers. "Not only requests for our assistance," Tissa said. "You'll never guess who this is from."

"Who?" I nearly jumped out of my chair.

"You're not going to guess?" She waved the letter teasingly. "Come on, Kaelyn. You're going to freak out when you find out."

My mind was racing. We had gotten a lot of attention recently from potential donors. A manufacturer from Surrvul called Veeln-Co, the company that built and distributed visins, had approached us about partnering for an ad campaign meant to raise awareness about workplace harassment and workplace safety. I wondered if the letter was from them.

"Is it Veeln-Co?" I asked. I was on the edge of my seat.

"Even better." Tissa was grinning fiendishly. I marveled at how adorable she was. She and Nnati were old friends from Nurlie. Nnati was only a few years older than Tissa, who was closer in age to me. Being in such a metropolitan city, the capital of Geniverd, I liked all the different faces, light and dark eyes, and complexions.

"Tell me!" I said. "Please, Tissa, tell me."

"See for yourself."

She handed me the letter, and I screamed when I saw whose name was on it. "No way!" I leaped out of my chair, doing a celebratory dance even though my head throbbed. "Is it real? Did you read it?"

"I was waiting for you," Tissa said, enjoying my excitement. "For you and Nnati. I think we should all be here to see what Lordin has sent to us in the letter."

That was when Nnati walked into the room. "Did someone say Lordin sent us a letter?" He looked nearly as excited as me. He readjusted his glasses with a huge smile on his face, glancing between Tissa and me. "Well, are we going to open it?"

"Yeah we are!"

I didn't even use the letter opener. I clawed the thing open with my nails and pulled it out, then read it aloud.

"'Dear Kaelyn, I am writing to you on behalf of myself and my partner, Prince Zawne, regarding your foundation, GMAF. We have been following your work closely—how you have been building new schools, quietly campaigning in the capital for social change among the lower classes, beseeching the clan heirs for their support in using Decens-Lenitas for the betterment of the people, assisting in natural disasters, and organizing wildlife protective services. And honestly, we are amazed at what you have accomplished. We are beyond impressed. I must say, Kaelyn, as the First Daughter of Gaard, you have gone above and beyond your station to help the people of this great continent, and indeed the world. Prince Zawne and I would like to invite you to Sud Cottage for dinner. We have a proposal for you. We hope to see you tonight at six p.m. sharp. Yours truly, Lordin.'"

The three of us were speechless. I placed the letter gently on the table and looked at my friends. "What do you think?" I asked.

Nnati nearly screamed, "You need to buy a new

dress and get your Gaard butt over to Sud Cottage tonight! That's what I think!"

"Me too," Tissa said. "This is such an incredible opportunity. Lordin—I mean, Lordin! We have watched her on our visins since she was a little girl working with the rural farmers of Gaard because she wanted to help others. This is the girl the whole world watched blossom into a beautiful young woman with a kind heart. Lordin, who was courted by the most eligible bachelor in Geniverd, and then tamed him. This is the person we are talking about, Kaelyn. We're talking about *the* Lordin. It's sure to be one heck of a proposal."

My legs bounced restlessly under the table. I was excited, nervous, intrigued, scared—all the emotions at once. "What kind of proposal do you think it is?"

Nnati considered my question as he rubbed his chin, clean-shaven and professional in a bow tie, as always. "Lordin said she has been following GMAF's work, and we all know the kind of humane causes she supports and projects she runs. It must be a merger or a funding campaign. Maybe she wants to help us reach more people. Our views are basically the same as hers. We both want to help make a better world."

Then Tissa's face lit up, and she leaned over the table. "Do you think Prince Jaken will be there too?"

I laughed, seeing the heat in Tissa's face at the mention of Prince Zawne's older brother. "I'm not sure, Tiss. Maybe."

Tissa settled into her seat, and a dreamy look dulled her face. Tissa was a girl born under the most common of situations in the most common of places, and maybe that was why she had a deep reverence for the princes of Geniverd. When her eyelids fluttered and she sighed at the thought of Prince Jaken, I knew it wouldn't have mattered which prince we were talking about. Sometimes I thought she was attracted to the royalty more than the people themselves.

"I know Jaken is married," Tissa said. "Even so, I'd love to go on a date with him. Just one date, nothing serious, no physical contact. He's just so handsome. I just want him to treat me like a princess for one day. Just one."

Nnati raised his hand. His smile was devious. "I'd also like a date with Prince Jaken," he said, "but can mine have touching?"

We all laughed. "Nnati," I said, "you're such a dog!" But I didn't mean it. Nnati was great, playful, classy. Hiring him and Tissa had been the best thing to happen to me since moving to the capital and starting GMAF. I loved them both like family. Well, I saw them more often than my own family. I didn't know what I would have done without Nnati and Tissa. I didn't feel like royalty when I was with them. They made me feel like just another person, like another normal citizen of Gaard. It was, in a way, a vacation from my pampered life back in NordHaven.

"But in all seriousness," Nnati said, deepening his voice and raising an eyebrow, "I like the idea of working with Lordin, and at the same time, I don't. It will be great if she agrees to work with us on our terms, but I don't want to get too tangled up in the upper-class workings of Decens-Lenitas. My pardons, Kaelyn, I know it's your foundation and your rules. It's just the whole paradox of the more 'esteemed' points of the moral code upsets me. I don't want to start helping the upper-class people. You built this foundation for the commoners, for the wildlife, and to keep your mama's memory alive."

"I understand," I said, "but I don't think it will be a problem. I, like everyone else in Geniverd, have been following Lordin's work for years. Even though she is now marrying Prince Zawne, her dedication to the homeless, the needy, the lost children, it hasn't changed. Her programs are still running. Perhaps she wants to join forces."

I stopped, a sudden look of bewilderment in my eyes. "Could ...?" I licked my lips nervously. "Could it be that Lordin wants to pass the torch? She may become queen next year." I blinked at Tissa, totally shocked by my revelation. "This could be huge!"

Tissa and Nnati beamed at me.

"You better get ready," Nnati said. "Take the day off, Kaelyn. Pick out your dress. It better be a cute one. You have a date with Lordin and Zawne tonight."

* * *

I WAS SWEATING in the courtyard of Sud Cottage that night, not only because of its grandeur—though it was only a quarter of the size of NordHaven—but because of my nervousness at meeting Lordin. I, like so many others, had revered her for so long. Now I was moments away from finally meeting her.

The door swung open, and Prince Zawne stood in the threshold. We had met before as younger people. Not much about him had changed. He still had a handsome smile, a full head of hair, smooth bronze skin, and a certain warmth about him. Zawne was just like the man I constantly saw on my visin, the man in love with Lordin.

"Welcome," he said. "Lordin is waiting in the parlor for us. She is a touch tired. I guess she didn't sleep well last night. But come in. Our home is your home."

"Thank you, Zawne," I said as I followed him into the foyer. He was polite, and I liked that about him.

As we moved through the hall, he made small talk to make me feel more comfortable. Maybe he had noticed how nervous I was. "Sud Cottage is not so grand as VondRust Palace, where I grew up," he said, "but it is cozy. Lordin and I love living here. Because there aren't a zillion rooms, we feel more connected, closer to each other at all times."

"That's nice," I said, recalling the tour of VondRust that his brother, Jaken, had kindly given me just before I'd moved into the lavish apartment in its grounds, provided for me by the king and the queen. It was their principal residence and administrative headquarters with at least ten music rooms, fifty grand ballrooms, twenty-six kitchens, and hundreds of offices and meeting rooms for councillors and other important people. "It's such an honor to be invited here. Congratulations on your engagement!"

"Thanks. We're thrilled," Zawne said. "How about you? Are you seeing anyone?"

"Nope. I've got too much on my plate right now with the company."

Zawne talked about being with Lordin as though it was all he cared about in life. I found myself a touch jealous that I didn't have that same love. And like so many times over the past year, I found myself thinking about Roki. I wondered where he was. I wondered if he had found somebody new.

Inside the parlor, Lordin lay on a large, plush sofa with her eyes half-shut. I was surprised when she perked up at my entrance, shone her bright white teeth at me, and said, "Welcome, Kaelyn. I am so glad you could come."

"Me too," I told her. Then I bit my lip hesitantly and said, "You're even more stunning in person," feeling an instant wash of embarrassment after I said it. But it was true. With her strong jaw, pointed chin and big blue eyes, Lordin was as cute as a button. No wonder Zawne was crazy about her!

"I appreciate you saying so," she said. "Please, Kaelyn, take a seat."

Lordin gestured to a chair across from her sofa, and I sat down. Zawne sat down beside Lordin, and I smiled as she slithered into the nook of his armpit and nuzzled her head against his chest. It looked cozy there. I thought for sure she would fall asleep.

"Are you all right?" I asked. Lordin looked fatigued beyond reason. I noticed her eyelids were a touch red, as if she'd been crying.

"Yes, I am quite all right. Sorry, Kaelyn, I just didn't get enough sleep last night." Lordin spoke with heavy eyelids, purring into Zawne's side like a cat. "But you, dear." She smiled. "You are beautiful, a true daughter of Gaard."

Now I was the one blushing. Could she mean it, that I was beautiful? Had Lordin never looked in the mirror?

"We should get to business," I said, suddenly

awkward and clumsy. "You sent a letter saying you have a proposition for me. What is it?"

Lordin tried to speak but was arrested by a long yawn. Zawne answered in her stead.

"We have been watching what you're doing with GMAF," he said. "And truth be told, we love it. We love it a lot. With Lordin's new position as my betrothed ..." He squeezed her thigh, so intimately that it made me blush.

"Sorry." Zawne cleared his throat. "With Lordin as my wife-to-be, the fact is we may be raised to the status of king and queen. There is also a chance that I will become the next clan leader of Shondur. If that happens at the coronation next year, Lordin and I must relocate out of the capital and back to my native land."

I could already feel where this was going. I was anxious. Could they really want me to ...?

"We need someone strong, capable, and upholding of Decens-Lenitas to take over Lordin's charitable works," Zawne explained. "As the head of your own foundation, with your high-profile lineage and the fact that you're unwed and, sorry to say it, have a low chance of being queen, we want you to begin transitioning Lordin's beloved projects over to GMAF. This means a ton more funding, more manpower, a bigger office, more responsibility, and more ways you can change Geniverd for the better."

"Yes," Lordin said, sounding so weak I was surprised she had the energy to speak, "my work must continue. It is imperative that you take over from me as the lead on all my charity projects and volunteer organizations. I want this very badly, Kaelyn. It is important to me that you make the decision now. I need to see you're

committed to helping the people. Only then can I ..."
She licked her lips and choked back emotion. Something was definitely bothering her, something other
than lack of sleep. "Only then can I rest well tonight,"
she finished.

Whatever bothered Lordin had no effect on Zawne.
He was all smiles, caressing Lordin's back, stroking her
hair. He loved her so much!

"I say yes!" I declared, way too loudly. I was nervous
and had lost control of my voice. It cracked as I said, "I
mean, that would be acceptable, Lordin. I really appreciate the opportunity and your trust in me. As the most
beloved woman in the kingdom—and the most
visinized—your belief means a lot to me. Really, it
does."

"I'm glad," she said. "I feel that our interpretation of
Decens-Lenitas is the same. I feel, Kaelyn, that we are
of the same heart, the same cloth."

I couldn't believe what Lordin was saying. She and I,
of the same cloth? Could it be true? And the whole
time, Zawne was petting Lordin and smiling at me. Was
I in a freaking dream?

"We need you to sign the papers right away," Zawne
said. "I've prepared the necessary documents to transfer
ownership, funds, and other technical details from
Lordin's private work over to you." He gestured to a
small stack of papers on the table between us. "Will you
sign them?"

I beamed widely. "Do you have a pen?"

* * *

45

"I<small>T</small> <small>WENT</small> <small>WELL</small>," I said to Tissa. We were in the office the morning after I had accepted Lordin's offer, going through the insane amount of paperwork that had flooded in overnight. "Lordin was different in person. She was tired. Like, really tired. It made me wonder if something more hadn't been going on behind the scenes."

"Like what?" Tissa asked.

I crinkled my nose. "I'm not sure. It was just a gut feeling, you know? Something felt off."

"But how was Zawne? Is he as handsome in person as he is on the—?"

I rolled my eyes at Tissa. "I can't answer that, not with the way he and Lordin were totally in love with each other. It would be inappropriate of me to call Zawne handsome ... which he was!"

She giggled. "I knew it!"

"Seriously," I said, "Zawne and Lordin are the most lovey-dovey duo I have ever met. At one point, after I had signed all the documents, Lordin fell asleep, and Zawne quietly told me about their first date. It was so magical!"

"Magical how?" Tissa asked. She had forgotten all about her work. "Tell me. I must know!"

I straightened up. "Okay, here's the deal. Zawne told me they first met at Prince Jaken's homecoming cere-mony, two years ago, after his Aska training. Zawne was in the crowd, and Lordin came out on stage with the Grucken. He told me how beautiful she had looked to him, speaking into the microphone, congratulating the bold warriors on their hard years of struggle and training. Lordin was showering the warriors with praise, telling them all how proud Geniverd was of them. But all that Zawne could concentrate on were the blue oceans in her eyes."

I sighed, getting soft at my own telling of Zawne's story. "Once Lordin got off the stage, Zawne scrambled through the crowd, looking for her. He completely ignored the throngs of young women and heiresses keen on trying to seduce him and found Lordin on the other side of the room. He was out of breath when he got to her. Zawne pulled her aside and said, 'I know this is inappropriate. You might not even know who I am, so I apologize. But your beauty has arrested me. I must see more of you, Lordin. Can we meet?'"

I was giggling now. "Isn't that great, Tiss? It was love at first sight. Obviously, Lordin agreed to the date, but they kept it secret. They met at Lithern Shrine in the Grucken's training complex early one morning. Zawne arrived in his blue steel flyrarc like an action hero. Lordin made him tea. They lingered around Lithern Shrine all day and were in love before nightfall. They continued to see each other in secret for over a year."

"That's kind of hot," Tissa said, getting all flustered. "I wish I could have a secret romance ... Well, any romance would do. A secret romance with a rich prince would do better."

"You will have your time," I assured her. "Your day is coming. Actually, I wanted to mention something to you about my brother, Raad. Maybe if—"

"Be careful, Tiss." Nnati entered the room and cut me off. "You could find yourself on the throne!"

Tissa and I winked at each other. I'd save that conversation for another time. I knew that Tissa would absolutely gush if I told her my brother was interested in a date with her.

Later that evening, when I was alone in my apartment, my mind returned to Lordin's moist eyes and her sunken body. I turned my visin on and flicked to the celebrity channel, hoping to catch a glimpse of her looking more cheerful. I flipped onto the news channel for a moment first and saw that there had been another fire, this time a huge inferno that had swallowed some nobleman's nine-story castle in the northern Lodden mountains, where he and his family went skiing in the winter. The fire was so strong it had melted the stones and left a brown spot in the snow, but somehow there were no casualties at all. The reports on the news were starting to call the arsonist "the Gurnot Dragon."

I finally reached the celebrity channel and gasped at what I saw on the screen.

Lordin has been found dead on a walkway near Sud Cottage, where she lived with Prince Zawne. There are reports that she was decapitated with a cleaver.

CHAPTER 4

I was still in shock at the funeral a month later. It was hard to comprehend that Lordin was dead. I had watched her for so many years on the visin, then finally been invited into her home and embraced as a friend, only to have her gone the next day. I had spent the last month in shock. The only thing that had kept me sane was focusing on the overload of work that she had passed on to me. It made me wonder, *Did Lordin know she was going to die?*

"Bad way to go, huh?" Nnati asked. He stood to my left, Tissa on my right. We were watching the crowd of mourners cry as everyone readied themselves for the traditional Gaard burial. We were to walk Lordin's remains one mile to her ultimate resting place on land acquired by VondRust Palace on Zawne's behalf.

"Yeah," Tissa said. "I can't believe someone cut her head off. It's just so ..."

"It's brutal," I said. "The way she was killed makes me sick. And what's with the groundskeeper who told the police a swarm of bees had killed Lordin? That's really weird."

I sighed and gave my head a shake. "Anyway, Lordin's a martyr now. The people of Geniverd are furious, especially here in Gaard. She's been elevated far beyond what she was in life. I've heard the Gurnots are cycling rumors through the capital that Lordin was killed by the upper class to stop her from meddling with Decens-Lenitas. I mean, she was highly versed in the teachings, but I know she opposed some of the more controversial aspects regarding the monarchy. The rumors have sparked outrage. I know that there was some serious division between the classes before, but this has incited some real trouble. Have you guys seen the riots?"

"Yeah," Tissa said. "People are throwing themselves from roofs. They're marching in the streets and demanding justice. The higher-ups still won't give out any information on who killed Lordin, or why."

"They should," Nnati said with a peculiar edge in his voice. "I was never one of Lordin's followers, but she was still a human being, and people deserve answers. I'll be the first to admit she seemed genuinely benevolent, like she really helped people. It's not right to cover up what happened. Why won't they tell us anything?"

"I don't know," I said. "That sort of thing is way beyond the station of a mere heiress. Papa hasn't said anything to me about it."

"It's suspicious," Nnati said. "And it's causing problems. I've heard the Surrvul are vying for the throne now. Word on the street is that they have six heirs going to the coronation next year. They're hoping to steal the seat. It's been two hundred years since the last

Surrvul rulers, and they're peeved about it. It's funny, actually, maybe even ironic, that the richest continent is the most desperate for the throne."

Tissa nodded in agreement. "With Veeln-Co in their territory, Surrvul has enough money to fund a war."

"Hush," I snapped, not meaning to. I hated hearing about wars. I hated hearing about how viciously Lordin had been killed. What kind of monster could harm such a perfectly radiant being? And what would happen now at the coronation? Poor Zawne. He must have been in tatters.

"Sorry." I hung my head. "I'm just upset—maybe because I had thought I could never be as morally upright as Lordin; then she came into my life and showed me I could try. She trusted me." I sighed, fighting back tears. "Then someone cut her freaking head off! She handed me the torch and died the next day. Who's going to change the world now?"

Tissa and Nnati remained quiet, sullen. The mood was bleak. Thousands of mourners talked in quiet whispers all around us. We had all come to bid Lordin a final farewell, people from every continent. It was one of the greatest pilgrimages Geniverd had ever seen. I had known she was popular and loved, but this was crazy. It seemed like the whole world had come to say goodbye.

"Death is a thief," I said. "It steals hopes, dreams, experiences. Death is the robber of life, happiness, family. Death takes everything and gives nothing. Death is the most unjust sentence ever passed."

* * *

THE PROCESSION BEGAN. We joined in the thousands of people marching slowly through the fields of Lordin's mother's estate. Lordin was to be cremated and placed inside a newly constructed mausoleum.

As we marched, drummers beat on their drums, and the Ava-Gaard sang out in painful bellows. Nnati and Tissa joined in as best they could, since they were Ava-Nurlie and didn't know the words. I belted out the words as loud as I could, danced the dance of the dead, and surrendered my body, swaying to the beating of the drum as we marched through the field. By dancing, the Ava-Gaard promised Lordin a peaceful rest with our ancestors in the afterlife.

We danced and chanted and marched all the way to the cremation site, to the mausoleum Raad had helped construct, since he was the soon-to-be clan leader. He had been practicing the duties, and he stood near the front of the crowd, wearing full Gaard-Elder garb. It made my heart swell to see my brother looking so regal.

And I wasn't the only one. Tissa couldn't keep her eyes off Raad. Or was she looking at Zawne? The two men stood beside each other, roughly the same age. Zawne was thinner beside Raad. He had suffered a month of grief, and it showed in his baggy clothing, his dark eyes, his sunken cheeks. Zawne looked half-dead. I supposed he was less alive without Lordin, his shining light.

Zawne stepped forward onto the podium and took the microphone in his hands. The hundreds of P2 camera drones buzzed around him like locusts, transmitting the tragic event to the whole kingdom. Zawne didn't seem to mind. He was probably used to them in his life of royalty and fame. It made me glad to be away from that boring life, constantly swarmed by cameras and press. Before Zawne spoke, he turned to look at a veiled woman standing alone at the back of the stage. Lordin's mother, I guessed. Her skin glowed the same pale white as Lordin's had, the porcelain complexion so rare for an Ava-Gaard.

"I'd like to recite a poem," Zawne said, his voice shattered by loss. "I loved Lordin more than words can describe, and I have written this poem to try to commemorate her. Maybe in death she will hear my words."

The crowd melted. I could feel them soften and whisper. Who could blame them? Zawne was the perfect model of a bereaved lover. Even Tissa said, "He's so romantic. I wish I had a man like him."

Zawne cleared his throat, then read his poem from a scrap of paper. "My love. Our love. I thought I knew what living was.

"Until I met you.

"Through the fog. I couldn't see. Every breath I took.

"You saw.

"Every smile or frown.

"You foresaw.

"I soared. We soared. I saw the birds for the first time and learned their songs.

"Heard their vivid tales, their blitheness, their misery.

"I saw all people beneath the surface.

"I was free. We were free. Our trees stand tall in the quiet of the night.

"Quiet to the untrained ear.

"Innumerable stars shine. Buzzing, purring, humming, rumbling, hissing.

"Thick gray clouds pour.

"Our branches and leaves sway. The winds are strong and cold.

"I never yield. We never yield. The darkness around us is perfectly lit.

"The abyss, a heavy universe.

"This season is a mirage. All seasons are none. We are forever one.

"I rest with you.

"Geniverd rests with you."

Zawne bowed his head, and a respectful silence permeated the gathered thousands. I had tears in my eyes. So did Tissa. Even Nnati had to wipe his cheeks. The poem was beautiful. Lordin deserved it.

Once the moment of silence was over, Zawne looked back at the crowd and said, "I have one more thing to say. Without Lordin, my life is worthless. I've spoken with the Grucken, and he agreed it would be a good idea for me to strengthen my inner soul and find a new purpose through becoming an Aska. I'm not doing this for publicity. I'm doing this for Lordin, so that she may be proud of me in the afterlife."

Zawne paused, waiting to hear reactions in the crowd. People were gasping and chatting among themselves. I heard Nnati say, "He'll never make it. My left foot says he drops out after the first day."

Zawne went on. "My brother, Prince Jaken, believes I have the strength to make it through. My parents, the king and queen, are also supportive, and I know Lordin, if she's looking down upon me from some ethereal plane, is also behind me. I want to thank the people of Geniverd for coming on this solemn day to mourn the bright life of our beloved Lordin. Goodbye."

Zawne passed the microphone over to the Grucken and retreated to the back of the stage. He gave the veiled woman, Lordin's mother, a brief glance, then hugged his brother. I watched him shake Raad's hand. Then Zawne was gone and the Grucken was speaking.

"Geniverd," the Grucken said, "thank you for coming. I'll keep this short. A child of Decens-Lenitas is committed to ashes on this day, and it is too sorrowful for speeches. I will say only that Lordin has not truly died. She has merely transcended her body and mind and all things physical. Lordin is still with you in your hearts, in the souls of every living creature in Geniverd. And Geniverd will never forget. Farewell, Lordin."

The men of Gaard boomed, "Gaard to Gaard."

And then the women said, "Breast to breast."

* * *

My friends and I spent the night at NordHaven. Papa had gone to bed early after three glasses of wine, and the hour was late. I sat on the sofa next to Nnati so that Raad and Tissa were forced to sit on the opposite sofa together. The room smelled of fresh daisies, of spring and renewal. After living so long in the city, I had forgotten what it was like to live inside the bubble of NordHaven, surrounded by pleasant smells and perfect weather. Tissa looked more comfortable here than I was. She looked quite at home on the plush sofa next to Raad in his royal vestments.

"Have you considered seeing anyone since you moved to the city, Kaelyn?" Tissa asked me. The talk had turned to dating.

I immediately flushed. "No way! How could I have

time for a boyfriend with all the work we've been doing?" Then I scoffed at her, trying to get the spotlight off me. "Isn't this an inappropriate time to be talking about dating, Tiss?"

"It's the perfect time," Raad said. He was sitting rather snugly against my friend. "With all the death surrounding us, we deserve a bit of happiness. We all deserve special people in our lives. It's what Mama would have wanted. Besides, Kaelyn, we both need to be married by next year for the coronation ceremony."

I rumpled my nose. "And what if I'm not?"

"Then you won't ascend to queen. If I'm chosen for king, you'll have to become a solitary leader of the Gaard Clan. You'll have men chasing you like crazy!"

I sighed, sagging deep into the cushions on the sofa. "I don't want any of the other heirs. There's only one man I really want."

My words came out too fast without me thinking and suddenly everyone in the room was staring at me.

"Who?" Nnati asked. "Who is the one man you want? I can't believe it. Kaelyn has a crush!"

Even Raad was grinning at me. I noticed his fingers getting awfully close to where Tissa's hand rested on the sofa.

"I ... He's no one ... He's just ..." I sighed, defeated. I couldn't lie to my friends. "Fine," I said. "His name is Roki, and we were, dare I say it, on the fringes of love."

Tissa was bug eyed. "When? Where? How? Spill the beans, Kaelyn!"

"It was over a year ago," I told them, "before Mama's passing. We spent every day together. I had never felt so in sync with anyone before. I was sure we could have ruled the world together. I may have wanted to become queen if I had Roki as my king. He was amazing."

"So it wasn't just an infatuation," Tissa said. "It was intense."

"Yeah." I nodded. "It was emotionally powerful. We were bonded. But then Mama died. I couldn't bear to see him in the state I was in. Then, well ... we drifted apart."

Nnati was grinning mischievously. "So," he said, "drift back together. Why don't you reach out to him, explain that your heart was broken and now you're ready to date again? Things happen; life happens. It doesn't mean you can't get back together."

I blinked at Nnati, totally dumbfounded by his totally perfect rationale. I suddenly wanted to ditch my friends, run to my bedroom, and try to call Roki on my visin. Did I still have his number? Could I bear to hear his voice again? Would he even still want me?

"You're thinking about it," Nnati said slyly. "I can see the gears turning in your head. Just do it, Kaelyn. Life's too short. We could all be killed by a superbug at any minute."

I laughed. Nnati was cheering me up with his typically grim demeanor, talking about superbugs as if there had even been one in the last five hundred years. I was also cheered to see Raad and Tissa giggling in their own little bubble across the room, their fingers entwined. She really did look right at home.

"But enough about you, Kaelyn," Nnati said, dramatically flipping his wrist. "Let's talk about me. I need a man too. Now that Zawne's single, maybe he'll come play for my team. What do you think?"

Raad answered for me. "I think Zawne is currently

on his way to Gaard's southern coast. By tomorrow night he will be paddling two hundred miles across stormy, shark-infested waters. If he doesn't get sucked into a whirlpool or eaten by a giant squid, he will be trekking through a merciless wasteland for the next eight months. After that he'll have serious training in Lodden for nearly one and a half years. I think dating is the furthest thing from his mind right now."

"Right," Nnati said, pouting his lips. "Do you think he'll make it through?"

Raad thought seriously about this, his eyebrows furrowing. "I think he has what he needs to get through it," he said. "If Zawne can embrace the pain of Lordin's death, draw strength from it, and let the pain and hurt guide him, then yes. Yes, I believe he can make it."

We all quieted then. I'm sure we were picturing a grief-stricken Zawne shirtless and sweaty in the desert, trudging along with dull resolve, battling leopards with the anger from Lordin's death. I could see by Nnati's raised eyebrows he liked the idea. As for me, I felt sad for Zawne. He had adored Lordin, made a home with her. Now Zawne was alone with himself and the wilderness. His only company would be the other lost souls desperate for purpose, and the hungry vultures circling above.

$\mathscr{I}$ was immersed in a sea of white arum lilies, my body buoyant on the current. I ducked below the canopy of white-spotted green leaves and swam among their impossibly long stalks. The petals brushed me softly, sublimely. Their musky scent filled my nostrils. I was alive, floating in a flowery paradise.

A new scent came to me: earthy, herbal. It was a sweet fragrance accompanied by a presence, a construct of pistils, a thousand flower eyes. It was a hot gaze that made my body shake, and I came to a stop amid the field of lilies. I felt naked here, bare and contrite. The large orange petals were reaching out for me. I let them brush against my skin, the flowery presence making me feel secure, filaments blown about me on a sudden breeze. I lifted my face, and there he was.

Roki in the flesh. The scene changed, and we were two bare souls in the field of arum lilies. He had a smile on his face. I realized I was crying, solid in my body. We were hugging. My tears streaked down his bare chest, slithered between his abs.

"What do you want, Roki?" I said against him. He held me tightly and allowed me to weep before I leaped back in anger. "Why are you here now?"

"Because I love you, Kaelyn. I need you to come back to me."

Roki's words were honest in this sacred dreamscape. I hadn't realized how much I had longed to hear his voice. It was like honey. I wanted to drown in it.

But I was still angry! So much time had passed without him to comfort me. "Why should I love you?" I demanded. "Why should I return to your embrace? You left me, Roki. In my hour of need, you were nowhere to be found!"

He took the brunt of my anger. He seemed to understand it and shook his head sadly. "I never left you. I've been here all along. I can't let go. By the world, I have tried. Yet your spirit lingers in my mind, in my being. I need you."

I hated how much I wanted to shrug off my anger and kiss him as if we had never parted. His words were sweet, yet they held no meaning for me.

"Where were you?" I asked. "When I was sad, beaten, crushed, and powerless, where were you? I was certain my grief would swallow me alive, and you weren't there to console me. I was hopeless. I had betrayed my mother for you, and in my time of need, you were gone."

He lowered his face close to mine. Roki, so handsome, so strong. How could I fight him? I was supposed to hate him, yet I wanted to touch him. My legs buckled, and I dropped to my knees.

He knelt beside me and pleaded, "Please, Kaelyn. You must believe that I was right there with you in your days of misery. I sobbed with you. I shared your pain and tried to comfort your soul. Maybe you felt me, smelled me. I was there. I could hear your mind, hear your thoughts of anger, and sense your grief. I respected your pain and your frustration, and kept my distance. I wanted so badly to stay away and let you grow on your own. You deserve a full life without me to drag you down. But now ..." Roki paused, swept his hand across my moist cheek. "But now I've heard you. I've listened to your heart and understood that you need me. I will be here from now on. I'm here, Kaelyn. I'm yours."

I had no words. I was so confused. Roki lifted my chin delicately. His fingers, his touch—they were perfect. "I love you," he said. And in his eyes was truth.

I caved, closed my eyes, and reached with my lips ...

* * *

"ROKI!" I screamed into my empty room. I sat upright in bed, sweating and hot.

"Just a dream ..."

I was disappointed and more than a bit confused. The dream had been so vivid, so real. Even Roki's scent continued to linger. It seemed like the universe was trying to tell me something. Did I need Roki back in my life?

I shook my head, trying to shake the dream from my system. It felt insane that he would appear to me in my mind on today of all days. I hadn't seen Roki for three years. I hadn't been back in NordHaven since Lordin's funeral two years ago. Yet there I was, in my old bedroom, my brother married to my best friend the previous night, and Roki's ghost was playing midnight tricks in my head. I already knew it was going to be a strange day. I could feel it in the air.

The service had been splendid. Tissa and Raad exchanged Gaard-Nurlie vows, and the massed crowd went nuts. Nurlie was happy because their chances of having an Ava-Nurlie queen were exceptional with Tissa's marriage to my brother. Gaard was happy because they adored Raad and figured he was sure to be picked by the Crown of Crowns. But Surrvul was displeased. They craved the throne with dangerous ambition. I was beginning to wonder what any of it meant for the common folk. What did the coronation mean for the people?

"Morning, newlyweds," I said as I entered the kitchen. Raad and Tissa were eating breakfast. The whispers of new lovers permeated the space.

"Morning, sister," Raad said. "Did you sleep well?"

"Yes," I told him, moving to the platter of strawberries on the counter. "Did you?"

"Hardly," Raad said, and he and Tissa erupted in secret giggles.

I was happy to see them like this. The past year had seen a lot of courting, a lot of travel back and forth between the capital and NordHaven. Now Tissa and Raad were finally wed. They were radiant together. I felt ashamed for being a touch sad that Nnati and I would soon fly back to the capital in our flyrarc while Tissa remained in NordHaven. She deserved some rest after the hard work she had put in over the past two years at the foundation. But for me, it felt like the end of an era. I could only hope everything would turn out well in the end.

"I have to talk to you about something," Raad said while chewing his eggs. "It's quite a serious something ..." He looked to Tissa. "Do you mind, wife? It really is rather private."

"Of course." Tissa bowed to Raad in the humble fashion of an Ava-Gaard wife. Then she came to me and kissed my cheek, squeezed my arm. "We're sisters now for real. You'll never get rid of me now, Kaelyn."

I laughed and said, "I'd never dream of it," and Tissa went into the hall and left Raad and me alone.

"What is it?" I asked him. He was squirming uncomfortably.

"As you know, sister, Prince Zawne had his homecoming two days ago. He survived the brutal trial of Aska training and made it home in one piece."

"I do know," I said. "I watched the ceremony on my visin. Zawne looks ..." I bit my lip. "Improved."

Raad flashed his teeth. "You mean he looks hotter, more muscular, tanned, and totally kissable?"

"No!" But my protest was useless. It was all true. Zawne had become a hunk from his two years of training. He had transformed from a prince into ... well, into a man.

"It's encouraging that you feel that way," Raad said, "because nearly two years ago I made a pact with Zawne's brother. I'm sure you're aware of the trade conundrum between Gaard and Shondur right now. People are scared that once the Shondur-born king and queen step down and a different clan takes the reins, the already shaky trade deal between our continents will crumble, and chaos will erupt."

"I've heard reports," I said, not at all liking where Raad was steering the conversation.

"Good. It's something you should be concerned about as the heiress to Gaard. I am. Papa is. Jaken too. It's why Jaken and I made the pact. We want to keep the balance between our prosperous domains. The best way to do this is through marriage. Since Jaken married a high-class lady from Krug to keep that alliance strong, Zawne is the only way. And you are the only daughter of Gaard. Get what I'm saying?"

My mouth opened and closed like a fish's. I had no words. Raad wanted me to marry Prince Zawne. Was he crazy? Zawne was Lordin's ex-fiancé. Might as well be her widower. Their bond was legendary. I could never fill such shoes.

"Are you serious?" I asked. "You're acting like Mama, trying to sell me off to a stranger."

"Don't be silly," Raad said, still chomping away at his eggs. "Zawne isn't a stranger. You're acquainted. I can tell by your reaction to his new physique that you're attracted to him. What's the issue?"

"I barely even know him!" I was irate. Sure, we had met, but I didn't *know* him. "And I could never replace Lordin. She put her entire faith in me, gifted me the prosperous foundation I have now. Who knows where GMAF would be if it wasn't for Lordin? For me to marry her living fiancé would be … it would be treachery!"

"Nonsense," Raad said. "People move on. It's neces-sary. It's also one of the things you learn during Aska training, that the world continues to spin without you when you're gone, that people continue with their lives. Zawne surely learned the same thing through his ordeal in the desert and in Lodden. I'm sure he will be happy at the thought of keeping our kingdom intact. I doubt he will have any qualms about marrying you, sister."

"You don't understand!" I protested. "Lordin and Zawne were truly in love. *Love* love, Raad. Love times a thousand! And the people. Oh, the people loved them as a couple. I'll be a new face and an utter disappointment next to Lordin."

"Don't sell yourself short, sister. You are ..." Raad squirmed. "Pretty. And men desire you. I have no less than twelve requests for your hand in marriage from the noble families in Gaard alone. You're a hot ticket."

"I don't want to be a ticket," I said. "I want to be loved. Can you imagine what the people would say about me dating Lordin's Prince Zawne?"

He looked at me incredulously. "Zawne was never Lordin's to keep, and Lordin wasn't even of noble birth, and ... she isn't even here anymore! Why are we even talking about her?"

It wasn't the idea of dating Zawne that provoked me the most. It was the feeling that I would be betraying Lordin and the sanctity of their relationship in Geniverd's eyes. Didn't he understand what Lordin meant to people, what she represented? What she'd always represent?

I knew Raad's mind was made up and there was no talking him out of it. So I changed tack. "He worshipped the ground she walked on, Raad. She owned him. I also don't think Zawne will ever love anyone as much."

"None of that matters," he said, waving his right hand dismissively.

"He might not even want me," I said. "How could

any man want to marry me before he knows me? It's absurd."

"It's strategic," Raad said bluntly. The business of taking on more and more Elder duties had hardened Raad, made him deathly serious when he needed to be. "It's for the people and for our family. Mama would have wanted this for you."

"Still, you're asking me to marry someone I hardly know before the coronation, which is in three weeks." I was thinking of Roki now, the dream that had molested me in my sleep. I wanted to see him again, but he was gone. Maybe it was time to move on.

Raad said, "Zawne will love you in time. That's how these things work. He intends to marry you, if you're also interested in him, and he'd like to meet with you as soon as possible. Please don't be selfish, Kaelyn. The Ava-Gaard need you to be strong for them. There's more at play here than love and affection. Your feelings may have to suffer, and I am sorry for this."

"I hate you." I crossed my arms and frowned. "And I also love you, so I can't be mad. I know what could happen if the trade agreement falls flat. More expensive food for Shondur from our farmers, more expensive leather and gems for us. There could even be a currency collapse. It would be chaos. And this is on top of all the other madness going on right now. People are suffering, more and more every day, it seems, and they don't need another reason to suffer."

Raad nodded. "Exactly. This is for the good of Geniverd."

I conceded. I always felt timid and weak before Raad, and this morning was no exception. "Fine," I said.

"I'll go on one date. One! If there is no connection between Zawne and me, then there's nothing I can do."

Raad wiped egg slop off his lips. "I knew you'd understand." He smiled at me. "And I know you'll do what's right, both for your heart and for Gaard. We are the leaders of this society, and we must be role models. We must be moral. We must uphold Decens-Lenitas."

* * *

IT WAS a pretext for us elitists, Decens-Lenitas. It always had been. It was a tool used to keep those on top firmly placed above the rest, to give those beneath something to aspire to. It had good roots, but over time, these roots had been forgotten, corrupted, then rotted into something ugly. I wanted to break that cycle. I wanted to make our moral code moral again. I saw nothing moral in the suffering of millions while a small portion of privileged people dictated the fate of the world from atop their castle ramparts—the ones not burned down yet by the Gurnot the news had titled "the Dragon." And for what? Most of the rich and the clan leaders were so bloated with the wealth of the world, all they could do for entertainment was play their game, fighting for the crown, for more power. They'd forgotten about the rest of the world.

I thought, *If I'm ever to become queen, that's what I'll do. I'll fix it all. I'll fix everything.* It was a reason to make the date with Zawne go well.

Nnati and I were in the flyrarc on our way back to the capital when I told him about it. "The part I can't believe is that Zawne wants to marry me. Me, over all the other girls in Geniverd."

"Why not?" Nnati screwed up his face. "You're gorgeous, well connected, smart, virtuous. Everyone wants to marry you."

I rolled my eyes. Compliments never sounded real coming from Nnati. He was like a second brother to me; he had to be nice. "You're just saying that," I said. "I've struggled with Decens-Lenitas my whole life. I'll never be as respectable as Lordin was. I'll never be as beautiful."

Nnati fixed his eyes on me. It was an angry look, like he wanted to scream at me. "Are you joking? You can't be serious, Kaelyn. Do you even own a mirror? Men stumble just to look at you when we walk in the street. They smash face-first into signs, trip off the sidewalk, crane their necks in their flyrarcs. You're gorgeous, Kaelyn. And as for being humble, being a good servant for the Decens-Lenitas fanatics—well, who cares? Lordin's just a myth now. You're real and virtuous in a meaningful way. Anyone can see that."

I thought, *Roki saw that. He saw it when no one else could.*

"Thank you," I said, feeling silly. Twice already today I had been judged as stubborn for ignoring my looks. I supposed it could have been true. Roki had liked me. Zawne was interested in seeing me. Maybe I wasn't a ghoul after all.

I swallowed my doubts and said to Nnati, "Do you remember the guy I talked about the last time we were at NordHaven? Roki?"

Nnati nodded. "I do."

"Okay. Well, do you think that by dating Prince Zawne, I would be betraying him? It's just ... I know it was three years ago, but I still feel connected to him somehow. Do you think I've waited long enough?"

Nnati stared at me like I was crazy. "Um, yeah," he said. "Kaelyn, you waited for him through your prime teen years. He never showed. You're eighteen now. You're a woman, and the coronation is in three weeks. You did all you could for that boy, and he left you high and dry. Go on the date with Zawne tomorrow and see how you feel. If it's good, move ahead. Move on. You deserve it."

"Thanks," I said, but I didn't feel like I deserved anything. I'd never be able to ignore the fact that I had left Mama with cruel words instead of love before she died. It would gnaw at me for the rest of my life.

"And Gaard deserves it," Nnati went on. "The Ava-Gaard deserve you at your best if you're to be their leader, maybe even their queen."

"Oh, come on," I said. "Now you're the one being silly. The Crown of Crowns will never pick me. Not even if I marry Zawne. Over the years, several eligible heirs have either trained with the Grucken or become Askas. All I have is the foundation."

"That might be all you need," Nnati said, "your kindness and your heart—oh, and the marriage to Zawne. Just remember, Kaelyn, marry in haste and repent at leisure. Keep the kingdom in mind on your date, but also follow your feelings. You'll know what to do."

* * *

I THOUGHT it was crazy that we hadn't even talked first, Zawne and I. Raad and Jaken had been the orchestrators of our little date. They had even decided on my apartment as the venue, which seemed a bit too intimate for my liking. I reasoned that it may have been improper to meet there, but I didn't want to be caught in a public place with Zawne, in case nothing came out of the meetup. The main VondRust Palace buildings were also risky, since too many people could see us. And so there I was, standing at the threshold of my apartment while lightning flashed across the black sky and Zawne stood on the stoop, smiling, rain washing his handsome face. Thunder rolled in an ominous boom as he said, "May I come in?"

"Of course." I gestured him inside. "Get out of the rain. How rude of me."

As I closed the door, I whispered to myself, "Just one date. Be strong, Kaelyn."

I had thought throughout my childhood that Mama and Papa would marry me off to a foreign heir. I had never imagined that when the day came, my brother would have a hand in it. And I never imagined that the man would be Zawne. When one of the Gaard councillors once suggested to me that Zawne and I would be a good fit, I had instantly rejected the theory. I was fifteen, and I thought we were too different. He seemed extroverted and cheerful, whereas I gloried in my solitude. If it had to be a prince, Jaken was much more to my liking. But so much had changed since then. Jaken and Raad had gotten married, and Zawne was now an Aska. I found myself asking: Did Zawne really want me, or was he going along with it just because it was expected of him?

On the plus side, the potential marriage could also be the answer to my anxieties about Roki's invisible pull. I wondered if it was because I thought about him so much that I was starting to dream about him. It was time to cut the cord. All this thinking only made me restless, and Zawne was shaking the water from his hair like a dog. "What was that?" he asked.

"Nothing," I said. "It must have been the wind. I have the fireplace roaring," I told him. "Let's go into the sitting room and get you warm." I gulped, seeing his wet shirt clinging to his muscles. "You're soaked."

I led the way, modest yet alluring in the silk dress I had chosen to wear. A slit in the skirt showed off the sheen of my calves, and I could feel Zawne's eyes fixating on them as he followed me into the sitting room.

"Are you cold?" I asked.

"No, not really. I swam and paddled for weeks through the frigid waters off the coast of Surrvul. I spent half a year with no shelter in the wasteland. It's a hot nightmare during the day but a cold and miserable place by night. I've stopped being cold."

"Oh." I didn't know what to say. I knew the Aska training was tough; people were killed by beasts and ravaged by the elements. I tried to sympathize with Zawne by saying, "Raad never talked about his time out there. You make it sound like a harsh and unforgiving wild."

"It is." Zawne took off his wet shirt and hung it on a peg above the fireplace to dry. His skin was moist, body chiseled like a sculpture of an ancient warrior. He had scars on his ribs and on his chest.

"Are those claw marks?" I asked.

"Huh?" Zawne inspected himself, looked at the scars on his right pec as if he had forgotten they were there. "Yeah," he said, "but I don't know which scar is from

71

which leopard. I battled two of them. Or was it three? It happened so fast. My apologies, but my memory is fuzzy."

I had a vision of Zawne on a hot desert while three leopards circled him, snarling, baring their teeth. "No one thought you would make it," I said, not meaning to be blunt. "But you did. You battled leopards, survived the wild, trained in Lodden, and came back a changed man."

"Only three days ago," he said, with a dazed look in his eye. "It is strange being back." Even though Zawne had been a pampered prince all his life, he seemed somewhat uncomfortable on the dainty sofa in my living room, surrounded by frilly throw pillows. He probably never saw a pillow during his Aska training. It made me appreciate what I had. I understood how fortunate I was, especially compared to the rest of Geniverd.

"I'm curious about one thing," I said. "Why was your first order of business to have a date with me?"

I wanted to cut through the formalities right away, no mucking around. I needed to know Zawne's intentions before we proceeded. He had had a reputation in college, bedding girls by the dozen, playing the field, and never settling down. I was sure Lordin had changed him for the better. But without Lordin, after being pummeled by the Aska training, who was Zawne now? Who was the muscled man bent in front of my fireplace, drying himself by the fire as if still in the wild?

"Can I be honest?" he asked. His eyes were dark and mysterious.

I gulped and nodded.

"Good," he said, "because if we are to be man and wife, we should begin with honesty. I don't know you well, Kaelyn, and you don't know me, but Lordin trusted you, and that makes you my number one choice for a wife. You're also beautiful, one of the most breathtaking women I have ever seen in my life. I caught myself thinking of you on occasion while I labored in Lodden. I would be at the watering hole, wondering to myself, 'Where is Kaelyn right now? I wonder what she's wearing.'"

I blushed. Surely he was lying. He could not have been thinking about me in Lodden!

"There is also the power of our alliance to consider," Zawne said, casting his gaze into the fire and glowering. "I hate the idea of arranged marriages. I really do. I would prefer people marry for love rather than power. Yet it is my responsibility to lead. That is what it means to be an Aska and an heir. I must be a leader of men. With the coronation ceremony only three weeks away, I must cast aside foolish pride and seek a wife. I must at least attempt the throne."

Zawne's honorable words were making me feel guilty. All I wanted was to follow my heart, while he was willing to sacrifice his personal feelings for the good of the people. I found myself thinking, *Of course Lordin loved him. He's selfless. He's a hero.*

My mouth moved without consulting my brain. "If the future of Gaard is at stake, I should also attempt the throne. I have a vision for this kingdom, and I would like to see it realized. It's taken your bravery to rouse my own. Yet all the same, I cannot marry a man if there is no chance of love. I refuse to be an emotional outcast in a loveless marriage."

73

"I understand," he said. Then Zawne smiled for the first time. In the glow of the fire, he was rugged and tanned, sultry, like a romantic lumberjack. And so defined! His muscles were hard and rippled as he moved. I wanted to touch them ... just a little.

"If that's the case," he said, "then I better make you love me tonight. I'm talking about here and now, Kaelyn, for the sake of Geniverd. Just give me the night to make you see that we can be lovers."

I gave him a warm smile and said, "I'd like that," meaning it sincerely. It was kind of what I had planned, anyway—one date to see if love was possible, then shirk my usual timidity and dive headfirst into a relationship for once in my life. He was rugged, handsome, and apparently caring. If Lordin could love Zawne, why couldn't I?

"Do we have a deal?" he asked through his grin.

I nodded. "Yes, Zawne, we have a deal."

"Great!" He rubbed his hands together. "This is going to be a perfect union. Mama and Papa will be so proud."

Zawne stood up, brushed his hands on his pants, and stepped closer to me. He was so tall. I had to tilt my head to look in his eyes. "You'll see," he said. "I will be a great husband. I can protect you, love you, care for you. I can be an ear, a friend, a partner. It will be fantastic. Lordin always used to say ..." He trailed off. He must have seen the subtle crinkle in my brow at the mention of her name. Of course, he would always think fondly of Lordin, but this was our first date. I preferred not to talk about Zawne's true love. I didn't want to picture Lordin rolling in her grave as her fiancé tried to seduce me.

"It's all right," I said, moving away from Zawne and plunking myself down on the sofa, crossing my legs. "You mourn her still, I'm sure. But it's something we can get past. My wise brother told me yesterday how it's all part of life. I never expect you to forget Lordin, but while you're with me, could we at least not talk about her?"

"Of course." He bowed to me. "My apologies, Kaelyn. Please forgive me."

His seriousness made me giggle. When he bowed, his abs were more defined, water droplets weaving through his coarse body hairs. "You are forgiven," I said. But he was more than forgiven. I already liked Zawne a lot. His muscles, his charm, his determined soul. In that moment, I wanted them all to be mine.

* * *

WE WEREN'T EVEN HUNGRY. At least, neither of us admitted to being hungry. I poured two glasses of wine, and we curled closely together on the loveseat in front of the fireplace, listening to the wood crackling, to the rain pelting the rooftop.

"This is a nice place," he said. "It's nice company."

We clinked glasses and drank. "It's a bit lonely here by myself," I admitted. "Sometimes I have bad nights."

Zawne swished wine around in his mouth, swallowed, and said in a husky voice, "Sud Cottage is like a graveyard. So silent and creepy. I feel like a dead man walking through it. Maybe when we get married, we can move in together. We'll have a much bigger place, of course."

"Who said we're getting married?" I asked, gasping and pretending to be offended. "I haven't agreed yet."

Zawne got closer to me, looked straight in my face. "Yes, you have. I can see it in your eyes. I can feel it in your body language. You've already agreed to be my wife."

"Maybe," I said, and immediately averted my eyes. Zawne was intimidating with his lips two inches from mine. Not in a bad way. Mostly because his breath was sweet. His manly scent was invigorating. If we stared into each other's eyes for too long, I feared that I would …

No! I told myself. *Not yet. You're a respectable woman. You are the daughter of Gaard-Ma. Control yourself!*

I took a gulp of wine and began to hum nervously. Zawne chuckled. I half heard him say, "I always suspected you were timid."

But I interjected, blurting out in a panic, "Tell me about Lodden!"

He eased back in the sofa and scrunched his face. "There's not much to tell that you don't already know. Lodden's horrendous. Earthquakes, the most recent volcano, tiny tremors daily. The people who live there are almost completely disconnected from the rest of the world. They refuse to pack up and go someplace else. Instead, their lives revolve around building and rebuilding. They live in squalor, in the mud, in small houses built of volcanic rock. What you may not know is that Lodden is the last place in Geniverd where the people still worship false gods. It's why they stay. They once claimed to be in everlasting servitude to Gomorogha, the fire god who lives in the volcano."

"Wow," I said. "That's news to me. Someone told me

once about how the world used to be very different, about how ..." I trailed off, wondering if Roki was on a date too, huddled in the rain with some cute girl he had found in another noble's mansion.

"You all right?" Zawne asked.

"Yeah, sorry. Tell me more."

"That's pretty much it," he said. "My friends died. I battled leopards and furious temperatures. I allowed my pain to encapsulate me, to numb me and guide me forward. It was how I survived the harshness of it all. In the end, my pain led me to you."

His last words caught my breath in my throat. I choked on my wine. Could Zawne seriously be this romantic to me? I still wasn't convinced. His words were so pretty, so flattering. I had to be sure he wasn't playing me for a fool, trying to put the moves on me and then call the engagement off tomorrow morning. I was all too aware of the ladies' man Zawne had once been. I needed to be certain he was committed to me before I opened my heart, that the loss of Lordin hadn't made Zawne revert into a primal beast.

"You talk the talk," I said once I had finished choking on my wine, "but can you walk the walk?"

Zawne smirked. "Why don't we find out?" And he slithered close to me.

"No," I said, knocking the cocky smirk off his face. "That's not what I mean. What I'm trying to say is that you have been sweet and seductive with me all night, but will you follow through? I need to know your intentions are pure before this goes any further. I need you to give your word to the king and queen that we are to be wed. Only then will I open my heart to you."

I felt childish saying this, but it needed to be said. I could never give myself up so easily.

I had expected Zawne to crumble at my ultimatum, give up and go home or find another girl to be with, who was easier than me. I was shocked when he put his glass of wine down on the table and said, "I'll do you one better."

I didn't have time to react. Zawne had touched his wrist to activate his visin. He swiped this way and that, then directed the holographic screen at himself and made sure I wasn't in the shot. "Get ready to look happy," he said to me. Then he hit the livestream button.

"Hello, citizens of Geniverd. It's Prince Zawne here, streaming live to the entire world, all six continents on all four billion active visins. Some of you may know that I am now an Aska warrior. What you may not know is that I'm engaged to be married."

Zawne paused for dramatic effect while I freaked out next to him, mouth dry, eyes wide, heart palpitating. I couldn't believe it!

"That's right," he said to the projection. "I'm getting married to Kaelyn of Gaard. We will be wed just in time for the coronation."

Then he maneuvered his visin's screen, showing four billion people the dumb expression on my face. He put his arm around me and pulled me close. "Here she is, my bride-to-be. Everyone, meet my new wife."

I guessed I had my answer.

CHAPTER 6

*E*verything happened faster than I could have anticipated. Before Zawne's livestream had ended, my visin was bleeping in my ear. Then Raad was screaming at me, "You got engaged in less than four hours? Did he even bed you yet?" His face was huge on the screen, as if he could open his mouth and swallow me.

"Whoa," I said. "Back off from the camera. You look like an angry giant."

"Sorry." Raad moved back. He was grinning triumphantly. "I'm so proud of you, sister. Finally, with three weeks before the coronation, Gaard has a fighting chance at the crown!"

"Calm down," I said. "I don't think I'm going to be queen."

"I'm just glad you listened to my advice," Raad said. "Queen or not, you agreed to marry Zawne for the sake of the Ava-Gaard and Geniverd as a whole. That really says something about you, Kaelyn. You're growing up."

Then he paused. "Or maybe I'm wrong. Maybe you only agreed because he's smoking hot."

Raad doubled over laughing, and that was when Tissa shoved herself into the frame of his visin. "Kaelyn, congratulations! Now we just have to find a man for Nnati! All three of us are going to reach such fabulous heights, Kaelyn. It will be like nothing we have ever imagined."

"Maybe," I told her. "Oh, and speaking of Nnati, he's calling me. Sorry, guys, got to go."

I ended the call and answered Nnati. Beside me, Zawne was being congratulated by noble after noble. His visin was ringing nonstop.

"You did it!" Nnati screamed. He sat in the darkness of his apartment, wearing pajamas. "How does it feel? What happened? Was he sweet? Was he gentle? Did you like it?"

Beside me, Zawne's laughter was insatiable. "Is that your friend?" Zawne asked. "He's funny! We'll have to invite him for dinner." Then he got up and began to pace the room. His features darkened, and I thought whatever call he had picked up on his visin was business related.

"We just talked," I told Nnati. "It was nice. I think I can do this. I really think I can. I feel like I'm evolving, Nnati. I feel like I've transformed from the bored, unruly girl sulking around NordHaven as a teenager into a woman who has a chance to make change in the world. I feel like I'm truly becoming a woman for our people."

"I'm happy for you, Kaelyn. This is great. Uh ... but your picture is all over the news. It's not a good one either. You look surprised and a little scared. They are playing Zawne's live feed on a loop. Questions are already being raised, comparisons between you and a certain dead fiancée. Brace yourself."

"I will," I said. I had already thought this might happen. The people still loved Lordin, and to some, I would seem like a shoddy replacement.

"Anyway." Nnati eased back into the shadows of his room and yawned. "I should go to bed. I'm sure you're not done answering calls. I'm happy for you. I hope you made the right decision."

I glanced at Zawne, pacing before the fireplace and yammering into his visin.

I said to Nnati, "I hope so too."

* * *

I LET Zawne sleep in my bed. It felt right, and it was worth every second. I felt complete when I nestled into his arms and drifted to sleep. I felt content.

And this was where things took a strange turn. I was sinking into slumber, head full of fluff, body heavy, when everything changed. My limbs started to tingle, but I couldn't open my eyes to look. I couldn't move a single muscle. I felt electrified, fuzzy with little vibrations like a thousand electric raindrops.

Then I was floating out of my body. I could see again—see myself, Zawne snoring gently beside me. I passed right through my ceiling and caught a glimpse of the capital, with all its bright lights and the flyrarcs zipping between skyscrapers. Still I ascended, pulled upward by some supreme force into the clouds, into the atmosphere. I could see the whole continent of Gaard like a pancake on the water. But I rose higher still. I rocketed into space at a thousand miles a second, through plumes of pink and purple space dust, galaxies of a billion twinkling stars. I zoomed through the cosmos faster and faster until it all became a blur and ...

I was in a void. My soul had been sucked right through the endlessness of space and into a place of nothingness. The floor was white and solid, but it looked like mist. All around me was endless and blank, yet above flowed a sky of peach clouds. It was tranquil and oddly euphoric. I wasn't even panicked. In the back of my head, I thought, *This is a dream ... yet it's not.*

"Queen Kaelyn, so nice of you to come."

"Who said that?" I whirled around. There was no one there.

"I did," the voice said. It seemed to boom from all around me. "You can call me Riedel."

Then another voice, a woman's, soft and sublime. "And you can call me Hanchell."

I gawked in every direction, but no one was there. "Where are you?" I said. "I can't see anyone."

"Settle down," Riedel said with great authority in his voice. "Be still and concentrate. You won't be able to see us with your human eyes. You'll have to use your other senses."

"Okay ..."

I closed my eyes and strained every muscle in my body, but nothing happened. Then I focused on listening. I listened, and when I did, I could hear the leagues of silence like subtle vibrations. It occurred to me my senses were enhanced in this spectral void. I took a deep breath and felt the air beyond my fingers. Every particle spoke to me, showed its existence. When I opened my eyes again, the air before me was shimmering. There were two shapes of light and motion. They were constructs of sound and spectral energy. Riedel was on the left—I could smell his manly, cedarwood scent—and Hanchell was on the right. I could also smell Hanchell's rosy odor, sweet and relaxing. Both were distinct to me now that I had focused my mind.

"Good," Riedel said.

"Very good," Hanchell echoed. "You can see that we are here, but you cannot see our true forms. No human can see the true forms of the Crown of Crowns. Only the Min can do that."

"I ...Who? What? Huh?" I blinked, confused and thrown off guard. The Crown of Crowns was a bird. That was what Papa had always told me. And what was a Min? Where in the world was I?

"It's understandable," Hanchell said in her delicate voice. "Humans are often shocked and awed by this place. It's called Shiol, by the way."

"It's like another dimension?"

"Kind of," Riedel said. "It's more of a spirit dimension. We are spirits, as are the Min. Only the Min may travel freely between spirit realm and human realm."

I kept blinking. I had no idea what Riedel was talking about. It was so strange watching their intangible shapes of light wriggle and sparkle before me.

"This is where we choreograph events in Geniverd and the other civilizations," Hanchell explained. "Right now you are in a protective bubble. The other spirits can't interact with you unless we allow it. Don't be afraid."

"I'm not," I said, which was strange, because I should have been terrified.

"Good," Riedel said. "There is no time for fear. We

83

have brought you here for a very important reason, Kaelyn. It is our practice to inform the new kings and queens of Geniverd of their positions before the coronation."

"Wait." I pinched the bridge of my nose, trying to digest all this information. "You're telling me Zawne and I will be king and queen? What about the bird Papa used to tell me about? If you are the Crown of Crowns ..."

"Yes," Hanchell said, answering my thought. "We take turns being the bird. It was Riedel last time, so I will be the bird in three weeks."

Riedel groaned. I could tell from his shifting light pattern that he was disgruntled. "I like being the bird," he said. "But fine, you can do it this time."

"This is all really crazy," I said. "No one is going to believe this!"

"We should hope not," both spirits said at once.

Then Hanchell said, "Kaelyn, you are forbidden to tell anyone about Shiol or our existence. We refer to this as the Great Secret. If you reveal the Great Secret to anyone, you and whoever you tell will die."

"Oh ..." My heart fell, but I supposed it made sense. People couldn't know there were spirits in an ethereal realm, pulling the strings down on Geniverd.

"It does make sense," Riedel said. "And yes, we can read your thoughts. But none of that matters. What matters, Kaelyn, is that we have chosen you and Zawne to be the next rulers. You two have a lot of work to do together. We need strong humans to lead Geniverd. Out of all the eligible minds and hearts we have searched, yours were the best. We were thrilled last night when your engagement was announced. We scanned your worthiness and couldn't believe it—leagues above the rest!"

I was more stunned by this revelation than by any of the supernatural stuff. "How is that possible?" I asked.

"We do not make mistakes, human," Hanchell said, very sweetly. "Your heart is the one we need."

"And Zawne's," Riedel added.

I thought Hanchell's light form smiled as she said, "But mostly yours. The truth is, Kaelyn, you are a strong and capable woman. We feel comfortable with the fate of Geniverd in your small human hands. We will help you, of course. You will need to see us five nights a week during your reign as queen, to be made aware of current events. This will exhaust you. Visiting Shiol takes a toll on the human body, but you will learn to cope."

"First you must decide if you want to be queen," Riedel said. "We shouldn't talk too much of your duties until you've decided to take the throne with Zawne by your side. But you must make the decision by tomorrow night."

"Why is it my decision to make?" I asked. "Why isn't Zawne here too?"

"It's a mercy," Hanchell said. "You see, if you say no, we have to kill you in a tragic and painful way. No humans aside from the Geniverd rulers may know the Great Secret. This way, should you not feel up to the task, only you must die. You'll be sparing Zawne's life."

"And if Zawne refuses the job?" I asked. "This seems utterly biased!"

"We're sure he won't," Riedel said. "He is a more basic human than you are. Your heart is complicated, like Lordin's was. We thought she would accept the job, but she didn't. We hope you will be different."

It hit me like a slap across the face. Lordin had been killed because she'd turned down the role as queen. But why? What would cause her to renounce the throne and be willingly butchered?

"It's true," Hanchell said sadly. She had read my thoughts. "Lordin turned down the offer to become queen. She thought Zawne didn't have what it would take to be ruler. Sad, really, the way we had to kill her."

"She's a Min now," Riedel told me. "Min are spirits that can move between our worlds. When someone who knows the Great Secret dies, they become a Min and work for us. This means we give them tasks, and then they are free to roam habitable planets, like Geniverd, and even inhabit another human's body. The only rule is that a Min may not influence people's ideas of their dead self, or ever reveal the Great Secret. If they do, they die an irreversible death."

I had so many questions, so many feelings. Two omnipotent beings were flipping my perspective of the world on its head. I stuttered, trying to ask everything at once. "So that means ... If I were a ... Does anyone else ...? What about my ...? Do you think ...?"

Hanchell laughed. "Calm, Kaelyn. All these questions will be answered in time. Firstly, yes, we do believe Zawne has what it takes to be king. And secondly, we don't seek overtly virtuous people. We instead search for pure and incorruptible hearts, like yours."

"Oh." That made me feel better. Maybe I wasn't as virtuous as Lordin was, but my intentions were certainly pure. I was more unnerved about Zawne discovering the reason for Lordin's death. I wondered how he would react, if he would turn on me or even turn on himself. I worried that he would hate Lordin for not having believed in him.

"I have another question," I said.

But Riedel cut me off before I could ask it. "Yes, your mother is at peace. But no, we cannot tell you anything more than that. The ultimate knowledge of what happens after death could alter your purpose in life."

"All right," I said. It was enough just to know Mama was at peace. "How will I get back to this place tomorrow night to give you my decision?"

Riedel said, "Spell Shiol over your heart as you lie in bed. Your ethereal self will be pulled into our mirror dimension. For now, when you awaken, you are going to hear glass shattering. Zawne will then come into the room with blood on his finger. The current king and queen will have invited you both for lunch at one p.m."

"This will prove to you that we are real," Hanchell said in her soft voice. "Now go to sleep, Queen Kaelyn. Tomorrow will be a hard day for you."

With that, the light of Hanchell and Riedel faded. The clouds above churned, and my vision got fuzzy. Everything went black.

* * *

I woke to the sound of shattering glass. My eyes burst open and I sat upright, the memory of my time in Shiol flooding my mind. "Zawne?" I called out. "Zawne, are you all right?"

He appeared in the doorway, blood trickling down

his finger. "Sorry," he said. "I cut myself on a wineglass. I'm trying not to get blood on my suit."

He looked good despite the blood, and it made me smile. I was glad we had spent the night together. Still, I was exhausted. My body was heavy, and there was an itchy burning in my eyes.

"You look beat," Zawne said, "which is weird, because you slept in quite late. It's almost noon. The only people I've ever seen sleep so late are my parents."

I wanted to say, *Because they've been visiting Shiol throughout their reign! They were being given orders on how to run the kingdom by the Crown of Crowns!* Instead, I said, "Do we have any plans today?"

"Yes," Zawne said, a little surprised. He was bandaging his finger with a roll of gauze. "How did you know? We have a lunch date with the king and queen in an hour. We're supposed to be there at one o'clock. I told them you were still asleep, and they both grinned at each other like they were in on some personal joke."

They know, I thought. *The same thing happened to them forty years ago.* "Cancel it," I said. "Your parents will understand, trust me. I have a lot of thinking to do."

And that was exactly how I proceeded to spend my day. Zawne didn't understand, and I didn't expect him to. Before he left my apartment, I probed him a bit. "Would you make a good king? ... What do you think of the current model of Decens-Lenitas? ... Would you allow me to change the world for the better? ... Could we reform the system of monarchy to better benefit the people, spreading the wealth throughout the entire population? ... Would you be up for promoting some of the older forms of tradition and society, bringing purpose back to the world and taking some of the overwhelming power away from the royal bloodlines?"

All his answers came back positive. "Anything you want, my love." His eagerness to help with my vision for Geniverd made me confident I could trust him as an ally. I was sure I would make a decision by the end of the day. I was getting more and more amped up at the thought of a new Geniverd, shaking the system to its very core!

I almost called Nnati to tell him the news, then remembered what the Crown of Crowns had said: *No humans aside from the Geniverd rulers may know the Great Secret.*

I couldn't risk telling anyone. I sat curled on my sofa and deliberated alone. Could Lordin really have thought Zawne so worthless? The thought made me bitter toward her. How could she have thrown away her life and jeopardized Zawne's chance at the throne? He had been so in love with her. Was Lordin not the woman she had seemed to be?

I forwarded all my calls from GMAF to Nnati, adding an apologetic message and informing him that we needed to double the staff immediately, but I refrained from telling him why. If I was to become queen in three weeks, the foundation would need a new boss. Someone would have to look after things while I busied myself with my royal duties and spent my nights in Shiol.

As I ate an early dinner and spun these ideas around in my head, that was when it hit me. Lordin had transferred her charitable works to me the day before she refused the Crown of Crowns. She had planned it all out. She had wanted her important work to go on but didn't want to take on the responsibility of queen, because she had thought her future husband was unfit. Instead, Lordin had entrusted me to look after things, and now I was in the same position, only I was going to make Zawne my king.

Lordin must have been blind. Zawne was the perfect man for the job. As I lay down for the night and spelled Shiol over my heart, I knew exactly what I was going to tell the Crown of Crowns.

* * *

"HELLO, QUEEN KAELYN," Riedel's powerful voice boomed. "We sense you have made your decision."

"I only have one question," I said. I was apprehensive. I needed to hear that the Crown of Crowns believed in me as much as I believed in Zawne. "How do you know I will be a good queen?"

"It won't be hard," Hanchell said. "We do most of the heavy lifting. Before we intervened hundreds of years ago in the choosing of Geniverd's rulers, men warred with each other, were killed constantly by infectious diseases, ravaged the countryside with pestilence, and even acted out genocides. They prayed to false gods and sacrificed children. It was chaos. Then we stepped in. Now everything is fine. We foresee immediate events and plan accordingly. You, Kaelyn, will be our commander in the physical world. You are here to heed our warnings and act accordingly. You are our adjudicator."

I pursed my lips and narrowed my eyes at the insubstantial light masses. "Which makes you the bosses?"

"Yes and no," Riedel said. "You can say no to us …"

"But we wouldn't recommend it," Hanchell finished.

"Okay." I took a deep breath. I had already made my decision. The needs of Geniverd were too great for me to ignore the call to the throne. Zawne was a good man and would rise to the occasion. We would do away with the corruption, the mass boredom, the uselessness of the strife. I couldn't wait to ruffle some feathers among the clan leaders. Even if Zawne wasn't as keen as I was for change, it didn't matter. I needed to fix the class system before our world regressed into peasants and kings, like in the ancient days. I needed to fix the dwindling middle class and bring peace to the agitated sections of the world, like on restive Nurlie Island.

Also, being queen next to Zawne, waking up in a palace every morning ... it couldn't be that bad.

"I agree," I said, back straight, eyes firm. "I will be the queen."

"Excellent!" Hanchell cried. If I hadn't known better, I'd have said she was clapping.

"The next step is to inform Zawne of your decision," Riedel said. "Do it tomorrow, when you wake up. We can bring you both back the next night for a debriefing. We don't want you coming back too often, Kaelyn. You will be too exhausted to complete your duties. Rest for tomorrow, tell Zawne, then come back the next night."

I nodded. "Got it, boss."

Hanchell tittered. "You don't have to call us that. Oh, and before you leave, there is a visitor for you. It looks like you have some friends in the spirit realm."

"Who?" I asked. "Is it Mama? Is it Lordin?"

But Hanchell and Riedel had vanished. Everything was still for about three seconds. Then I sensed a different scent, a scent I knew very well. My head lifted, my chin sticking out. My eyes searched as I spun. It was a man who answered me finally, his shape forming in the distance of the vast, clouded plain.

"Kaelyn." The voice was low as it danced my name.

I choked, overwhelmed with emotion. And then my tears brimmed over. "Roki?"

CHAPTER 7

e stared at each other for over a minute, unblinking, unflinching, utterly mute. I studied his hair, the soft handsomeness of his face, his muscular frame. Roki hadn't changed that much in three years. He was the same man I had adored before the world fell apart, back when I was an ignorant little girl.

What was he doing in Shiol?

Roki came to me, floating across the ground like a spirit. He took my hands in his and said, "I've missed you. I was looking for you just now. I saw your body lying in your bed, but you weren't in it. Your body was empty. I flew directly here and saw that the Crown of Crowns was speaking with someone. I couldn't see you inside their bubble, but I knew it was you. I signaled to them that I wished to meet with you. I told them we used to be friends."

"You were in my bedchamber?" I said, a little scandalized. "You were watching me as I slept?"

"Yes …" He made a face, probably realizing how creepy that sounded. "But it's not weird. I do it all the time. You see, I'm not a human, Kaelyn. I'm a Min."

I gaped at Roki, speechless. I would have torn away from him, but I liked the warmth of his hands over mine. I moved my mouth, but no sound came out. How could Roki be a Min? All our time together, and he was a spirit? I had given my heart away to a spirit!

"It's tough," Roki said with a laugh. "I get it, I do. I've been alive for a long time, and I have never once told a human being what I truly am. If I let the information slip, I would suffer a final death, and the person I told would be killed. I have always expected this kind of reaction. It's great seeing it from you."

"I'm funny to you now?" I had started crying. I was mad that he was here, mad that he had lied to me about being a spirit, mad that I loved the feeling of his hands enfolding mine.

"No," he said, becoming serious. "I'm sorry. You're not funny to me. You're adorable and radiant, even now when you're crying." Roki delicately wiped the tears from my cheeks. He had always been a gentleman. "It's just, I use laughter as a medicine, you know? It's why I always jested with you, always tried to make you laugh. It felt appropriate now, in this strange moment, you here with me in the spirit realm. I just want to make things right."

"Okay …" I sniveled, trying to hold back my tears. It was hard to stay mad at Roki. "But why now?" I said. "Why didn't you make things right before, when I needed you the most, when I was at my lowest low? If you're a spirit, you could have visited me anytime—"

"And I did!" Roki said, suddenly enveloping me in

his arms. He said in my ear, "I've visited you every night since the fateful day your mama died. I sat on your bed and watched you. I walked with you through the quiet halls of NordHaven. Then I followed you to the capital. Sometimes I watched you at work. I wept tears of joy when I saw how well you were doing with the foundation. You've helped so many people climb out of poverty. You've given so many young children meaning and a future. You even helped to save all those turtles and that coral reef."

"Then why didn't you reveal yourself to me?" I demanded. My face was pressed against his chest, and I clung to his shirt for dear life, as though he might evaporate. "I could have used a friend like you. I've spent so much time wondering where you went. You could have made it easier for me!"

"I wanted to," Roki said, "but in those first days, I felt your heart and heard your thoughts. You didn't want to talk to me. You blamed me in part for the way it had ended between you and your mama. You had chosen me over your own family, and then death came like a wrecking ball to demolish your emotions. It would have been wrong of me to go against your wishes."

I tore away from him, feeling dumb for crying like a child. "You could have tried," I said, hardening my expression. "It would have been nice knowing that you did everything within your power to see me again. Instead, you abandoned me. You left me alone."

Roki pouted, stepped back, and hung his head. "I stayed by your side. I followed you into your dreams. I let my scent linger in your room. I know it feels like I deserted you, but I didn't. I never lost my feelings. I never forgot about you. Instead, I let you grieve. I gave

95

you the space I thought you needed. I didn't want to ruin your life by getting you mixed up with a Min."

"I wouldn't have cared if you were a space alien!" I launched myself forward, pulled Roki's arms around me, and hugged him fiercely. "But I forgive you. I understand now you were doing what you thought was right. It's the reason I was so crazy about you, because your soul is pure." Then I laughed. "I guess it has to be. All you have is a soul!"

Roki smiled and pushed me gently away, looked down into my eyes. I knew right then I would believe anything he said. His eyes sparkled with sincerity. "I know you've changed," he said. "You're not the same naive girl who followed me, laughing, through the fake market. You've gotten stronger over these last three years. You've become wise and selfless. You've become a woman. You've also gotten engaged, so I know we can't be together like we used to be ..."

"Not necessarily," I said, hating myself as I said it, as I began to scheme in my brain. "It's true, I am engaged to Zawne. We are set to be king and queen in three weeks. It doesn't mean I can't have you for a friend. It would mean a lot to have you around. You know, giving me moral support, telling me jokes, letting me confide in you. It will be frustrating not being able to talk about Shiol with any of my human friends."

Roki brightened. He had an air of mischief about him, the same excitable energy I remembered. "I would agree to that!" he said. And right then I knew my life was about to change. Nothing could be simple anymore. Roki was back. This time, I knew he was back for good.

* * *

ROKI WAS RUBBING his hands together. "Let's start right now," he said. "Let's forget all the other stuff and start over. How can I be of service, my queen? What do you want to know about Shiol or about Min? I'll answer anything."

I thought about it for a second, stroking my chin. Then I said, "Tell me everything."

Roki was biting his lip, trying to contain his excitement. I now believed everything he had told me, about how he had watched over me, about how he had only wanted what was best for me. It made me think of him as my watcher, as my guardian. I wasn't mad anymore.

Roki said, "I'll start with where we are: Shiol." He waved his arms like a magician, and the emptiness of the void rippled and changed. I suddenly saw in the distance a land unlike any on Geniverd. There were tower spires of gold, cities nestled in the clouds, odd gaseous auras moving freely throughout the mystical empire, humans flying as if they were birds. It looked peaceful and divine, the radiant sun shining over the otherworldly civilization.

"Wow ..." I had no other words.

"It's just a fragment," Roki said, and waved his hand. The vision faded, and we were back in the endless void. "Where we are now is like a meeting hall the Crown of Crowns uses to parley with various monarchs. But that, what I just showed you, is the space Min call home when they aren't out on missions or goofing around in other realms."

"There were so many," I said. "How can there be so

many? Geniverd only has four billion people. And what were those weird electric auras I saw floating around?"

Roki laughed. He hunkered down on the ground and smiled up at me. "One thing at a time, Kaelyn. The universe is bigger than you think. There are worlds, dimensions, planets. There is more than just human life, and the Crown of Crowns presides over it all. They use Min as their servants of order. We keep the scales balanced in these different worlds. We all have assignments, and for the past five hundred years, I have been assigned to Geniverd. It was where I was born, died, and became a Min. But that's a story for another day."

My jaw had hit the floor some time ago. I felt woozy, overwhelmed by all the information. I kept picturing the Shiol city, the magnificent structures unlike anything I'd ever seen. Who had built such a place? How long had these spirits been pulling the universe's infinite strings? Could Geniverd evolve into such a futuristic place one day?

"As for the auras," Roki said with a smile, "those are Min without bodies. Like I said, we're just spirits. Most Min don't have a special upbringing. Some are created in Shiol, some on other planets, and some are born to other Min. Yet each Min has the ability to possess a life-form within his or her zone of assignment. In simple terms, we take over bodies and use them to do our jobs. We need them to infiltrate governments, become authority figures, influence the masses to keep civiliza-tion from imploding. In truth, most of the successful people on Geniverd are Min: the athletes, celebrities, serial killers, businesspeople. There are no restrictions on what we can do, and some Min have a mean streak.

Some of the worst Min like to murder because they enjoy the way it feels."

I was appalled. "And the host doesn't know what's going on, that they're being used as a tool for evil?"

"No," Roki said. "And yes, it sickens me too. Yet this is the way of the universe. The host's mind cannot know what's going on. They have no idea they're being controlled by a Min. The Min quashes fear, trepidation, anxiety. The Min makes them almost superhuman."

Then Roki chuckled. "But it's not all bad. We also use humans for fun. For example, when I inhabit the body of a human, I can feel despair, joy, love, anger, euphoria, and physical pain. The human senses become heightened. Oh, and the human still lives inside their body. They just take a back seat, like a passenger in the back of their mind." He saw my skeptical expression and assured me, "I never kill them. That would be cruel."

Then he went on, saying, "Sound, sight, hearing, smell." He gave me a look. "Touch. These sensations all become enhanced. Colors are brighter. Smells are more pungent. I find myself pausing for five minutes every time I pass a bakery. But touch is the big one. I can feel the air like it's water. I can feel the blood flowing underneath my human skin. And women ... don't get me started. When we hug, it's like we're—"

"Stop," I said. "I don't want to hear about the women you've been ... hugging over the past five hundred years."

"Sorry." Roki shifted awkwardly. "In truth, that was just physical stuff. I prefer deeply emotional connections. And in terms of minds, I have never interacted with a mind like yours. Never. You don't accept some-

CLARA LOVEMAN

thing without questioning it first, even if it sounds like the greatest opportunity in the world. You genuinely care about the consequences and everyone's welfare. Those other women were just bodies. You are both."

"Oh," I said, but stopped it there. I didn't want to start flirting. Roki and I had only become friends again five minutes ago, and I already felt like I was betraying Zawne. I tried to change the subject. "How have you kept your body for so long? What's the person on the inside doing? I know you said they don't know they've been possessed, but what's going on with them?"

"Ah," Roki said, nodding. "This is where things get complicated. See, a Min can possess a body either for a brief period or for the full course of the body's life. It depends on the assignment. My supersecret mission means that I am in this body for the next eighty years at minimum. The man inside is kind of dormant, at rest."

"That's like murder," I said. "It's like a mental murder."

"The man was dying when I possessed him," Roki said. "He had been infected by a pathogen and would have been dead within the hour. If anything, I saved him."

"Oh." Again Roki had twisted my judgment around and made me feel stupid. He hadn't killed the man. He had saved him. The man was getting to live it up with a Min for eighty years. I was more concerned that someone had been about to die because of a pathogen. I'd thought we were beyond such casualties. If there was one good thing about our society, it was that our medicine was top of the line.

"You're not stupid," Roki said. "And yes, I can read your thoughts. Sorry about that. I'll try not to. But

100

really, you're not dumb. You're worried and kind-hearted. I can already see that your core values haven't changed in three years. You're the same girl I fell for. It's no wonder the Crown of Crowns picked you over the other heirs. I've eavesdropped on their thoughts and can tell you this. Half of them are evil, a quarter are hubristic, and a quarter only want the throne because it's expected of them. Ninety-nine percent are just bored and looking for something to do. They think ascending the throne will give their restless lives some entertainment. You know how they are. These people have so much wealth and influence that life is border-line meaningless. But you, Kaelyn, you are driven by love and social justice. You are more righteous than them all."

"Thanks," I said. It was no use arguing anymore. I had heard this same thing from a dozen people in the last week. I was just going to shut up and start accepting that yes, perhaps I was fit to be queen.

"Speaking of queens," Roki said, "we'd better get you to sleep. You need to be well rested for tomorrow. You've got a busy day ahead of you, I'm sure."

"But I want to know more," I cried. "I'm not ready to go! Tell me more, Roki. Please."

"Fine," he conceded. "One more question. Then you need to get some rest."

I thought long and hard, mostly because I was distracted by Roki's soft lips curled into a smile. Then it came to me.

"Mama," I said. "Please, Roki, tell me who poisoned Mama."

Roki's face drained of color. He took one of my hands in his and said, "I'm sorry, I don't know. Min

101

CLARA LOVEMAN

don't pay too much attention to murders in Geniverd. I
asked around, but no one could tell me. And I was with
you when it happened."

Now I was sad. I didn't want to think about Mama's
suffering because of some rival leader's wrath. It made
me want to unleash a wrath of my own!

"You're tough in your thoughts," Roki said, teasing
me like old times. "Now get some sleep, Kaelyn. We will
talk more later."

"When?"

Roki flashed his perfectly white teeth. "When you
wake up." He waved his hand in front of me, hypno-
tizing me deep into a slumber.

* * *

IT FELT like I had slept for a whole week. I dozed
dreamlessly in a black nothing. When I finally awoke, it
was to the sight of Roki's bright eyes blinking at me.

"Good afternoon," he said softly.

Roki was kneeling at my bedside. I groggily reached
up and caressed his face.

"Afternoon?" I immediately took my hand back. I
was in the real world again. I couldn't touch Roki
without betraying Zawne. I had to keep this as a friendship, a very close friendship.

"Yes," he said. "It's already noon. And don't stress
about it. We've done nothing inappropriate."

Before I could respond, Roki vanished into thin air.
At the exact same moment, Zawne walked into my
room.

"Sorry to barge in like this," he said, "but I've been

102

calling you on your visin all morning. Are you all right?"

"Yes," I said, finding it hard to sit up straight. I was incredibly tired from my time in Shiol. "I must have slept in again. All the excitement has got me fatigued."

"That's understandable," he said. Zawne crossed my bedroom in four brisk steps, leaned over, and planted a kiss on my lips. He pulled back just enough to look in my eyes. "I've been missing that."

I needed more. The talk with Roki, the fact I was to be married—it had a fire burning inside me. "Again," I said, then grasped the nape of Zawne's neck and pulled him close. Our lips touched, then our warm tongues swished and pressed and tugged; I was lost in it. I knew then that Zawne and I could rule the world.

"That was unexpected," Zawne said as he sat on the edge of my bed, panting. "You're fiery for such a sleepy woman."

"I guess I needed the affection," I said, which was true.

Zawne gave me a smile. "You'll always have mine."

I wondered if that was true. Would we always be so close and loving? I felt ashamed all over again for allowing Roki back into my life.

Zawne said, "I'm going to have a quick shower, my love," and he went into the bathroom. The second he closed the door, Roki was right back at my bedside, and I was lost in his eyes and his wild hair, his cut jaw. I was pulled between two worlds!

"How did you do that?" I asked, trying to keep my voice low.

Roki grinned, devilish in the way he silently teased me. "Every Min has heightened senses and extrasensory powers. I can detect moods, changes in temperature, slight fluctuations in air molecules. It means I can sense when someone is coming. I can even sense what they are going to do. It's how I knew Raad was about to barge into your room with bad news that day. It was why I left, to let you and your brother mourn together."

"Wow," I said. "That's amazing. It must be so great to be a Min. No wonder Lordin gave up her human form."

"That's not all," Roki said. "We each have one special ability. It comes with the package when you're transformed. Mine is that I can mask presences. For example, I could mask my presence, and you would forget I was here. I can mask smells, feelings, even entire ideas. It's incredible."

I gawked at Roki. "All these you can do ... and you choose to visit me."

"You've sold yourself short for too long," Roki told me. "I'm happy to see you're coming into your own. You're turning into a splendid woman, Kaelyn. I'm eager to see what the next forty years of your rule have in store."

I opened my mouth to speak, but the bathroom door was opening. Roki vanished and out came Zawne, naked but for the towel wrapped around his waist. He was wet, bearded, and delicious. I suddenly felt like a very bad person, like a little girl and not at all like a queen. I motioned to him. "Come here. Sit close to me."

Zawne smirked. "I thought you might say that."

As he sauntered over to me, I remembered there was something important to tell him. My strange new obsession with his body would have to wait.

He sat on the bed, stretched one arm over me, and said, "So, now what?"

"Now we have to talk." It made me feel bad that his expression went slack. Zawne had had something else on his mind. The silly man would have to wait.

He sat up straight, suddenly a bit edgy. "Talk about what?"

I remembered what the Crown of Crowns had said about Zawne being a simpler person than me. There was no way he would deny the offer to be king. So I spat it out.

"Zawne, you and I are the chosen ones. We're going to be king and queen."

His expression remained unchanged. His eyes were locked on mine, but there was no emotion. Was this part of his Aska training, to be as cold as ice when he needed to be?

"Could you repeat that?"

"We're chosen," I said. "We are *the* chosen. The Crown of Crowns came to me—well, sucked me into their dimension. I know the Crown of Crowns is a bird, and they are a bird—well, they take turns. Anyway, they told me we would be selected as the next king and queen."

I told him everything from beginning to end, every rule and every crazy new universal truth I had learned over the past forty-eight hours. I even snuck in some of the stuff Roki had told me. When all was said and done, I sat panting on the bed, and Zawne stood by the window, the afternoon light slashing across his rock-hard abs.

"I always had a feeling," he said distantly, as if talking to himself. "I always knew there was something strange about my parents. They slept so often, and always like they were dead or in comas. They even had rules about not being disturbed. Whenever I woke with a nightmare, I just crawled into bed with my brother."

"So …" I gulped. This was the moment of truth. "So, do you agree to rule Geniverd with me?"

Zawne stared seriously out the window. It was one of the things that was totally in contrast to Roki. Where Roki was a charismatic jokester, Zawne could be stiff and severe. Yet it was one of the reasons I was so attracted to him.

"I agree," he said. "I agree in the name of Shondur and in the name of Geniverd, for my parents and for the people." Zawne turned to me, a smile finally breaking through. "If I had said no, would you have been killed?"

"Yes. I was quite nervous. We both would have been killed."

"Not to worry," Zawne said, swooping across the room to sit with me on the bed. "We will survive, prosper, and rule with compassion and courage. We will face this trial together as man and wife. When do we go to Shiol?"

In that moment, I was proud to be Zawne's fiancée. I wondered if Roki was watching me. I wondered if he was there in the room, listening to my thoughts. Was Roki jealous?

* * *

THE FOLLOWING EVENING, as Zawne and I lay down to sleep after a busy day of wedding planning—our wedding was to be held the day before the coronation— we both spelled Shiol over our hearts. Seconds later we were being zipped through the eternal cosmos.

"What a ride!" Zawne said as we materialized into the Crown of Crowns' bubble. "The gaseous bursts of space, the huge planets, the interdimensional tear into a pocket of the universe. I could get used to that!"

"I already am," I said, laughing. "It's amazing how fast the human brain adjusts to a new experience. This was my third time, and it didn't even faze me."

"And it never will again," came Riedel's voice. I had to concentrate and reach out with my senses to see his twinkling form standing beside Hanchell.

"I can't believe it," Zawne said. "You are built of light. This is amazing."

I supposed Zawne didn't need to focus to see Riedel and Hanchell. He was an Aska. His training would never leave him. Still, it made me feel inferior. Zawne was already better at this than I was.

"I see you've made your decision together," Hanchell said. She sounded pleased.

"Yes." Zawne took a bold step forward. "I agree to your proposal, Crown of Crowns. I agree to become king of Geniverd."

"Good for you," Riedel said. His voice was an earthy boom, perhaps to try to put Zawne in his human place. "But there are things we must go over before we proceed. This will be our last meeting before the coronation, so you must understand all the rules before you leave here today."

"Got it." Zawne folded his hands and stepped back. I touched his arm, trying to show some solidarity between us, but Zawne was at attention, as if he were listening to his squad leader.

"The first rule is that you must come here to Shiol five nights a week," Riedel said. "We suggest you take shifts, split up your time here. That way one of you is not constantly tired."

"When you come to Shiol," Hanchell said, "you will be given our recommendations on how to adjudicate the following day's council meetings. You will be ruling over disputes and issues between two or more clans. These are important, and we highly suggest that you adhere to our recommendations."

"But we don't have to?" I asked.

"No," Hanchell said. "You don't have to, but no one in hundreds of years has ever gone against us. We suggest that if you wish to make the business of governing four billion people on six continents easier, you listen to what we say."

I nodded, but Zawne wasn't convinced. "Where do you get the information for your recommendations?" he asked. "How do you decide?"

"Irrelevant," Riedel boomed. His voice shook the void with authority. It left no room for debate.

"And you cannot discuss our findings with anyone," he continued. "Not with the ex-queen or ex-king. Not even with the dead! If you do, you and every person you've revealed any part of the Great Secret to will be killed brutally and painfully within the hour."

That was enough to shut Zawne up. He stood straight and didn't say a word.

"Should you need to speak with us urgently," Hanchell said, "you may take a power nap. Drift quickly here, ask for what you need, then return to Geniverd. This will wear you out, so please don't do it too often."

Good, I thought. *If I get overwhelmed, I have a place to go.* However, I could always ask Roki for his opinion. It was going to be nice having a Min at my disposal while I was queen.

"Our recommendations will also come with physical evidence for your human eyes," Riedel told us. "You may read through reports, flick through video, and listen to audio recordings here in Shiol. Then you must return to sleep and make your judgments the following day. This will be a stressful process. Ready yourselves over the coming weeks."

"One more thing," Hanchell said. She was audibly giddy. "Whose head would you like me to land on at the coronation? I'm so excited!"

Zawne and I exchanged a glance. "I'm okay with it being Zawne," I said, smiling at him.

For once in the meeting, he smiled back. "Thank you, my queen. I appreciate it."

"It's settled!" Hanchell said. Her blob of light was agitated, sparking with excitement. "I will land on Zawne's head in two weeks' time. Now go to sleep, humans. You have a wedding and a kingdom to plan. We will see you soon."

Hanchell and Riedel fizzled out, leaving Zawne and me alone in the endless vacuum of the bubble. I kept thinking of the marvelous city just beyond the illusion. I wondered if Roki could take me there one day.

"Are you ready?" I asked Zawne.

He nodded. "We can do this, Kaelyn. We can rule together with the help of these beings."

Then he took my hand and kissed it lightly. Zawne's unexpected romantic side was always a treat, and it made me giggle. "I'll see you in the morning."

We closed our eyes and entered the blackness.

CHAPTER 8

It was two weeks of mayhem. Dress shopping with Tissa, planning the ceremony with Zawne and his royal parents, sorting out the Ava-Gaard guest list with Raad, and spending countless hours gossiping with Nnati. The toughest part was keeping my mouth shut about Shiol and the secret Min living among us. I wanted to tell someone so badly! This was where Roki came in handy; he was always around, leaving a trace of his scent like a signature to let me know he was watching. We'd talk sometimes in the space between meetings. He'd visit me on the rare days I went to the office. Roki even promised to be there at my wedding, masked somewhere at the front of the crowd. He was a good friend to me, and it sometimes hurt that he couldn't be more.

You're getting married! I had to remind myself. *You wouldn't betray Zawne. You wouldn't!*

But hadn't I already?

Tissa and I were in the dressing room before the

ceremony, a space the Grucken had set aside for me at Lithern Shrine, inside his training complex. Through the walls, we could hear the intense clamor of singing voices outside, the banging drums, the wild chanting. It was a Gaard tradition that the attendees chanted and danced frantically for up to four hours before the bride revealed herself. It was meant as an enticement for her to be wed, to arouse passion for her and the groom's union in the hearts of the people before the wedding began.

We had been listening to it already for two hours when Nnati came into the room.

He stopped just inside and gaped at me. "Wow ... Kaelyn, is that you?"

I laughed. "Of course. Who else would it be?"

"You're ..." Nnati was tongue tied. I'd never seen him like this before. "You're beautiful," he said. "Your dress, your hair, your glow. I can't believe it's you."

"Thanks," Tissa said for me. "I helped with the design of the dress. It's pure white to match Zawne. I thought the diamonds and white silk were a nice touch. I also gave her a scoop neck and a sweeping train. And what about my outfit, Nnati? Being married to Raad sure has its perks. Check out the diamond necklace my hubby bought me just for his sister's wedding. Look closely—these are real diamonds embedded in the gold."

Nnati gave her a look with one eyebrow raised. "You're sure getting comfortable in your new life, huh? I suppose it's understandable. Nobody where we come from could have purchased you such a gift if they had saved all their money for forty years."

Tissa grinned, mostly to herself. She was fiddling with the necklace.

"Anyway," Nnati said, charging across the room to give me a hug. "You look amazing!" He stopped just short of me with his arms spread. "I want to hug you, but I also don't want to wrinkle the dress."

"I appreciate it," I told him bashfully. "And thanks for your kind words. They mean a lot."

Nnati blew me a cheeky kiss. "Anything for you, darling." Then he turned his attention to the window. "They're acting like lunatics out there. It's like that mad parade for the dead at Lordin's funeral. What's going on? Why do the Ava-Gaard commoners have their faces painted like birds?"

"It symbolizes the Crown of Crowns," I told Nnati. "It's meant to be good luck for Zawne and me in the upcoming coronation. It's supposed to raise our chances of being the chosen ones."

I thought, *If only they knew the truth. I wish I could tell my friends!*

"I doubt you'll need luck," Tissa said as she put the finishing touches on my dress. "You're as benevolent as they come. Your work with GMAF says it all."

I said nothing. I was afraid that if I spoke, all the truths would come spilling out. I didn't feel like accidentally getting my friends killed because I wanted to gossip.

Nnati was still peeking out the window at the crowd below. "I don't see a lot of clan leaders," he said. "No one from Surrvul or Krug. No one from Nurlie. The usual Gaard folk and some emissaries from Shondur are here, the king and queen, your Aska bro. But none of the other main players. What gives?"

"The coronation is tomorrow," I told him. "They're all busy. The clan leaders are getting their heirs ready. All the families have a thousand things to do before the coronation."

"Gotcha," he said. Then Nnati broke out laughing. "Your Gaard traditions are comical, Kaelyn. I love how enthusiastic the Ava-Gaard are. Will you and Zawne be jumping over the borehole?"

"Borehole! What borehole?"

Tissa shot Nnati a look. "They don't do that here. That's only in Nurlie, Nnati. Not even at my wedding to Raad. And honestly, it's a little diminishing for such royalty."

"What is it?" I said, ignoring Tissa's weird attitude. "Tell me. It sounds fascinating."

Nnati always loved telling stories about the solemn and archaic traditions over on the Nurlie continent. He clapped his hands together and said, "Before two people can be wed, they must jump over a borehole hand in hand. If they miss and fall into the hole, not only could they get a broken limb or a black eye, but their wedding is considered cursed. Many who fall into the borehole cancel their wedding on the spot."

"That's insane," I said. "You guys don't actually believe that, do you?"

Nnati shrugged and Tissa made a face.

"Who's to say?" Nnati said with his usual pessimistic flair. "Some couples have good marriages. Some don't. The ones who don't, they blame the borehole."

I was starting to wonder what would happen if Zawne and I were to jump over a borehole. Would we fall in and be cursed? Would we become king and queen?

"But enough of this Nurlie talk," Nnati said, coming close to me. We stood in front of the oval mirror, all three of us in the frame. "This is a happy day. Happy for you and happy for the whole of Gaard and Geniverd!"

"And your dress is finished," Tissa said, a pincushion and some thread clutched in her hand. "It's time for you to go, Kaelyn. They're chanting your name. They're cheering for their new Gaard-Ma."

Queen, I wanted to correct her.

I didn't. I smiled instead, stood between my two best friends in the most beautiful dress I could have imagined. It was my wedding day. Tears of joy spilled down my cheeks. "Thank you so much," I said. "Thank you for being my best friends. I promise we will never part, no matter what. Nothing will ever change between us!"

* * *

STANDING on the podium next to Zawne was a dream come true, a dream I had never known I had. He was handsome in a snow-white tuxedo, dashing with his hair gelled and his teeth whitened. Strong, tough, unbending, and yet he was gentle and loving. We held hands while the Grucken began the wedding ceremony. The crowd silenced. I looked out and saw Papa's face shining in the front row beside Raad and Tissa. Papa was so proud of me. Mama would have been too.

"Love prevails," I said, Zawne and I facing each other to do our wedding vows. "Ava-Gaard, we call on you all to help us to abide by Decens-Lenitas."

Then Zawne recited his Shondur verse. "Love prevails. Ava-Shondur, help us to abide by Decens-Lenitas."

And together we said, "Only love until the very end. May Mother Geniverd help us to abide by Decens-Lenitas."

"When asked to choose a human quality you both possess that you place above all else for my blessing, you chose love," the Grucken said. "Let all who've gathered here bear witness. Prince Zawne, why love?"

Zawne pasted his eyes onto mine. "When I look upon Lady Kaelyn, I see love. Her love is honest, kind, respectful, caring, and empathetic. Her love listens, shares, and has integrity."

The Grucken turned to me. "What about you, Lady Kaelyn?"

"His love is brave and does not fear pain or danger. His love is faithful, sincere, and resilient. He is love."

* * *

WE WERE MARRIED. Zawne and I kissed, and the crowd went crazy. He picked me up and whisked me offstage to the cheering of our clanspeople. He carried me all the way to our flyrarc, and we were gone, the merriment below like a rioting crowd at a music festival. Zawne put the flyrarc on autopilot, and we kissed all the way to Sud Cottage. It was romantic, dreamy, everything I could have hoped for.

He kicked the door open with me cradled in his arms in my wedding dress. We were both giggling. "Take me to the bedroom," I said. "I want to kiss my husband."

Zawne carried me through the halls of Sud Cottage as if I were weightless. It was funny, because we would only live in the cottage for one night. After tomorrow's coronation, we would be moved into VondRust Palace. It was only a brief honeymoon.

Everything was great until Zawne dumped me on the bed and I saw half-packed boxes stacked by the closet. Lordin's things had been crammed into them. Jutting from one of the boxes was a framed portrait, a picture of her wearing a diamond tiara and looking very much like a queen. It made me think, *Did I usurp her? Have I stolen Lordin's place?*

Then, *Is she watching us right now as a Min?*

CHAPTER 9

*E*very forty years the world stopped. Four billion people held their breath as the heirs of Geniverd gathered in Coronation Square and awaited the Crown of Crowns. It was something many of us were experiencing for the first time. It was something the older generation would experience for the last.

P2 camera drones hovered above the square like silent metal hummingbirds. They were broadcasting the coronation throughout the kingdom. They were the paparazzi, technological eavesdroppers. The people were gathered below them by the thousands. Six distinctive creeds mixed in the enormous lower court-yard of Coronation Square. Anyone who owned a flyrarc hovered in the sky and watched with binoculars. The sky was so full of them it looked like an invasion. The streets were packed. No one was at work.

I was on the raised podium above the masses, surrounded by a barrier of Protectors. We heirs were an island above the people, eighteen pairs kneeling in a

wide circle. The air was tense. I knelt on a cushion next
to Zawne and Raad, with Tissa very near to us.
Directly across the square was Jaken and his wife,
Kyna, representing the Ava-Shondur. To the left was
Surrvul's insane cluster of heirs. They were all married
to other noble Ava-Surrvul. It was a real nationalist
offering, and they glared angrily at everyone else, pale
faced and blue eyed. They wore bright pink hats with
sawtooth points along the brims. They were kind of
creepy.

The Grucken stood center stage. He wore a long
robe of many colors and leaned on his jeweled staff. We
were all waiting for the Crown of Crowns. Everyone
was nervous except Zawne and me. The Grucken was
deadly serious as he turned slowly in a circle, scruti-
nizing the heirs, acting as though he was judging our
hearts, as if the Grucken were a Min and could hear our
thoughts.

I suddenly realized how paranoid I had been
growing over the past two weeks. I was seeing Min
everywhere I looked. I sometimes whispered Roki's
name so he would appear. I would ask him, "Roki, is
that a Min?" pointing through a window in the palace
residence at any person who I thought was suspicious.

"No, Kaelyn," Roki would say. "Not everyone is a
Min."

But how could I know for sure?

The Grucken's words reverberated as he summoned
the flight of the Crown of Crowns. He was saying, "We
implore you to choose wisely from these couples
offered by Geniverd, the elite, the wise, the moral.
Whomever you choose will be named the Most Courageous, the Shielded Ones, the Most Supreme Majesties.

They will rule unquestioned for forty years. They will lead Geniverd into the future."

The Grucken bowed his head to the current king and queen. "We thank you for your service, the Queen Emerita and the King Emeritus," he said. "Geniverd thanks you for your service. Please step down."

As per tradition, Zawne's parents rose up from the twin thrones at the far end of the square and stood nobly beside them, ready to pass over control of the kingdom. They looked happy, watching Zawne and me with subtle grins. I had to remind myself, *They already know!*

And that was when the bird appeared. The Grucken raised his jeweled staff and cried out, "The Crown of Crowns has come!" Silence washed over the crowd. The hairs on the back of my neck stood on end. It was a magical moment. Some of the heirs wore worried expressions. Lady Juni of Nurlie had her eyes shut and her arms folded over her sand-colored gown. The Surrvul heirs straightened their backs and tried to appear their most decent, their most righteous, as if Decens-Lenitas had any importance at this stage of the game.

The bird was just as Papa had described to me when I was a little girl. Its bill was straight and yellow. It had a long turquoise tail for such a tiny creature, yellow breasted with white feathers, and red sprinkles on its feet. It came streaking from the sky as if from Shiol, almost leaving a trail of color behind it. The heirs took a quick glance and then bowed their heads. No one breathed.

The crowd gasped when the bird landed on Zawne's head. There was a surge of whispers, shouts; every one of the Surrvul heirs cursed under their breaths and stood up angrily. I caught Raad's eye, and he grinned wider than I had ever seen. Tissa gave me a thumbs-up. Then the trumpets blasted. The cheers were deafening. We were in Gaard, after all, in the capital, and most of the crowd was local. The bird flapped off Zawne's head, circled the podium, then flew off into the sky.

Everything happened in a series of flashes, almost too much for me to handle. We were being ushered into the middle of the square by the Grucken, who congratulated us quietly while some of the heirs stormed off and some lingered on the fringe with big smiles, happy for us despite their loss. The Grucken said to the crowd, "May I present the Most Courageous, the Shielded Ones, Their Most Supreme Majesties, King Zawne and Queen Kaelyn of Geniverd."

The people lost their minds. Hats were thrown in the air, firecrackers, fireworks exploding above the city. Flyrarcs diffused special fuel mixtures to create spritzes of rainbow-colored exhaust overhead. Two royal clerics were draping me and Zawne in vestments of gold silk. I didn't even see who placed the gem-studded tiara on my head or the spiked crown on Zawne's. Then we were bowing to the roar of our people ... *our* people ... *my* people.

"Thank you," Zawne bellowed in his strongest voice. "We will serve Geniverd well."

I said nothing. I couldn't. My throat was tight, and I was having a slight panic attack. The Grucken led us to Zawne's parents, and hugs and handshakes were exchanged. Then we sat in the thrones while the ex-queen and the ex-king bowed to us. The King Emeritus and the Queen Emerita were bowing to me! Me, Kaelyn of Gaard! I wept tears of joy while the world worshipped me. The smell of earth and toffee filled my nose. Roki was close by, and it made me cry harder. Later I followed Zawne and the Grucken to our flyrarc with tears in my eyes.

* * *

WE LANDED at VondRust Palace to a welcoming committee of servants, Protectors, and a peculiar man who was short and balding. Greeting us with an enthusiastic smile, he said, "Congratulations," then got straight to business as we walked into the palace flanked by Protectors.

"My name is Torio, as Zawne already knows. I am the head of the council and will be assisting with the royal transition. If you have any questions, my number is already programmed into your visins. You may call me at any time of the day or night. From this moment onward, you will be escorted everywhere beyond the palace by at least five Protectors. This is for your safety."

I was trying to take everything in. Zawne was so calm, nodding and hemming as he rubbed his chin. But it was a lot for me. I tried to keep up as Torio led us through the grand mansion that was now our home. It was such an extravagant place. Everything was furnished in velvets and golds, the ceilings stretching high, and each corridor was a massive tunnel of portraits and archaic candelabras that must have been gold. The entire palace smelled faintly sweet. It was not a flowery smell, more of a refined scent, like cherry-wood or burnished copper. It was hard to define, though the smell of it was easing my panic. I wondered if the atmospheric bubble around VondRust infused a calming herb into its generated scents.

Torio talked quickly as we walked. "Your calendars are already full," he said. "You can check the schedule anytime on your visins. It's all been preprogrammed. Tomorrow you will be selecting your councillors."

"Thanks, Torio," Zawne said. They had known each other for twenty-five years. "Where are Mama and Papa? Where's Jaken? He's Shondur-Elder now, right?"

"Right," Torio said. He was articulate with his words. I could tell Torio knew his duties well and would be extremely useful in the weeks ahead. "Your parents have already left for Shondur ahead of Jaken. As you know, there are huge parties being held in all six clans. Jaken will be inaugurated as Shondur-Elder, with his wife being ushered in as Shondur-Ma. I'm afraid your parents won't be back for at least six months."

"They deserve a break," Zawne said.

I agreed with him, yet internally I was panicked. I thought, *Who's going to give me advice for the first few months if I can't talk to Zawne or Roki?*

At least Zawne was confident. He swaggered through the lavish halls beside Torio as if he had been born for the role of king. I guessed, in a way, he had been. But then again, hadn't I been raised for the role of queen?

"You'll have ten councillors," Torio said. "You may review the short list of names tonight and pick fifteen suitable candidates for interviews, then choose your final eight tomorrow afternoon. They are all eagerly waiting on standby. As for the other two councillors, you each get an independent pick. I'm sure each of you has a trusted friend you would like to make an adviser."

"I do," I said right away, thinking about Nnati. But then I remembered the foundation. It was my tribute to Mama's memory, and Lordin's dying gift to me. Who would look after it if Nnati was living in VondRust and advising me?

Torio stopped. We had been walking for five minutes through a labyrinth of hallways, and I was utterly lost. We were in a honeycomb of golden trim and red carpets. "These are your quarters," he said, gesturing to a huge open doorway. "There will be Protectors outside at all times." The Protectors who had been following us branched off and stood on either side of the doorway, silently menacing in their robotic armor. "There will also be Protectors below your windows outside. In total, there are about a hundred Protectors on the estate. They work through a hive-mind synapse system. Any sign of danger will be registered by the whole company. You've never been safer."

Except from Min, I thought.

Then Torio was bowing. "I will collect you in the morning. Get some rest, check over the files, and once more, congratulations. You are the new rulers of Geniverd. I bid you good night, Your Most Supreme Majesties."

Torio scampered off down the hall. Zawne looked at me, extended his hand, and said, "Shall we, my queen?"

I took his hand and let him pull me into the bedroom. This was it, my new life as a queen. Zawne shut the doors and carried me to the royal bed.

* * *

"SURRVUL ISN'T HAPPY," Nnati said. "They're saying the crown shouldn't stay in the same family, meaning Zawne. But really they're just peeved because they have to wait another forty years for another shot at it. People are saying they might inflate visin prices or even restrict their distribution. They could even shut them down altogether. Oh, then there are the Gurnots. They've made encrypted messages available for the public to let them know that they are watching. People are scared of what they might do."

"They won't do anything," I told Nnati. I was in the main sitting room of our royal mansion. Zawne was snoozing in the bedroom while I chatted with Nnati on my visin.

"They already have," Nnati said. "Didn't you see? There was another fire today, this time in Shondur. The authorities are saying it was the Dragon, the rogue Gurnot who keeps lighting wealthy people's estates on fire. This time it was the local retreat the ex-queen and ex-king were supposed to be staying in. Before their flyarc could land, the entire place went up in flames, even melting the Protectors that had been stationed there, melting them into nothing but metallic jelly. Nobody has a clue how the Dragon—or Dragons for all we know—are getting away with it. Some say secret Gurnot weapons technology."

"But the Gurnots are a minor threat to the kingdom," I said. "There aren't even that many of them. Where did all this damage come from?" I stopped to think, then said, "Maybe if I make it clear to the Gurnots that I have the interest of the people in mind, they will stop the fires. I've been thinking about bringing them into the fold. Maybe I can give them an official seat of power to stop their violent activities and their burning."

An idea was percolating in Nnati's head. He stared at me on the projected screen, gears turning behind his eyeballs. "Interesting ..." he said. "I'd like to see how that turns out. Maybe if you make a statement to that effect, you can alleviate some of the fear. Maybe the fires will stop. However, to side with Gurnots would mean public outcry. Be careful, my queen. Tread lightly."

"I will," I said. "You always give me such good advice. It's actually the reason I called you. I need you, Nnati. I have one free seat on the council, and I want you in it. Could you do that for me? Could you join me in VondRust as my loyal adviser?"

Nnati gaped. He had been doing a lot of that lately. Funny how much can change in three weeks. "Is that not a title held only by royalty?" he asked. "I'm only a commoner. I have no royal blood. And what about GMAF?"

I bit my lip, smiled at Nnati, and said, "I'm going to shake things up a bit. This won't be like the last administration. I'm really going to push for change. Noble blood or not, I want you as my adviser. In fact, I want to start bringing a lot more so-called commoner blood into positions of power. This government is going to be run by the people, for the people, just like it should be. As for GMAF, we've already doubled the staff. I trust you to find a suitable replacement."

Nnati was speechless. I had to goad him. "So, what do you say? Will you help me?"

Nnati fumbled for words, trying to be my friend while at the same time trying to speak to a queen. "Yes,

Kaelyn. I mean, yes, my queen. Yes, Your Most Supreme Majesty."

"Cut it out," I said. "We're alone. Can't we just be normal?"

He let out a massive sigh and sagged over himself. "I was hoping you were going to say that. I can't stand being fake, and I don't think you can either. Can we talk about something normal before bed?"

"Of course," I said, happy Nnati felt the same as I did. It would be nice to have a real friend on the inside. "What do you want to talk about?"

"How's Zawne?" he asked. "How is your relationship?"

I opened my mouth and paused. I didn't have an answer. We had been so busy the last few weeks that we hadn't had much time to be a couple. We slept in the same bed, went through the same routine, but were often very distant. I said to Nnati, "It's been a whirlwind ever since we got engaged."

"I bet," he said. "But what abou—?"

The smell of sweet toffee swirled into my nostrils, and my eyelids fluttered. Oh no! Roki was in the room! He was right beside me, masking everything except his scent.

I blurted into the visin, "Sorry, Nnati, got to go." I got a glimpse of the shock on Nnati's face as I hung up.

It was quiet, but I could feel his eyes watching me. I tried to steady my breath, my heart pounding wildly in my chest. I whispered, "Roki, are you here?"

CHAPTER 10

*N*ordHaven couldn't hold a candle to the absurd grandeur of VondRust Palace. Our private estate within VondRust was three stories tall, had eight sleeping quarters, twelve bathrooms, several large dressing rooms, two kitchens, a tennis court, a home theater, a vast wine cellar, an indoor pool and an outdoor pool, a gym, and a sauna. Not to mention the flyrarc pads on the roof for the king and queen's personal flying machines. We even had our own miniature atmospheric bubble, scenting the air, controlling the temperature, conjuring rain or sunshine at will. The place was epic. Wandering through its halls was dizzying, and I could hardly get used to it. I kept thinking, *Do I really deserve all this? Does any one person deserve such massive excess?*

Either way, it was ours. VondRust could have been a city of its own for all the various manors and structures, the guesthouses reserved for clan leaders, and the huge government building in the center of the flowery courtyard. Everything was connected via well-kept pathways. Zawne and I even had hover scooters so that we didn't have to use our royal legs. Spoiled is what I called it. I often missed my old apartment and my daily commute to GMAF. All the people I'd known in the city were probably still living in tiny pods stacked up like bricks, and there I was, in my own subcity.

But hey, the view was nice. I stared out the window of our bedroom the morning after the coronation, admiring the mountain peaks in the distance, the snowy inclines and patches of firs. It was a tranquil scene after such chaos. I liked listening to the water run through the pipes as Zawne showered in the other room. I felt introspective.

"Morning, beautiful," came Roki's voice.

I whirled around to see Roki sitting on the edge of my bed. I felt panic rise in my chest, then remembered Roki could vanish in a split second if he needed to. "What are you doing here?" I asked. We had talked for two hours last night while Zawne slept. I felt guiltier than words could describe.

"Don't feel guilty," Roki said, reading my thoughts. "We're friends, remember?" He looked sad as he said this, as if I had shackled him, made him a prisoner of friendship when we both wanted something more.

Then Zawne yelled from the shower, "Who are you talking to?" He had turned off the water and was likely toweling himself dry.

"Nnati," I said hurriedly. "I'm on a call."

Roki was grinning at me. He loved the thrill of being bad, of being in the same room with me while my husband dried his naked body less than twenty feet away.

128

"I had another reason for coming," Roki said, not even bothering to hush his voice. It was like he wanted to get caught!

"What is it?"

"I'll see you tonight in Shiol. I'll also be with you all day during your council decisions. It turns out I really love watching your lips move. I love watching you, giving you a whiff of my scent but not showing myself. It thrills me. I'm obsessed with you."

Zawne emerged from the bathroom. Roki was gone. "Finished your call?"

"Yes," I said, but I didn't sound very convincing. I swallowed hard and changed the subject. "You look wet."

Dumb! Who says that?

But it was true. Zawne wore nothing but black briefs, his muscled form moist from the shower. I wanted to consume him on the spot. Let Roki watch. Let him discharge his earthy scent while I shoved my tongue in Zawne's mouth and we became lost in a frenzy of love.

It was almost as if Zawne could hear my thoughts. He strode across the room without saying a word and scooped me up. He was so rough when he wanted to be. "I don't think I got all the way clean," he said, and carried me giggling into the shower.

* * *

BREAKFAST WAS LAID out in the main dining room downstairs: fried eggs, bacon, blueberries, pancakes, strawberries, and tea.

"Wow," I said to the chef, a short fellow in a white

smock. It was rare to see a human chef when so many were Protectors now. The palace must have been paying him a fortune. "How did you know what I like?"

"We know everything that will make Her Most Supreme Majesty happy," the man replied.

I looked to Zawne. "Is this how you grew up?"

"More or less," he said, casually chewing on a strip of bacon. "My mother and father were the rulers of Geniverd. Jaken and I had a ... cozy childhood."

"Cozier than mine," I said. I took a seat, and the chef left us to eat in private. There were two Protectors standing guard outside the kitchen door. Even though they were machines, they still made me uncomfortable.

"Listen," Zawne said, getting serious as he leaned over the table and found my eyes. "I have an idea. It's never been done before, but I think it could work. I grew up with my parents being constantly exhausted, and now I know why."

"Shiol," I said quietly.

"Exactly. So I was thinking that if we split up the council, call it the King's Council and the Queen's Council, we could get double the rest and double the free time. We would split the duties in half."

"That's a great idea," I said. "The only thing is that we have to"—I looked around, then said at a whisper —"follow the recommendations from our friends."

"We must," Zawne said. "That's not up for debate. But I'm sure they won't mind. It's a great idea."

It *was* a great idea. I found myself surprised by his gusto. Zawne wore the mantle of king well.

"Which subjects would you like to handle?" he asked me.

"Health," I said immediately. It was the first thing

that came to mind, since Gaard, my home, was known for manufacturing medicines. I had to open my visin and check the other categories.

"Industries," I said, flicking down the list. "I'll take ecosystem, preservation, human resources."

"Great," Zawne said. "That leaves me with trade, defense, and finance."

He made for the door, stopping to kiss me on my head. "Enjoy your breakfast, Queen Kaelyn. I'm going to get ready. We have a long day ahead of us."

I ate my breakfast feeling like a happy schoolgirl. I had my macho man, my Aska warrior, my husband, and I had my confidant, my spirit boy with the charming smile who always kept me on my toes. I couldn't tell if it was Roki I smelled or a spice from my toast. Either way, I was happy.

* * *

SELECTING the councillors was easier than I had anticipated. Zawne and I sat at the head of a huge room with a domed ceiling while one by one the applicants introduced themselves. We had no trouble picking eight of them. They were all noble-born or Aska certified. Besides, it was Geniverd law to have at least one adviser from each continent on the council.

In the end, I chose an additional Surrvul councillor, a young woman by the name of Shiru. She was an heir and too young to become clan leader ahead of her many siblings. Shiru needed something to do for the next forty years, and I was happy to oblige. There was nothing worse than a clan heir with eighty years of life, all the power and cash in the world, and not a single thing to do with any of it.

Zawne chose the other extra, a stern man by the name of Aska Nikhel. He was Ava-Lodden, a rare breed in the capital. Zawne said they had met during his training.

The most enjoyable part of the whole ordeal was when we called the selected councillors into the main chamber, including Torio, who had been reinstated as Head of Courtiers, and delivered the big news.

Zawne stood up and said, "We have an announcement to make," then paused for dramatic effect. He seemed to love doing that. "We will be splitting the council into two parts, the Queen's Council and the King's Council."

Everyone gasped. Torio looked ready to faint, his jaw on the floor. "You're sure about this, Your Most Supreme Majesties?" he asked.

"Yes," I said, standing up to take Zawne's hand. It was better that we appeared as a single unit of authority. "We have talked it over and agreed. This is for the better."

The councillors exchanged a flurry of confused glances. Then we split them into groups.

The Queen's Council consisted of Nnati, Master Widrig, Lady Katrin, Aska Nikhel, and Aska Xi.

Zawne's council consisted of Aska Stingl, Lady Shiru, Master Nokag, Aska Chu, and Aska Tatu. It was almost entirely made up of Askas.

* * *

AFTER SPENDING the entire morning and afternoon in the conference room, choosing our councillors, it was nice to attend the welcome party Torio had organized for them. Zawne and I showed up fashionably late, around six thirty. I didn't want to linger too long. I was eager to go to bed and transport myself to Shiol, where I could find out what Roki had to say. I was smelling him everywhere. I figured he was close by.

Didn't he have a job to do?

Zawne and I were seated at the head of the table, our councillors to either side of us. There were seven courses, endless bottles of wine, and lots of laughter. Lady Shiru loved to tell jokes, and everyone else seemed to appreciate her sense of humor. This made me feel confident about our decisions earlier in the day. We had to spend four days a week governing with these people for the next forty years. It was important that we all got along.

It was as Lady Shiru began to tell a joke about three Ava-Lodden and an unfortunate goat that Zawne whispered in my ear, "I want to go to Shiol tonight."

My heart sank. He couldn't be serious. Roki was waiting for me, and I wanted him to show me more of Shiol. There was no way I could miss our meeting! I had been thinking about him all day.

"Why?" I asked.

Zawne crossed his arms and pursed his lips. "I just want to," he said, no explanation given. He was acting like a stubborn baby.

"You can't." I had to make something up quick. My heart was racing and I was sweating. "It's my turn," I told him. "We need to keep to the schedule. I'm sorry, Zawne, but I won't budge."

His face warped into a scowl. I thought he was thinking of something mean to snap at me. Why was he doing this? It seemed so unnecessary. But then something occurred to me. I realized that Lordin was a Min. She could watch us, read our thoughts, follow us as a bodiless spirit. She could also visit Zawne in his sleep. Now that I was thinking about it, Zawne had been waking up around the same time as me every day. Had he been going to Shiol in secret? Had he been seeing Lordin like I had been seeing Roki?

I boiled over with anger. It was a good thing the councillors were distracted and half-drunk. No one paid me any attention when I hissed at Zawne, "I'm going to Shiol and that's final. And I better not see you there. I know you don't have an appointment with you-know-who, so I don't know what you want to do there."

I got up in a huff, pushed my chair back too loudly, and the whole party stopped to stare at me.

"I'm going to bed," I said flatly. "Thank you all for agreeing to work with me and the king as we mend our kingdom and push forward into the new dawn, but I'm tired. Good night."

Nobody questioned me—I was the freaking queen. They all bowed their heads, and I left Zawne at the head of the table, glaring at me as I stormed off.

* * *

THE FIRST THING I wanted to do when I got to Shiol was run my hands through Roki's silky hair and kiss him.

No!

I cringed, clenched my teeth, and squeezed my eyes tighter. I couldn't cheat on Zawne. It wasn't in my personality. But I kept thinking about Lordin. I couldn't help but wonder, was Zawne cheating on me?

All I could do was allow myself to get sleepy, sink deep into our cozy bed, and spell ...

S-H-I-O-L.

I zipped through space in my spirit body, landed in the Crown of Crowns' reception hall, and found them waiting for me beneath the cloudy, ethereal sky. They were sparkling light, the same as always. Riedel greeted me warmly enough.

"Queen Kaelyn, we're glad you've come. We have seen that you and Zawne split the duties in half. We were surprised. It's a wise move."

"You might even get some rest," Hanchell said.

I moaned, "Thanks, but it was Zawne's idea."

"We know," Hanchell said.

Riedel's laugh echoed through the void. "We know everything."

I just wanted to get the meeting over with. I wanted to see Roki. We had a lot to discuss. I wanted to ask him about Lordin, if he had seen her with Zawne. I needed to know if they were an item again. If so, it might seriously change my feelings toward Zawne. It might also open up possibilities between Roki and myself. I needed to see him!

"Can we get to it?" I said. "I have a meeting after this." I didn't mean to be blunt, but it seemed like recently I had been shedding the timid, awkward girl I used to be. I was becoming bolder. I didn't know if it was from age, stress, sleeping in bed with a man every night ... or from finding out there were entire worlds secreted just behind the fabric of our universe!

"Of course," Hanchell said. "You are a busy woman. Here, this is what's on the docket for today."

A blast of images, documents, video clips—all exploded from thin air and cycled around me. It was a lot to make sense of. All of it got sucked into the visin implant in my wrist.

"You may now access the files," Hanchell said. "Use your visin normally. It will function in Shiol, but the files will be immediately erased upon your return to the physical world. We can't have them slipping into the wrong hands."

"Okay." I was a bit excited. If there was one thing I knew how to do, it was to ignore my problems and bury myself in my work.

"One more thing," Hanchell said. Her electric form seemed to giggle. She was awfully excitable for an all-powerful spirit.

Then Hanchell's light fluctuated, and the space we were in changed. The clouds were gone, sealed off by a high ceiling. Four walls materialized, and within seconds, I found myself standing in NordHaven's study, the one Papa had always used for work.

"It's just a projection," Hanchell said. "We hope it helps you as you go through the material. Take a seat on the sofa by the fire. Relax. You have time to review the evidence."

"Thanks so much!" I said, but they had already evaporated.

* * *

I WALKED through the room in awe over how the Crown of Crowns could manifest NordHaven so accurately. It was my papa's study down to the last carpet fiber: dark, musty, more comfortable than any royal chamber at VondRust. It even smelled like old books and smoldering wood, just like Papa always programmed it to smell like. I plunked myself down on the leather sofa, felt the warmth of the hearth on my feet, and turned on my visin. It was time to get to work. I needed to absorb all the information and still have time left over for Roki ... and there were ten claims I had to go over!

At the top of the list was a request from Nurlie, asking for the Crown to stop a covert petition from Nurlie Island. The island was demanding independence from Nurlie. Over eighty thousand islanders had signed the petition, and the shadow government of the island wanted to push ahead with a referendum. The island represented forty percent of Nurlie's exports, mainly due to rich mineral resources. It was one of the few places where the mines were still operated by human workers. The Nurlie clan leaders were fearful that the shadow government might try a hostile takeover of the continent, fueled by anti-mech and anti-authority sentiments.

I scrolled down to see the Crown of Crowns' recommendation. It stated that I should side with Nurlie and put an end to the island's shadow government before it could do any damage. Then I watched some video evidence that showed the island's leaders plotting to transfer lucrative business contracts to some companies in Surrvul once they took over. This would infer a strong and dangerous relationship between Nurlie and Surrvul, not to mention total anarchy for the Nurlie continent.

I made a mental note to side with Nurlie and moved on.

Next was a breach of contract complaint from Gaard about the purchase and supply of antimicrobials. A large company based in Gaard had been providing antibiotics and antivirals to Surrvul, but Surrvul had canceled the contracts in favor of an innovative new company in Krug. Surrvul claimed their reasoning was a supply shortage. Gaard denied it. I was recommended to side with Gaard, forcing Surrvul to continue purchasing through the Gaard company.

When I read the third case, I began to see a pattern. Surrvul had lodged a complaint against Shondur. Surrvul needed phosphorus for fertilizer and the production of steel. The main source of phosphorus was in Shondur, and Surrvul claimed the Shondur government was being stingy. They wanted easier, ampler, and fairer access to the mineral. The recommendation was to rule in favor of Surrvul and force Shondur to give them what they wanted.

At this point, I made a mental note to speak with Lady Shiru and have a long discussion about what exactly the Ava-Surrvul and their rulers wanted. They seemed to be at the heart of every conflict.

I skimmed through and memorized the rest of the complaints and cases until I finally made it to the last one. I was wondering why Roki hadn't shown up yet. I had hoped he would massage my feet while I did my deliberations. A foot massage wasn't outside the realm of friendship, right?

The last case was a plea from Gaard, Lodden, Shondur, and Krug to commemorate Lordin formally. The idea irked me, and I skimmed through most of it. Basically, the Crown of Crowns recommended that I ask all clan leaders how they wanted to keep Lordin's memory alive. It made me wonder, *Why does everyone still care? She was just a woman!*

I closed my visin and sat back, glad to be done with the day's dealings. But where in the name of Geniverd was Roki?

"Roki?" I called out. I thought maybe he was waiting for me beyond the illusion of Papa's study.

I was surprised when an unfamiliar girl walked through the illusion like a phantasm and stood a few feet from me.

"Hello, Kaelyn," she said.

"Uh ..." I didn't recognize this girl at all. "Who are you?"

"It's me, Lordin."

It may have been the first time in my life that my tongue had literally slithered into the back of my mouth. I gaped at her in horror. I had no words. I wanted to scream at her, "Have you been seeing my husband?" But I also wanted to wrap my arms around her and thank Lordin for all the good she had done. It was a real quandary.

"I got a new body," she said, showing no signs of reading my mind. "That's probably why you don't recognize me. I know, I'm not as cute. But hey, I'm younger. And I have all the perks of a Min. Everything I do feels a thousand times better than it used to. Life as a Min is great!"

She was bubbly, petite, still pretty even though it wasn't Lordin's original body. Maybe it was her personality that made her so attractive.

"That's great. I'm glad you're doing well." It was all I

could say. I didn't have the strength to confront her. I also didn't have the strength to apologize for stealing her fiancé. I'd never felt like more of a fraud! I thought I was the queen of Geniverd. Where had my confidence gone?

Lordin hung her head and took a step closer to me. "I actually came here because I have some sad news."

Oh no, I thought. *Is she going to confess?*

"What sad news?" I asked.

"It's about Roki."

"Roki?" A thousand more questions bubbled in my head. How did she know about him? Had she been following us? Did she know about Roki's secret visits? Was I the villain here?

Lordin said, "Yes, your friend Roki." The word *friend* sounded sarcastic. Then Lordin came up beside me, held out her wrist, and activated her visin. The holographic screen bloomed in front of us. "You'd better see for yourself."

Lordin brought up a carousel of photos on her visin. Every one of them was of Roki. But not just Roki—not even just Roki and another woman. The photos were of Roki and other women! Plural! She showed me ten photos of him kissing other girls, all the while my heart hammered madly in my chest. I was getting angrier by the second.

Lordin pointed to the last photo and said, "That was taken today. I'm sorry, Kaelyn, but Roki has been playing you. That's why he's late for your date."

I was seething mad. Lordin turned off her visin and stepped back, leaning on Papa's oak bookshelf. It was so weird to be talking to a Min in the illusion of my old house.

"I just had to tell you," she said. "But I am sorry. Min are jerks. When you live for so long—"

"Exactly how long?" I asked. I needed to know how long Roki had been messing with girls' emotions.

"Min live for a thousand years," Lordin told me, "an extra three thousand if you get promoted to Crown of Crowns. We're basically indestructible. Other Min can kill us if they try hard enough, but that's rare. The only thing that can kill us instantly is the Seeing Water."

"The what?"

"Never mind," she said. "I have to go. Roki's coming. Remember, Kaelyn, trust no one."

Lordin vanished through the hologram of Papa's study just as Roki materialized in front of me. "Who was here?" he asked, sniffing the air.

"Go die," I told him. I had tears streaming down my face. I clenched and unclenched my fists, pacing the room and snarling like an angry bull. I didn't know what to do. I had put so much faith in Roki. I had betrayed my husband's trust to be with him. And now ... now he was a no-good liar and a cheat!

"Why are you thinking these things?" Roki asked.

I hated that he could read my thoughts, that he answered questions before I could ask them, before I could assault him with accusations. It was rude and annoying. He was annoying! What kind of pervert would continuously read my thoughts? It was another violation of my trust!

"Get out of my head!" I told him, screaming at the top of my lungs. My face must have been smeared with mascara, and I must have looked crazy. "You're evil!" I said. "You're an evil Min, and I hate you. I'll never forgive you again. I should have trusted Mama. I should have listened to my gut. This is the last time I ever go against my family, against my morals. Yet …" I paused, Roki looking at me as if I were the heartbreaker and not him. "I deserve this, don't I? I deserve it for my own treachery, for betraying Zawne. No honor among thieves, huh?"

"Kaelyn …" Roki reached for me.

I slapped his hand away. "You're just a filthy spirit," I said. "Geniverd is your playground, your sick human playground. Well, I won't be your toy anymore. I'm done, Roki. Don't ever watch me at night again, you creep. Don't leave your scent like some pervert's trail around me. Don't read my mind. Don't visit me in my dreams." I closed my eyes and screamed, "Stay out of my life!"

Roki was weeping. "You have to trust me," he insisted. "Kaelyn, I love you. I would never—"

But I was done. I let my body relax and dissolved into the blackness, away from Shiol and Roki's lies.

CHAPTER 11

$\mathcal{I}$ was mad at myself mostly. I was mad at myself for getting tricked. I had let it happen. I had let Roki use me. I had deceived myself into thinking he was a good spirit, a good Min, a good man —whatever he was supposed to be. I had dug my own shameful hole, and there was nothing left to do but suffer in it, drag myself through day after day with the unbearable guilt of what I had done.

Zawne noticed the change. I was gloomy, paranoid, always sniffing the air and looking around as if Roki might appear and club me over the head. It was frustrating, because I knew he could mask his presence. It came to be that every scent generated by the atmospheric bubble around the palace made me think of Roki. The smell of jasmine at sunrise, the scent of toffee in the parlor by night. I knew he could be watching me at any time. What I didn't know was what happened when you angered a Min. Could they strike back and hurt a human? Would Roki take out his anger on me?

143

I asked this one night during a meeting with the Crown of Crowns. "I know Min hurt people for fun, but can they hurt royals?"

Riedel answered, "As long as a Min fulfills their obligation to us and doesn't reveal the Great Secret, they are free to do as they please. This is the covenant between Min and the Seeing Water."

Again with the Seeing Water! Just what in the name of Geniverd was the Seeing Water? The Crown of Crowns refused to give me more information about it, and I left Shiol in a bad mood—again!

Later that day, Zawne called me out for my decline in attitude. "What's gotten into you?" he asked when I woke up, staring straight into my face. "You've changed this last week. You're grumpy and depressed. Have you forgotten that you're the queen of the world?"

"I'm just tired," I said, slipping out of bed. "I'm sorry that I don't have your Aska training. I'm not as strong as you. Okay?"

Zawne said something, but I was already in the bathroom with the shower running. I stood under the hot water and cried silently. Why had I been so quick to let Roki consume me? I hated how much I missed him. I hated what I was doing to Zawne. I felt like garbage, like a piece of trash. I had betrayed my husband, my vows, and worst of all, myself.

* * *

I HARDLY TOUCHED my food at breakfast. Zawne wouldn't talk to me. He got up as soon as I entered the dining room and left without looking in my eyes. What had I done? I had destroyed both my relationships in one fell swoop.

My visin was beeping in my ear as I poked cold eggs around with a knife. I saw it was Raad and hit ignore. I didn't feel like talking to anyone.

I got dressed, moving sluggishly through my closet. I had an important council meeting in an hour, but who cared?

I got there late. Nnati was pacing by the doors of the council chamber, waiting for me.

"Are you crazy?" he said. "You can't be late for these meetings, Kaelyn—you're the queen."

"Exactly," I snapped. "I'm the queen, and I can be late if I want."

I stopped, tears welling up in my eyes. "I'm sorry ..." I collapsed into Nnati's arms, hugged him fiercely. "I'm just so freaking tired. I ... I'm exhausted, Nnati."

He hugged me back and whispered in my ear, "I know, I know. But you're stronger than you think, okay? You can get through this. We're only at the beginning. Give yourself some time. You'll bounce back."

"Thanks, Nnati," I said, pulling away from him and wiping my eyes. "I knew it was a good idea to have you by my side. I couldn't ask for a better adviser."

He looked awkward then, biting his lip as if he had something terrible to tell me. I couldn't take any more bad news.

"Since I am your trusted adviser," Nnati said carefully, "I want to talk to you about some recent rulings."

"Oh?"

"Yeah." He leaned in close to me so that the courtiers walking through the grand hallway couldn't hear. "This deregulation case for Gaard's main medicine manufac-turer, I'm not sure we're doing the right thing."

"Why?"

"Well, we have already deregulated the sale of certain antigens twice, making it easier for the company to manipulate the market and potentially drive other manufacturers out of business."

"Oh ... yes, I remember."

But I only half remembered. It was easy to forget things when the Crown of Crowns was making deci-sions for me, pulling the strings, sometimes without giving me good reasons. I felt like a tool. I was also starting to understand how the social system had managed to become so skewed over the past few hundred years. With the Crown of Crowns running the entire world from an alternate dimension while the kings and queens dwindled their time away in Shiol and spent their days exhausted and sucked of their energy, it was easy to see how our world had become so upended without the monarchy fully realizing it. It was as if all of Geniverd were on autopilot.

"And there's another request for a different deregu-lation today," Nnati continued. "This one will make it easier for the company to absorb and acquire other properties and manufacturers. Essentially, they will have a monopoly on the best antimicrobials."

Now I remembered. The councillors had argued with me over the last two deregulations, but I had stuck to the Crown of Crowns' recommendations and allowed them through.

"I think I will allow it," I told Nnati. That was the recommendation, and I planned to abide by it. I was to let the Gaard company do whatever they wanted, even if it didn't feel right in my gut.

"Seriously?" Nnati was floored. "But, Kaelyn, it's going to have serious repercussions."

"They have a delegation coming, do they not?"

Nnati nodded. "They do."

"Then let's listen to what they have to say," I told him, trying to balance logic with the Crown of Crowns' ruling. "So long as there are still manufacturers outside of Gaard, and so long as they don't raise their prices, commit to not raising the prices, and ensure the medicine remains effective and safe, I see no reason to hold them back."

Nnati shook his head. "Yes, my queen." And he opened the door and gestured me into the council chamber.

* * *

MY SEAT WAS at the head of the wide room, covered in red and gold upholstery. My councillors flanked me, Nnati to my left and Torio to my right. We were silent as the delegation from Gaard took the floor and bowed to me.

"Your Most Supreme Majesty," they said in unison.

One of the delegation members stepped in front of her colleagues. She was tiny and young, shockingly beautiful, with radiant skin and golden hair. She had my attention immediately, and the attention of every man in the room.

"Your Most Supreme Majesty," she said, curtsying, "we thank you for seeing us. Shall we get straight to business?"

I nodded. "Present your case."

"Yes, Your Most Supreme Majesty. My name is Hagan of the Ava-Gaard, and I represent VBione Corp. Our proposal is for an acquisition of a Krug-based company called Medseet. This will be the biggest absorption of another manufacturer in twenty years."

Hagan took a deep breath. The councillors were hushed and attentive. She said, "The reason this case is being brought to you, Most Courageous, is because Krug is concerned that our acquisition of Medseet will mean all of Geniverd's antimicrobials will be made by one manufacturer in Gaard. The Krug council is upset, but Medseet is eager to be bought out. The money we have offered them is substantial."

Aska Nikhel raised his hand and looked at me. "May I speak?"

"Of course."

Nikhel cleared his throat. "The problem I see with this acquisition, Your Most Supreme Majesty, is that VBione Corp would be in possession of all the highest-value medicines. They would have the largest portfolio of medicine in Geniverd. If they chose, they could limit the distribution of said medicines."

"I see your point," I said, but it was moot. I had already made my decision. I had to obey the Crown of Crowns. I wasn't about to cause problems a month into my reign just because of some company acquisition. These things happened all the time. Companies in Geniverd were in a perpetual state of consuming one another, leaving workers scrambling to find new jobs and a handful of CEOs with their pockets bursting. I needed to fix the system but not today. Not with this ruling.

"Hagan," I said, "present your rebuttal."

"You are correct, Aska Nikhel," she said. "We do have a large portfolio. However, there are other valuable medicines not owned by us. Our takeover of Medseet means we will be able to create synergies to benefit everyone. We are not restricting innovative companies in other clans, or even here in Gaard. In fact, you will see that over time these other companies will produce transformational medicines that will benefit the world. Once our acquisition of Medseet is complete, production costs will be lowered, while the extra money will go into research."

"That sounds appropriate," I said, nodding in turn to my councillors. "Yet what do you say about job losses in Krug?"

"There will not be any," Hagan said. She was very confident. "The plant in Krug will be under VBione Corp management, but the workers will stay to help us. We will continue to employ all qualified workers."

"That is acceptable," I told her. There were some hushed whispers from my councillors, but no one could openly argue with keeping jobs and advancing research. Hagan's proposition was solid.

"Your time is up," I told her. "Are there any final remarks you wish to make?"

"Yes. On behalf of VBione Corp, we would like to thank you for your time, Your Most Supreme Majesty. We urge you to think of the future, of the cooperation between Krug and Gaard. With the extra money placed into research and development, we will be even more capable of combating the ever-mutating viruses and bacteria that threaten our society. With our innovative data repository, linking with Medseet will enable fast-paced antiviral development and response time, should an outbreak occur."

"Councillors," I said, "any final thoughts before I pass judgment?"

"I don't like how powerful VBione Corp will become after this acquisition," Nnati said, defiant as always. It was nice to have someone with Nnati's commoner upbringing on the council. He always called it like it was when the noble-born council members sucked their thumbs and remained quiet. I respected Nnati for that, but it didn't mean I had to agree with him.

"Noted," I said.

Aska Xi spoke up. "I think it's a good thing. Super-bugs have been a threat since the beginning of time, and our defense against them is tenuous at best. Our medicines are regulated no matter what happens here today. To have more effort put into the development of new drugs to help our citizens is an opportunity we can't ignore."

"Thank you, Xi," I said. Then I looked down at Hagan, standing patiently and with supreme confidence, as if she already knew her case was won. "I side in favor of VBione Corp," I announced. "This case is closed."

Hagan didn't whoop or smile. She simply said, "Thank you, Your Most Supreme Majesty," and walked backward from the room with her burly associates, bowing deeply.

I could feel Nnati's anger. He had his arms folded, staring straight ahead. I wanted to comfort him, to say it was the right decision and I was sorry, but Torio spoke up in his loud voice. "Next on the docket," he said, "the commemoration of Lordin. The clans would like to build a monument in the capital. People could visit, see her work, remember Lordin for—"

"Skip," I said. I didn't want to think about Lordin. I was sure Zawne was visiting her binightly in Shiol. I had resolved to speak with him about it but hadn't found the time. I'd been too upset about Roki and too busy being queen.

"Skip?" Torio sounded confused.

"Skip," I repeated. "On to the next, Torio. I'll deal with Lordin later."

* * *

ZAWNE and I ate dinner quietly that night, nothing but the sound of our knives scraping against our plates. I needed to broach the subject of Lordin without coming across accusatory. I started with something neutral.

"What do you think of the rulings?" I asked. "Do you ever consider ruling differently from what the Crown of Crowns recommends?"

"I wouldn't dare," he said, very matter-of-factly. Then Zawne did something I hadn't expected. He got up and moved around the table, hunkered down next to me, and cupped my face in his hands. It made me feel delicate, priceless, like he did still want me.

"I'm sorry we have been so stressed," he said, and kissed me on the lips. "I want us to be okay together." He kissed me again, his breath delicious, his voice raspy.

"Me too," I said. I was lost in his voice, spellbound by his beautiful eyes. It felt like forever since we had spent quality time together. I still hardly knew him, yet

I was drawn to him nonetheless. I wanted to explore this draw, explore our relationship together. But I was worried about Lordin. I needed to know ... was our marriage authentic?

I moved to kiss him more deeply, helpless in the moment; Zawne had already gotten up and moved toward the door. "I have to go," he was saying.

And I just blurted it out. I had to say something before it drove me to insanity. "Have you seen her?"

"Who?" His face was scrunched up.

"Lordin," I said in a mousy voice. I was fearful of provoking Zawne's wrath. I didn't want to cause any more problems than we already had, especially now that Roki was out of my life. My husband was all I had left.

Zawne's demeanor grew cold. He stomped across the dining room, grabbed a chair, and dragged it loudly across the floor, flipped it around in front of me, and sat down, leaning and glowering into my face. "I don't know," he said. "Have you seen your boyfriend, Roki?"

My heart stopped. I bumbled, "I ... Roki ..."

Lordin must have told him about Roki and me! No wonder Zawne had let me be depressed the last week or so. He had known the whole time.

"That's what I thought," he snarled. "And yes, I have seen Lordin. She was my fiancée before you, remember? She came to me one night after we were crowned. She told me about you and your sweetheart. She told me everything."

"We never touched!" I said, feeling humiliated. It was worse because we had touched. I had touched Roki's sweet face, held his strong hands ...

"It looks like we both have secrets," Zawne said.

152

I felt I needed to explain myself. Maybe if Zawne heard the truth from me, we could get past it together. Maybe we could still salvage our relationship. "Roki was my first love," I stammered. "I never knew he was a Min. He came to me around the time of the coronation, and I agreed to be his friend. But nothing else happened. He's not my sweetheart, as you say. I haven't even seen him in almost two weeks."

"Sure," Zawne scoffed. He didn't believe me.

I knew it was unfair of me to demand anything from Zawne, but I had to know if he had gotten back together with Lordin. "Are you done with me?" I asked. "I know I screwed up, so I understand if you've gone back to Lordin. Just please tell me, have you? Are you seeing her again?"

"I'm not going to answer that," Zawne said, standing up angrily and moving across the room. He stopped at the door. "You knew what had happened to Lordin this whole time, about her death, about how she had chosen to become a Min over ruling the kingdom. But you hid that from me just like you hid Roki from me. How does it feel to be kept in the dark?"

I started to cry. I had never imagined Zawne could be so icy, so heartless. Yet it was my own fault. I had lusted after two men, and now I was paying the price.

"I didn't betray you," I said, but my words came out weak. "I'm not going to see him again. I am yours, Zawne. I am only yours."

But a part of me wondered, *Am I only saying this because Roki turned out to be a scoundrel?*

Zawne saw my pain, and his anger faltered. His expression changed to one of compassion. He wasn't so heartless after all. "We will work it out," he said, his

153

voice softer. "We are set to be king and queen for the next forty years. We will be together."

"When?" I asked. I hated how I seemed to be begging my own husband for time together.

"We'll find opportunities," he said. He sounded sad, unsure. "We're both busy between council meetings and visiting Shiol, but we will find time. We'll find a way."

Then Zawne left. I was alone, tears spilling onto my untouched meal.

* * *

I NEEDED TISSA. I had Nnati available to me every day, since he lived on the other side of VondRust in the advisers' mansion, but my sister-in-law was on the other side of Gaard, ruling the Ava-Gaard alongside my brother. It had been ages since we'd talked. One night, after a long series of council meetings, while Zawne drifted off to Shiol, I fired up my visin and called Tissa.

"So good to hear from you," she exclaimed. "It's been too long. How are things?"

"Things are things," I said. I was ready to unload. "It's a bit chaotic. Everyone in the kingdom is waiting for me to rule on Lordin's commemoration, the monument they want me to approve in the capital. It's been weeks and I'm still undecided. All I can say is that I'm glad the ex-queen and ex-king are coming home early from Shondur. They decided to live in VondRust, and they'll be back tomorrow."

"It's good to have a confidant," Tissa said, reminding me of how Roki had been just that before the betrayal. "But why are you so undecided about Lordin?"

I groaned into my visin. How could I possibly

explain to Tissa that I was competing for my husband's love with a dead woman? "It's complicated," I said. "I'm just unsure what to do. I don't know if Lordin really deserves a monument. It doesn't seem very humble, if you ask me."

"No," Tissa said, "it doesn't. What does Nnati think?"

I laughed. "You know Nnati. He wonders how we can spend all that money on such a thing. He doesn't think one person deserves to be raised up so high. She was righteous and fluent in Decens-Lenitas, and people all over Geniverd looked up to her, but Nnati questions the morality of the project."

"As he would," Tissa said with a smirk. "We've always known Nnati thought Lordin was too self-righteous, using her fame to reach for the stars. Sometimes I wonder if he isn't a secret Gurnot."

"As if!" I said. "Not in a million years. Besides, Nnati has too much work to be running around with those scoundrels, setting fires and wreaking havoc. Not to mention he's loyal to me. There's no doubt about that."

Tissa nodded her agreement. "No doubt at all."

"Anyway," I said, "the clans want a monument, so I suppose I will have to build one. Really, there are too many important things I need to focus on besides Lordin. It's a relentless barrage of problems here. It seems like everyone has a grudge with everyone else. And Surrvul is always involved in one way or another."

"It's the same here, on the other side of Gaard," Tissa said. "Every day is something new. Raad and I try to deal with the problems as quickly as possible, but even with our council, decisions are tough."

We both went silent then, letting the gravity of our new appointments weigh upon us.

Then Tissa said, "By the way, I meant to introduce you to Rein and Forschi." She shifted her visin from her face to her bed, where two big dogs with puffy white coats and little black eyes sat quietly. The dogs lifted their paws and waved at me. They were adorable.

I waved back. "Hello!"

And then Tissa's face zoomed back in. "Aren't they just the cutest?" she said. "Raad had them made specifically for me. I got them yesterday. You'd never guess they aren't real, right? They are smart replicas. They understand everything I say; they can dance; they can cuddle me; they can follow complicated orders. Plus I can turn them off when they get annoying! They don't even need to use the toilet. I'm supposed to keep them clean, but I just make one of the Protectors do it for me. I really can't be bothered with cleaning anything but myself."

"Do people have real pets?" I asked.

"People do, Kaelyn, not nobles. Nobles get smart replicas. They're better than natural animals, which can be unpredictable and stinky. The last thing I need are muddy paw prints all over the new carpets in our chamber. That would be a disaster, and I simply don't have time for it."

Tissa sighed. It was as if the mere notion of a dirty carpet stressed her out. "Things were so much easier, huh," she said, "back when we worked from our office in the city. Our only concern then was helping the less fortunate. Now a whole new team is running GMAF. I'm ruling over Gaard with your brother while you try to mend the world with Nnati whispering in your ear. Things sure have changed."

"They sure have," I said. Things were tough. Even

with the Crown of Crowns' recommendations to guide me, I repeatedly had trouble making firm judgments. I worried that my council was beginning to question my indecision.

I began to ask, "How's Raa—?" but my visin bleeped in my ear. It was Torio. He had never called me so late before. My heart dropped like an anvil. What could Torio possibly have to tell me in the middle of the night?

"I'm sorry, Tiss," I said, "I've got to go. It's Torio on the other line."

She made a sad face. "Okay, I understand. Duty calls. We'll talk later. Raad is missing you."

"And I'm missing Raad. Please tell Papa I love him. Bye, Tissa. Bye, Rein and Forschi."

The dogs yipped in the background as I ended the call and picked up Torio. His face appeared on my holographic screen. He looked agitated.

"Torio, what's wrong?"

"People are dying," he said—no pause, no formalities, straight to the point. Torio didn't beat around the bush. "Twenty deaths in Nurlie since yesterday. Five deaths in Surrvul. Three deaths in Krug. It's an outbreak, Kaelyn. It's a viral illness unlike anything Geniverd has ever seen. We're hours away from a pandemic!"

CHAPTER 12

"What do you mean, an outbreak? What's going on, Torio?"

I was suddenly very awake, hunched on the edge of my bed, shouting at the screen of my visin. Zawne was sprawled out behind me in la-la land, probably in Shiol with Lordin.

"It starts as a fever," Torio said. "Then it escalates into vomiting, hallucinations, and eventually death. We think it began two days ago. As of right now, there are three hundred people hospitalized."

"Why have they not received medicine?" I asked. "Tell me there's a plan, Torio. I can't have widespread disease in my first year as queen!"

Torio made a face, ran his tongue across his teeth, and said, "Well, Your Most Supreme Majesty, the sick people have indeed received antivirals. However, the ones they need—the ones that can combat this virus—are not being delivered. This is also a mutated strain. We need an antiviral to be produced."

"So," I asked, "what's the holdup?"

"We are still waiting for word from the manufacturer. You might remember it: VBione Corp."

I gasped. "Don't tell me ..."

"Yes," Torio said, a look of deep remorse on his face. "They bought out the other companies. The only other manufacturing plant that could have engineered the right vaccine or produced antivirals was Medseet. VBione Corp absorbed them after you gave them permission. They shut down the plant in Krug, pending change of ownership."

A wave of nausea swept over me. I got out of bed and stumbled through the darkness of the apartment. Had I made the wrong decision? Why had the Crown of Crowns made me rule in favor of VBione Corp?

"Is there no one else?" I asked Torio. "What of the antimicrobial producers in Gaard? There must be some way to stop this before it spreads."

"We've started to quarantine," Torio said, "but it may be too late. I'm not sure that you gauge the scope of VBione Corp's influence. They've gobbled up every large antimicrobial manufacturer across the six continents. We're relying solely on them to fix this, and they aren't delivering."

I was chewing on my lip. I had no idea what to do. How was I supposed to solve a global pandemic?

"Set up a meeting," I said to Torio. "I want everyone in my private council chamber in thirty minutes. Got it?"

"Yes, Your Most Supreme Majesty."

Torio ended the call. I paced for thirty seconds in the dark, wishing I could wake up Zawne. But no, he was flirting with his dead fiancée in Shiol. To heck with it, I could run the kingdom myself. I was the daughter of a Gaard-Ma. I had to keep her strength alive!

Then I remembered Raad. My brother was Gaard-Elder. I figured if anyone had access to the Gaard medical companies, it was him. I dialed his number on my visin while trying to get dressed in my massive dressing room.

"Kaelyn?" Raad was red eyed, half-asleep. I must have woken him. The light from his visin made him look like a ghostly silhouette. "What's going on? It's the middle of the night."

I spoke in bursts, trying to jam my legs into a pair of pants. "Disease spreading across Geniverd. Emergency. No medicine. People dead."

"Whoa," Raad said, sitting up and rubbing the sleep from his eyes. "What are you talking about? Slow down, sis."

I stopped, took a deep breath, and explained as best I could. I told Raad everything Torio had told me.

My brother gave me a look of resolve, but I could see the fear in his eyes as he said, "You need to stop this outbreak right away, before it gets out of control. Get ready for your emergency council meeting while I make some calls about VBione Corp. I've heard about their recent acquisitions, but I also heard you gave them the go-ahead. That's why I didn't make a fuss when they swallowed the last of their competitors here in Gaard. After Medseet, VBione Corp was simply too big. No one could refuse an offer from them."

I was having serious reservations about my decision regarding VBione Corp. I couldn't help but feel like I had been played for a fool. Yet it was what the Crown of Crowns had recommended. Did they have a divine plan regarding the outbreak? I needed to have a chat with Riedel and Hanchell as soon as possible. Something here didn't smell right.

I thanked Raad and ended the call.

* * *

I WAS on my personal hover scooter, zipping through the dimly lit pathway toward the government building with Protectors gliding behind me, when Raad called back.

"Any news?" I asked. There was no projection, just Raad's voice in my ear.

"Yes," he said, "and it's not good. First off, the spokesperson for VBione Corp claims they are having stability issues with the antivirals. They can't send them out, because they're not ready to be administered to humans. There is a batch undergoing testing as we speak. I don't know. It sounded fishy to me."

"Do you suspect foul play? Do you think their takeover of the industry was a precursor to the outbreak?"

"I don't know," Raad said, "but I don't like it. When I tried to figure out who the owner of VBione Corp is, I got lost in a web of fake names and addresses. There are backdoor dealings signed by twenty different people. There are mailing addresses in Surrvul, Krug, Shondur. I even found an address in Lodden that was devastated by an earthquake three years ago. It doesn't even exist anymore! Whoever owns VBione Corp has put a lot of effort into not being found."

"I don't like the sound of that," I said. "Not one bit."

"Neither do I. It seems orchestrated to me," Raad

said. "I'm going over to VBione Corp with Protectors and some of my best Aska councillors straightaway. We're going to get to the bottom of this. You work on containing the infection."

"Got it," I said. I was coming up on the government building.

"And one other thing," Raad said. "I checked the news before I called. More people are dying. Five hundred people in Nurlie, fifty in Lodden, and thirty-eight in Surrvul. You need to get a message out and advise people to stay indoors. You can't let this thing spread to the capital."

* * *

TORIO GREETED me as I entered my private council chamber. "Your Most Supreme Majesty, I have requested Dr. Weintag be sent for straightaway to assist in the emergency meeting. He should be arriving shortly. Dr. Weintag is an expert in airborne infections and viral mutations."

"Excellent," I said. I took a quick look around to make sure everyone was present. All five of my councillors sat red eyed in their respective seats, waiting for me. "Let's get started," I told Torio. "We have no time to waste."

"The king?" he asked. "Shouldn't the king and his council also be here?"

"He's busy," I said, moving past Torio to take my chair. "All you've got is me. Now let's get started."

We squabbled for a few minutes over the best way to proceed. Master Widrig suggested stifling the news so we didn't cause a panic, but I quickly squashed that idea. I ordered Lady Katrin to put out a public warning for people not to go outdoors without breathing masks and to leave their homes only if there was an emergency. I had Master Widrig authorize huge overtime payments to doctors and nurses for the extra work, then had him order every able-bodied medical professional to their nearest hospital. "We need to be fully staffed and prepared," I said, "even here in the capital."

Next, Torio sent out orders to the Protectors to begin door-to-door safety checks and take any infected people straight into quarantine. Special bubbles were already being put into use all over the globe to try to contain the virus. Still, I had Aska Nikhel put out a travel ban. No flyrarcs, no boats, no trains. As of that moment, travel between continents was off-limits.

And that was when Dr. Weintag entered the room. He was an older gentleman with white hair and a dusty lab coat.

"Good morning, Dr. Weintag," I said. "Please take the floor. Tell us everything you know."

Dr. Weintag cleared his throat and activated his visin. He began talking us through the images on his screen.

"We're dealing with a sudden mutated strain of the flu virus, which we're calling KS3. It's airborne. That's why we're having trouble containing it. As far as we can tell, it has spread to all continents. We now have a global pandemic. This is a red-alert situation, Your Most Supreme Majesty. Testing from the last twelve hours indicates KS3 is continuing to mutate and evolve. None of our medicines are working. Upon entering the human system, KS3 bypasses all antibodies and attacks the central nervous system, causing fever, chills, nausea, vomiting, delirium, and ultimately ... death."

"What's the death toll at now?" I asked. "Someone check the damn reports!"

Master Widrig said, "Four thousand in Nurlie, eight hundred in Krug, four hundred in Surrvul, two fifty in Lodden, one hundred in Shondur, and fifty in Gaard. The capital is no longer safe."

No one even gasped. They just blinked, eyes huge, breathing shallowly. Lady Katrin said, "At this rate, the world could be gone by tomorrow night."

"Not all of it," Dr. Weintag said. "We will live, and the clan leaders, I'm sure, have already retreated to their secret underground bunkers. None of the clan leaders dare retreat to their remote lodgings or private sanctuaries, because of the Gurnot pyromaniac on the loose. The ones who will suffer seriously from this disaster are the commoners, all the people in the street who can't escape the devastation of KS3. As for you, my queen, I suggest wearing a breathing mask from this point on."

A Protector then entered the room with a box full of sterilized items. My councillors and I each put them on, then exchanged frightened looks through our masks and visors.

"We need an effective antiviral," the doctor said, "and we need it now. This is the most potent flu we've seen in our time, much like the Great Destroyer Bug, which wiped out over half our population five hundred years ago. The basic reproduction number is very high. By our calculations, over five hundred million people will be dead by next week. We have roughly forty-eight hours to put a lid on this."

"What can we do in the meantime?" Nnati asked. "How can we protect ourselves and the people?"

Dr. Weintag ran his hand through his wispy white hair. He was visibly trembling. I could understand why. This outbreak had the potential to end the world. "We need the Protectors to begin handing out antiviral sprays," he said, "breathing apparatus, gloves, sterile wipes, and even flimsy bodysuits to keep the masses relatively safe. As for the nobility, I highly suggest refraining from touching or even being in the same room with others."

"Got it," I said. Then I addressed my councillors. "From now on, all meetings will be held through visins. I want my staff barricaded in sealed rooms behind sterilized barriers. Everyone, take extra breathing masks with you when you leave and only let the Protectors into your rooms to deliver supplies."

I turned my attention to Torio, who had been listening while swiping the channels on his visin and responding to messages. "Any news of VBione Corp?" I asked.

"They claim the test batch failed. They're starting trials for another batch. They hope to have it ready within two days."

"Damn it!" I smashed my fists down on the table. "We don't have two days! I want everyone on their visins right now. I don't care who you have to call, who you have to pay, who you have to threaten with banishment—I want the old Medseet lab up and running by noon today. I want every available scientist, biologist, pathogen specialist, and medical expert in that factory working on a cure by tonight. Do you understand me?"

"Yes, Your Most Supreme Majesty," they all said, scrambling to get to work.

I realized then that my breathing was erratic. I was all jacked up on adrenaline. It was the intensity of the moment, the whole world threatening to implode while my team and I scrambled to fix it. And where was Zawne during all this? He was hanging out in Shiol with his mistress. Maybe Lordin had been right in assuming Zawne was unprepared to be king.

I pushed my chair back and stood up, feeling more like a fierce queen than I would have thought possible three years—no, three weeks ago! "And someone find out who owns VBione Corp," I said. "I want a name within the hour!"

* * *

"I JUST DON'T GET IT," Nnati was saying over the visin. We were both in our private quarters, waiting for the Protectors to finish sanitizing everything and lock us inside until the KS3 scare was over. "These are profit-making companies. VBione Corp should want to make money. Why are they being so stubborn about getting the product to the people? They could be making a fortune!"

"I don't get it either," I said, sagging into my couch. Zawne had been placed in another part of the mansion under his own quarantine. If neither of us showed signs of infection after forty-eight hours, we would be allowed to rejoin each other. "I just really hope they're being honest. We haven't seen this kind of outbreak in a long time, so it's understandable if they were unprepared, what with so many people having immunity and the mandatory vaccinations. There shouldn't even be a superbug!"

"Yet there is," Nnati said with a sigh. "I feel bad. I've been joking about it for years, and now ..."

"Don't think like that," I told him. "We are going to work this out. The councillors are hard at work containing this, while Raad is investigating VBione Corp, and Dr. Weintag is helping to get the Krug medicine plant back up and running. Together we will come through."

Nnati gave me a confused look. "Where the heck is Zawne? What is the king doing in all this?"

Canoodling with Lordin, I wanted to say. But that wasn't entirely fair. Zawne was trapped in a private quarantine, just like me. I was sure he was working with his own councillors to mend the situation. "He's working tirelessly," I told Nnati. I wasn't about to start slandering the king, my husband. Not yet, anyway.

"Good," Nnati said. "I was beginning to think you were the only one ruling around here."

Just then Raad bleeped in on my visin. I told Nnati, "Got to go. Raad's calling," and switched lines.

"You have news?" I asked as my brother's sweaty face filled my screen. He looked crazed, stressed, totally frantic. I'd never seen him like this. I wondered how disheveled he would have been without the Aska training.

"A lot of news, and none of it good."

Raad wiped sweat from his brow, closed his eyes to steady himself, and then said, "Someone's out to incite global chaos. I can't tell you why. It could be because they're angry about you and Zawne taking the crown. It could be an idea that's been fermenting on one of the

167

continents for a long time, maybe a shadow government, maybe the Gurnots. I really don't know. But listen to this, I got nowhere at the VBione Corp main factory. They have batches of the antiviral being made on the assembly line but claim they're not ready. They claim it isn't potent enough to halt the virus from spreading. They need to create an entirely new compound. I saw their scientists busy in labs, so they do appear to be working on a cure. Meanwhile, it's not ready and people are dying."

Raad sucked in a gulp of air. "And it seems like no one is in charge. Or at least, no one knows who's in charge. There are factory foremen, but the higher-ups all respond to a computer, to messages sent to their visins. I have my best techs working on triangulating the signal. However, it's being bounced off satellites. It's like we're up against a supervillain or something. I don't know what to make of it."

I didn't either. A freaking supervillain? Why did disaster have to unfold under my watch? All I wanted was a peaceful kingdom. But no, I had maniacs unleashing viruses, polluting the planet with toxins, killing thousands. Never had I wanted to be in Zawne's embrace more than in that moment, to have him hold me and tell me everything would be all right. But I couldn't even do that. We were under quarantine for another forty-eight hours. I didn't even care about Lordin anymore. I just wanted Zawne.

I slumped into my chair. "Thank you, Raad. Will you let me know when your techs find a name? I want this person brought in for questioning and VBione Corp destroyed."

"You've got it, sister queen. But ..." Raad hesitated, lips twisted in a scowl. "But that's not all. There's more."

"Oh dear." I whacked myself in the forehead. "What is it? Give it to me straight, Raad. Things can't get much worse."

"They can," he said dourly. "They can and they have. Remember the dispute between Nurlie and the rogue islanders? Well, it's elevated into rioting. The entire island is in upheaval. People have taken to the streets, burning vehicles and smashing windows. It's anarchy. They're demanding a referendum while the shadow government is gearing up for an invasion of the mainland. Nurlie is scared."

"Can't we send in Protectors?" I asked. "Can't they put a stop to the riots?"

"Maybe," Raad said, but it sounded a lot like a question. "The problem is that too many players have come onto the stage. With the KS3 virus ravaging Nurlie, all the little weasels have come out of their holes. The Gurnots have taken up arms on the mainland and on the island, inciting both sides of the conflict to all-out war. They've brought tech with them, high-end stuff that they shouldn't have. I'm talking laser clubs, proton beams, mobile incinerators. We sent a legion of Protectors to the island, and they were disabled in just a few minutes, their circuits fried by camouflaged Gurnots with laser clubs."

Raad groaned. "And don't even get me started on the fires. Whole squads of Protectors have been melted into mercury by an unknown assailant while the last few luxury retreats in Surrvul have gone up in flames, all of them belonging to clan heirs or heiresses. I know the media calls the arsonist the Dragon, and I'm starting to wonder if it isn't true, if it isn't a flesh and blood dragon."

While Raad explained, I divided my visin screen in half and turned on the news. P2 drones were recording the pandemonium in the streets of Nurlie and on the island. There were flyrarcs crashing and smoldering in buildings, waves of demonstrators waving the island's flag and throwing bricks at the barricade of Protectors, sick people dying in the streets. It was absolute carnage.

"I can't believe this," I said. "Who's responsible? Who's given them such high-tech weapons? I thought weapons were reserved for the Askas and highest level of Battle Protectors, the P5 Protectors."

"They are," Raad said, and I could tell he was mad by the growl in his voice. "But one of my inside sources told me Surrvul's new clan leaders are funding the rebels and maybe even the Gurnots. It sounds to me like this could have been in development for a long time. It could also be an opportunistic move by the eldest of the Surrvul Clan, who took power last month. Everyone knows they want the crown with a violent passion. I wouldn't be surprised if they're trying to cause so much global turmoil that you and Zawne are forced to step down. Or worse, they could be planning an invasion of the Gaard continent and global war."

"They'd never," I said. I was aghast. Not only was a deadly virus on the loose, but now I had enemies, and they were mobilizing. They could be coming after me and my husband. I had never even wanted to be the stupid queen. It was supposed to have been Lordin's job!

"They might," Raad said. "And there's another issue. The Protectors. Their armor plating is produced in—

yup, you guessed it—Surrvul. They've been stockpiling the phosphorus we need to manufacture the armor, and the mines in Shondur are almost all dried up. There's nothing left. If Surrvul has been giving anti-Protector weaponry to the rebels, and the rebels start to win the fight, we won't be able to build any more Protectors. It'll be like ancient times. It'll be war like the world hasn't seen in five hundred years. The streets will run red with the blood of our people."

"Unacceptable," I said. "All of this. It's all unacceptable. We need to put an end to the referendum in Nurlie before they start a war. We need to start restricting Surrvul's access to our precious minerals. We need to take away the Gurnots' weapons. We need to put a stop to whoever is burning down half the world, before they reach Gaard and burn down the palace. And we need to find a cure for this disease before it wipes out everyone in Geniverd."

"All in forty-eight hours," Raad said with a hollow, hopeless laugh.

I thanked him for the information and ended the call. I was at my wits' end. Where did I go from here? I had to save the world, but how? I couldn't even get my own husband to look me in the eye!

CHAPTER 13

*E*verything had spiraled out of control. It was about time I made it back to Shiol. By the time I ended the call with Raad, it was only four in the afternoon, but I recalled that the Crown of Crowns had told me I could take an emergency nap if I ever needed to speak with them. Well, if this wasn't an emergency, I didn't know what was.

I lay on the sofa, let fatigue overtake me ...

And Zawne called me. My visin bleeped, and I saw his name on the display. "Oh, great," I said. "Here we go. Hello, Zawne," I said, sitting upright so we could talk face-to-face.

He looked upset. I could tell he was emotional. He said, "I'm sorry," and I was taken aback. Really, Zawne was sorry? Sorry for what?

Then again, if Zawne wanted to make amends, I was okay with that. "I'm sorry too," I said. "I'm sorry I kept secrets from you. It was wrong, I know."

"And I'm sorry I was distant," he said. "I'm sorry I

lashed out at you. It wasn't right. Our ex-lovers showed up as Min. We were both confused and conflicted, torn between two worlds. The fact is, Kaelyn, I love you. And we're both here in the real world. It took this whole KS3 fiasco for me to realize how important you are to me. The world's falling apart, and all I can think about is you."

Zawne had left me speechless. I moved my mouth, unable to make a sound. I wished he were beside me so I could reach out and touch him. Damn the blasted quarantine! "I ... I love you too, Zawne."

We held each other's gaze for a full minute, peering through the visin's display into one another's eyes. It was romantic. I wanted to somehow slither through the screen and kiss him.

I eventually said, "It's nice talking to you like this. We've been at odds, and it sucks. I wish we could be a team in this terrible time."

"We are," he said. "You and me, king and queen for life. We're the best team in Geniverd."

I chuckled. "Yeah, and we're trapped in separate apartments for the next forty-eight hours. The world will be on fire by then."

"I've started to put the fire out," he said with a cocky smile. "I sent a delegation to Nurlie to try to calm the rebellion. There will be a meeting held later today between all parties to come to an agreement. If the fighting continues, we'll use force."

"Force ... What do you mean?"

"The underwater weapons system," he said. "It's been dormant for hundreds of years. The clans have been at peace, so there hasn't been a need for it. But it's still there, waiting to be used. We have enough firepower to wipe out Nurlie, Surrvul—every continent except Gaard if we need to."

I was appalled. I had known there were weapons, but I hadn't known how powerful they were. Torio had planned to give me a tutorial but had never gotten around to it, because we had been so busy.

Zawne saw my shock. "What did you expect?" he asked. "Did you think the rulers of the world wouldn't have a fail-safe, a means to maintain power? People may have forgotten because generations have come and gone, but the Crown still has the power to wipe out ninety-five percent of Geniverd with the push of a button. We've come this far because of war. From the ashes of destruction, we built this peaceful civilization. I promise you, Kaelyn, there will not be an invasion of the capital."

"What about Decens-Lenitas?" I asked, frantically making up excuses. "What about the public? They would surely hate us for the next forty years if we unleashed weapons."

Zawne shook his head. "The public are not the ones in power; we are. In times of trouble, we must maintain our image before the other clan heads to keep their respect. That's what Decens-Lenitas is all about, Kaelyn, respecting the monarchy, the upper class, the system, obeying the orders of those in power. And do not be mistaken, even though we have councillors and *you-know-who* pulling the strings, we are the ones who rule the world. Our word is law. The people must obey."

"I don't care," I said. "I couldn't wipe out millions of human souls. Not ever. When did Decens-Lenitas become a means for retaining power within the upper echelon of society? Does it mean nothing for the rest of our people, for the ninety-nine percent who are at our mercy? It's not fair, Zawne. We can't butcher our own subjects just to save face with a handful of spoiled nobility."

"Would you prefer a long and bloody war?" Zawne asked. "The alternatives are worse, Kaelyn, much worse."

"I ... I won't let it come to that," I insisted. "I refuse to resort to weapons! I will stop this before it goes too far."

"How?" Zawne asked. "We can't even leave our living quarters! We still don't know who's in charge of VBione Corp. We can't even catch the elusive Gurnot who's been torching our residences. There are almost no retreats left in Surrvul or Shondur for the wealthy to take vacations." Zawne snarled and furrowed his eyebrows in frustration. "It doesn't even matter. I just want to be with you, Kaelyn. We should be solving this mess together."

"I know," I said.

It was weird. As the apocalypse bloomed on the horizon, Zawne and I were finally coming into our own as a couple. The fights were behind us, the secrets, the betrayals. If only we could survive the next week. If only ...

A message popped up in the corner of my screen. It was from Raad. While Zawne went on boasting about his love for me, I opened the message and read it.

KAELYN, *triangulated origin of signal. Boss of VBione Corp is Emell—Lordin's mother. En route to make arrest. Seek ex-queen for answers. Remember the story Mama told us when*

*we were young, about the king and his mistress. Don't tell
anyone. Trust no one.*

* * *

IT TOOK LONGER than I would have liked to get off the
call with Zawne after reading Raad's message. Zawne
kept babbling on about our union and our future
together, which was sweet, but I had priorities. I had a
mystery to solve. A whole new set of clues and
misshaped puzzle pieces had fallen into my lap.

I sent a discreet message to the ex-queen, requesting
a secret meeting in the evening, somewhere on Vond-
Rust grounds. I would have to be sneaky to get out of
my quarantine and past the Protectors. I figured if I
could do that, then I could sneak into Zawne's private
apartment and spend the night with him, feel his
strong, calloused hands, full lips, tight abs ... Yeah, that
was a good idea.

But first I had to get to Shiol. I had to start asking
the important questions. Lordin, Emell, VBione Corp,
KS3, Nurlie rebels, Gurnots, Surrvul's greed—was it all
connected?

I lay back and closed my eyes. Before I knew it, I
was standing in the spatial void with Riedel and
Hanchell glittering before me.

"What gives?" I said. I was in no mood to screw
around.

"What gives with what?" Riedel asked, his blob of
light fluctuating. I had the sense he was being purposely
coy.

"Oh," I said, rubbing my chin sarcastically. "I don't
know. Maybe the fact that because of your recommen-

dations regarding VBione Corp, and against my better judgment, the kingdom is now on the brink of war. Not to mention the thousands of people dying as we speak. All of Geniverd has gone to the dogs in the last twelve hours."

"Oh," Riedel said, "that. Yes. We have been watching."

"So?" I asked. I was on the verge of hysterics. "What's the deal? How could you not foresee this? Aren't you omniscient? Or did you know beforehand? Are you behind VBione Corp? Are you friends with Emell?" I sucked in a deep breath, looked between their flashing masses. "What gives?"

"Well," Hanchell said, "we can see the future, but not so well. Our capabilities are restricted to somewhere between twelve and twenty-four hours. We had no idea humanity would break out in disease or conflict. In fact, the whole reason we ruled in favor of VBione Corp was because one of our Min convinced us it was the smart move for Geniverd. She told us that by siding with VBione Corp, more potent and effective medicines would be put into mass production. She showed us convincing evidence, and we passed the order along to you. We take full responsibility for the poor recommendation. That was our bad."

"Your bad?" I was furious! The Crown of Crowns was not supposed to make mistakes.

"Let us remind you," Riedel said, "at the end of the day, our recommendations are just that: recommendations. We picked you as queen because of your wise mind and questioning heart. Had you felt strongly enough to disagree with our suggestion, it was your decision to make."

"Now you tell me," I said sourly. I felt deflated, as if the Crown of Crowns had just smooshed the air out of me. *My decision to make?* They were trying to blame the entire mess on me, say everything was my fault because I didn't listen to my gut! The Crown of Crowns was acting like a couple of cowards!

"We do apologize," Hanchell said. "And we wish we could fix it. However, we are unable to directly interfere with humanity. We have our Min working to keep the balance, but we oversee everything from the spirit dimension. The future of Geniverd is in your hands, Queen Kaelyn. There's nothing we can do."

"You're saying I'm on my own?" I asked.

"You have all the resources available to a queen," Hanchell said chipperly.

"But I need your help! Can you at least tell me why Emell has done all this? And who was the Min who gave you the suggestion to side with VBione Corp? Was it Lordin? If you could at least fill in some of the blanks, it would make it easier for me to save the world from my quarantined apartment."

Hanchell and Riedel both fizzled strangely. I thought they were uncomfortable, which was odd considering they were thousands of years old and had seen this sort of thing before, war and death and disease.

"We cannot divulge information about our Min," Hanchell said. She at least sounded sad about it. "We do want to help you, Queen Kaelyn, but we cannot give up the secrets of the Min to a human. Our bond is sacred and may not be broken. However, we can tell you that Emell is currently being taken into custody by your brother. She is the head of VBione Corp, and she is very angry at the seat of power and seeks vengeance. As for the Nurlie conflict and the virus, it's almost too late. Without the distribution of a full cure in the next thirty-six hours, the world will be consumed by disease."

"Great," I said, all hope sucked out of me. "The world is doomed, and there's nothing I can do about it."

"No," Riedel said, "not doomed. The world will not end; it will merely regrow, like a forest burned to the ground that takes a long time to grow back. Humanity will flourish once again."

"But four billion lives will be lost!" I screamed. "I can't have that. I must save my people. I must protect the six clans!"

"I have an idea," Hanchell said, her gaseous light brightening to a fantastic hue of yellow. "What about your friend Roki? He's a good Min. We may not be able to give you information, but he can. I suggest you seek out Roki. He may be your only hope."

* * *

THE CROWN of Crowns had proved more useless than I could have possibly imagined. I supposed they didn't care. I couldn't blame them. If ninety-five percent of humanity were wiped out, they would just watch and wait while society regrew and restructured itself. We were nothing to them, a kingdom of ants who could rebuild if our nest was destroyed. Time was irrelevant to such beings. Five hundred years went by in the blink of an eye.

I woke from my nap supremely exhausted, eyes red and bleary. I sat up and checked the news on my visin.

Twenty thousand more deaths around the globe. It was already more death than anyone in my generation had seen. It was too much, too devastating. I had to stop it. But that meant ...

Roki.

What had the Crown of Crowns meant when they told me he was a good Min? What did that mean to them? So long as Roki did his job in Geniverd for them, he could be considered good. But I knew better. Roki was an evil womanizer. Yet lives were at stake. The world was at stake. It looked like I was going to have to swallow my pride and call out to him. I just had to promise myself it would be strictly business. Then, after we saved the world, I wouldn't speak with him anymore. I also had to promise myself that when I saw him again in the flesh, I would refrain from getting emotional. No matter how badly I wanted to, I could not touch him. Not even a friendly hug!

I got off the couch and stretched, almost too exhausted to think. It was a quarter past seven, the time sifting away from me like grains of sand. Only thirty-four hours left to free the world from disease.

I checked my messages while pacing in a circle, trying to get my energy back. Raad had left a message saying he was escorting Emell to the security compound outside NordHaven but that she insisted she was guilty of no wrongdoing. As if to spite her arrest, VBione Corp had finally issued antivirals that could slow down the effects of KS3, though they claimed the full cure was still in development.

There was a message from Torio saying the delegation to Nurlie had been involved in a fist fight, and another message five minutes later saying that war between the island and the mainland was now imminent.

Nnati had left messages asking to call him back; so had Tissa. But they didn't have information relating to the salvation of Geniverd. They just wanted to make sure I was okay.

"Sorry, guys," I said to myself. "We'll have to catch up later. I've got to save the world."

Then I saw my final message. It was from the ex-queen. She had agreed to meet me in a secluded corner of VondRust's southern gardens at eight o'clock, in forty-five minutes. I scrambled to find a disguise and get ready, snuck from my room, and slipped through the halls of my mansion, out into the heat of the night, then farther into the garden.

* * *

UNDER DIFFERENT CIRCUMSTANCES, the garden meeting with Zawne's mama, the ex-queen, would have been pleasant. Under the moonlight, the flowers appeared moist, the strong scent of jasmine and hyacinth filling my nostrils, the beautiful twilight of the atmospheric bubble around VondRust painting the night in deep blacks and blues, like a fairy-tale garden. But as it was, the meeting was grim.

The Queen Emerita emerged from the shadows, wearing a black robe, her face covered by a thick scarf. I myself wore a gardener's outfit with my hair hidden beneath a cap.

"Good evening, daughter-in-law. What can I do for you in the midst of this unfolding tragedy? You clearly didn't bring me here to talk about the flowers."

"Sadly not," I said. It sucked, because I would have preferred to welcome the ex-queen back home under better circumstances, with a grand feast and much wine and laughter. "I asked you here because the kingdom is under siege, and I have a feeling you're familiar with the attacker."

"Is that so?" She came close to me, and I felt right away how warm a woman she was, kind and gentle. "Tell me, child," she whispered. "Tell me of this attacker. I trust you took a nap today."

It was funny. We both knew of the Crown of Crowns yet were sworn to secrecy, even with each other. I had to choose my words carefully. "I did have a nap, but it was not useful. I woke up more confused than ever."

"That may happen from time to time," she said with a sad smile.

I paused, wondering how to bring up Emell. I thought of Raad's message, him reminding me of the story Mama used to tell. I was sure Emell was the mistress in the story and that the king was the King Emeritus, Mama the Gaard-Ma in the scenario. I just came out with it.

"I heard a story once," I said. "In the story was a mistress of pale skin and light eyes. She had the king's ear, and the king of the time was very greedy for the land of Gaard. Gaard-Ma beseeched the mistress for her aid but was shunned. As a result, Gaard-Ma started a rumor that eventually drove the mistress to be condemned and banished to the farthest corner of Gaard. I've recently discovered who these players were, their true identities."

The ex-queen smiled at me. "You're a clever girl. It's

easy to see why my son fell for you. To answer your question, yes, I was reigning queen during this debacle. And yes, your mama was Gaard-Ma. And Lordin's mother was the banished mistress. Imagine my surprise when Lordin began to gain fame throughout the kingdom. I couldn't believe it when she ascended all the way to Zawne's bedchamber. He never did know the truth of her mother, and the king and I kept our mouths shut."

She regarded me curiously. "But considering the severity of the current plague and turmoil, why bring this to me now?"

"Because Emell is the owner of VBione Corp," I said. "Raad has arrested her on suspicion of genocide. I am merely trying to determine how involved she is in everything. I'm trying to find a motive. I also need to know if Lordin is involved. As I'm sure you know ..." I had to remind myself to choose my words carefully. "She's dead, but not forgotten."

"Oh, I see." The ex-queen nodded, her face pinched in a contemplative expression. "That is troubling."

"It would help if you could explain what happened," I said. "My brother suspects this disaster was premeditated. If I can find motive, perhaps I can stop it."

"It was twenty-five years ago," she said, "but I will do my best to recall everything clearly."

She took a deep breath and told me the story.

"Emell was always a vindictive woman. She cared only for power, and the young king was drawn to her because of this. They wanted to rule the kingdom with an iron fist. The whole reason the king sought extra land from the Gaard farmers was to build a lavish estate for Emell, his whimsical mistress. Why do you think Emell refused to help Mama with her request to stop the land acquisition? Anyway, after the rumor began to circulate, the king was distraught. He held meetings with his councillors to try to fix it, but there was no way around Emell's banishment. It was the only way to save face with the other clan leaders, lest they try to oust him as king. He bid Emell farewell with a heavy heart, sending her to the frigid north of the continent, where she stayed.

"Yet Emell vowed to get her revenge against the Crown. Before she left, she cursed us. Emell was mad with hatred for the king, hatred for me, hatred for Gaard-Ma. She said, 'Your kingdom will collapse one day. Gaard-Ma will choke on her slanderous tongue. The king and queen will suffer horrible loss. And as for the kingdom ...' Emell cackled sickly, the Protectors dragging her from the palace. 'The kingdom will burn, and the people will vomit and die in the streets. I vow this with my life!'"

The ex-queen sighed. "I never took the curse seriously. Even with this virus sweeping the world, I never imagined Emell could be responsible. But you say it's true, daughter queen?"

"Sadly, yes." I had never heard that part of the story. I had never considered Lordin's mother to be a corrupt and jealous woman, cast aside and hungry for vengeance against the entire world. I was wondering about something now ... something I had wanted to know for a long time.

I asked, "Do you think it was Emell who poisoned Mama?"

Her face turned glum, and she put her arm around me. "I am sorry for your mama's death," she said.

"Gaard-Ma was a good woman, a good friend." She bit her lip, deep emotion moistening her eyes. "As for Emell ... it is possible she was involved. Perhaps she poisoned her. Perhaps Emell has been plotting the destruction of Gaard and the rest of the world for the past twenty-five years."

I gasped, staggered backward through the grass. "Which could mean ..."

"Yes," the Queen Emerita said. "It could mean Lordin has been helping her since day one. With Lordin's death ..."

She couldn't say it, but I knew what the ex-queen was thinking. She wanted to imply that with Lordin's transformation into a Min, Lordin would have ultimate power throughout Geniverd. She'd be able to pull strings, push the pieces where she wanted, maybe even get Zawne and me elevated to the throne. That was when I remembered Hagan and her mannerisms, her confidence. In a split second, I knew it had been Lordin inside Hagan's body, controlling her, securing the deal for VBione Corp. Yet how could Emell interact with Hagan-Lordin without knowing the Great Secret? Could it be Lordin was helping her mother from beyond the grave, using the cover of a businesswoman from Gaard?

It suddenly felt like I was in the center of a great conspiracy, a family rivalry that had trickled down through the years and left me to suffer in its fallout. It wasn't fair. It didn't make sense. Lordin had been such a good person in her life, so noble. Could that have been the plan all along? Could Emell have twisted Lordin and made her impure?

"I thank you for your time, but I must leave," I told the ex-queen. "I need to get to the bottom of this."

I also needed to confront Emell. If she had killed Mama, I wanted to look her in the eyes and hear her confess. I wanted justice.

CHAPTER 14

I was at a crossroads. To my left was the cobbled path to my mansion. To my right was the path to Zawne. I wanted more than anything to be cradled in his strong arms, to tell him everything I had discovered. I needed advice, and I needed it badly. I couldn't go to Nnati or Tissa, or even to Raad. I couldn't discuss the Great Secret with them, but I could discuss it with Zawne.

On the other hand, I was a little nervous of Zawne's allegiance. I was sure in my heart that he was fully unaware of Lordin's deception. Yet I couldn't risk it. I needed a mutual mind to help me. I needed …

"Roki."

I whispered his name, standing in the dark between the two mansions. I was out of options. He was the only one who could help me, even if I did hate him for betraying my trust. "Roki," I said, "I need you now. I need your help. I have nowhere to turn. I'm alone in the world."

I dreaded the thought of him appearing in front of me. I could still see the images of him and those other women tangled in lustful embraces. It made me sick. Yet deep in my heart was a longing for Roki. I had to trust my instincts, that summoning him was in my best interest.

His scent came to me on a breeze. I closed my eyes and felt the wind stir. When I opened them, Roki stood before me. Unlike in the past, he wore no smile. He had a sad and beaten quality to him. There was blood on his shirt.

"Are you bleeding?" I immediately threw away all my hardened resolve to keep things impersonal and rushed to Roki. I lifted his shirt and looked for wounds. I was checking him all over, Roki sagging where he stood as if drained of energy.

"No." He took my hands and gently pushed them against my chest. "But thank you for the concern. I have been helping in Nurlie, dragging the wounded from the streets, trying to protect the innocent. It's insanity there right now. Reinforcements are on their way, but right now it is violent. With Surrvul in the mix, flaunting their money and providing weapons, things look grim. The Gurnots are trying to help, but there is only so much they can do."

"The Gurnots? I thought they were terrorists!"

"Hardly," Roki said. We began to walk along the left path, toward my mansion, through the sweet night air. It was dark and no one could see us. "The Gurnots fight for the people of Geniverd. They despise the way Decens-Lenitas imprisons the lower classes. Everything they do is for the liberation of humanity. Sometimes they must use violence or intimidation tactics. It's why they released the Dragon. Just look, Kaelyn. Look at what the greed of the clans can do!"

Roki activated his visin to show me an overhead view of the nighttime violence in Nurlie. Buildings aflame, laser beams zipping between the ruined towers, wounded and dead stuck between two walls of opposing soldiers. The soldiers weren't even soldiers. Not really. They were ordinary men and women fighting for their cause. It was horrendous, and in their hands were weapons.

"I can't believe it has come to this," I said. "And on top of it, the virus is spreading. Why fight in the streets when people would be safer inside?"

Roki said, "They believe in their cause. That's stronger than the fear of death."

I had never thought about it like that before. I had never truly understood how devoted people were to their clans. Not until I saw them fighting, losing their lives for their beliefs. Only now did I realize the power the upper class and the media had over the masses. Quite frankly, it made me sick.

In the video, words on the bottom of the screen read: *Surrvul Clan denies involvement in Nurlie war. Claims soldiers are rebels and not endorsed by Surrvul.*

They had said this to save face, I figured. The clan leaders needed to keep up appearances, keep up their moral standing in the eyes of Decens-Lenitas. It was all blindfold politics. It wasn't for the people. It was all an act for the other illustrious families!

On Roki's screen, a massive ship came from the sky above the Nurlie capital. The back hatch opened, and P5 Protectors spilled from the ship by the dozen and used their booster systems to hover toward the ground.

They immediately started using their built-in supersonic artillery to push back the invading islanders. It was mayhem. People were blasted back into buildings, against flaming cars. I could hear the screams.

From the rooftop were blasts of light. "Oh no!" I said. "The rebels are using remote plasma cannons!"

"Yeah," Roki said.

We both watched the green particle beams launch off the rooftops and dissolve entire groups of P5 Protectors like they were made of butter. It was a barrage of laser fire back and forth. Human and robot, rebel and defender, Gurnot and Nurlie and Surrvul— they all fought and died in the ruined city, the P2 camera drones recording all the action for the people watching in their homes, one last bloody show before they died of the KS3 virus.

"The humanity," I said. "I can't watch it. Please, Roki. Please turn it off!"

He deactivated his visin. We were entering the mansion, and I said, "Can you mask our presence until we're in my apartment? I'm supposed to be under quarantine."

"I already am," he said, giving me his sweet smile. "I've been masking us since I heard your call and zipped across the world. I'm tuned in to your voice. If you say my name, I will always come."

"But—"

"Don't worry," he assured me. "I haven't been listening to your thoughts. I'm still not. I guess I don't really need to. I can tell what you're thinking without listening. I guess it's because of the bond between us."

"I guess so," I said. But I didn't want to fall back into our old ways. I was still mad. I couldn't let Roki's charms seduce me. I had to ask, "Is it possible for a Min to control a person to get what they want? I need to know if Lordin entered the body of a woman named Hagan. I also need to know if Lordin is conspiring with her mother. What I'm asking is, has Lordin used being a Min to bring about all this destruction to get her mother's revenge?"

Roki let out a sigh. We were in my room now, and he plunked himself down on my sofa while I sat on its arm, observing him. "Yes," he said. "It's what Min do best. They invade bodies to manipulate events. I've been a little busy these last few weeks and didn't really have my eye on Lordin, so I can't say for sure if she is involved. But it is possible. A Min can do pretty much anything."

An idea burst into my head like a bomb, shaking me to my core. *A Min can do anything. If I were a Min, I could save the world!*

It was a good thing Roki had stopped reading my thoughts. He would never have let me consider dying to become a Min. My friends, my family ... my husband. I would be abandoning them all. Yet how else could I stop the virus? If Lordin was the kingpin of this terrible design, I could never stop her in my useless human body.

"Thanks anyway," I said. "The Crown of Crowns is no help. I don't know if I can trust Zawne. I've recently found out Emell killed Mama. And now—"

A message blipped onto my visin. "Sorry," I said to Roki while I opened it. "It's from Raad. Oh no ..." I gasped. "Raad says they had to let Emell go free. There was no evidence to suggest she had designed and unleashed the virus, nor that she was withholding the proper medicine. He says an antiviral is in the works but won't be ready for approximately thirty hours. That means Emell is going to distribute the cure just in time to avert mass extinction."

"It's not enough," Roki said. "The virus is spreading too fast. Thirty hours will mean at least two million casualties." He buried his face in his hands. "I can't believe it. I thought humans had a handle on these viruses. How could one woman have done all this?"

"The scorn of a loved one," I said, catching Roki's eye. "It's amazing what a broken heart can do."

"Kaelyn ..." he said. I could see the yearning in his eyes. He wanted to touch me, to explain himself. I wasn't having any of it.

"Don't start," I said. "I saw the photos. I'm not blind." I shook my head. "Thank you for being here, Roki, but I think I need to be alone now. I have a lot of decisions to make."

"I'll always be here," Roki said. And then he vanished. Not even his scent lingered when he was gone.

* * *

I HAD LIED TO ROKI. I only had one decision to make. I needed to decide. Was I going to give up my life to become a Min?

The first thing I did was call Raad.

"Brother," I said when he answered, "you've made a terrible mistake letting Emell go."

"I know," he said. "I could see the guilt in her eyes when we arrested her, but there was no physical evidence. Plus VBione Corp had already started to ship the inhibitor antivirals to slow the virus. They've promised a cure within thirty hours. We had to release her."

"Thirty hours is too long," I said. "That's two million human lives, Raad. I'm positive Emell is biding her time until the very last second. She must want maximum casualties to make Zawne and me look incompetent."

"I figure the same thing," Raad said. "But my troops searched the VBione Corp main lab and factory. There was nothing. Protectors searched Emell's home, her known places of affiliation. They didn't find a single thing."

"What about the reopened plant in Krug?" I asked.

Raad shook his head. "It was a dud. VBione Corp had the Medseet factory stripped. It would take at least two weeks to rebuild the proper systems and get new machines online."

"Darn," I hissed. Then I looked to Raad. If I was going to become a Min, I needed to be sure he would chase Emell to the far corners of the planet. I needed to know he would get justice for Mama. "Raad," I said, "I talked to the ex-queen, like you suggested. And, well, we both figure it must have been Emell who killed Mama. We think she's been planning her revenge for twenty-five years."

Raad's eyes grew huge in anger. "What!" he bellowed. "I had Emell in my flyrarc! I had her in custody. And now you tell me this? Had I known she was responsible for Mama's death, I would have ... I would have ..."

"I'm sorry," I said, "but I just found out. It turns out Emell has a vendetta against our family and Zawne's family. She's poisoned the world to rid the throne of us.

193

She killed Mama to get revenge for being banished all those years ago."

"I knew she was the mistress in Mama's story," Raad said. "But I never suspected murder. I can't—"

"I'm sorry," I said, "but I have to go. There's something I need to do, and every second I stall means more lives lost. I love you, brother. Get justice for Mama. Find the truth."

I ended the call with tears in my eyes. How could I say goodbye to Raad for the last time? He would be so upset when my body was found. I was thinking about what the Crown of Crowns had told me: a painful and tragic death. It scared me, but I needed to be strong. Strong for Mama, for Gaard, for my friends.

My tears only worsened when I called Papa, Nnati, then Tissa. They all knew something was wrong, asking me a thousand questions.

"Is it Zawne?"

"Is it the virus?"

"Is it the images of war on the news?"

"Why are you crying?"

I wished I could tell them about Shiol, Min, my plan to save millions of lives. All I could do was thank them for their friendship and tell them I loved them. Then I sat in the dark and wept. Only one person left on my list.

"Hello, Zawne."

"You're still up too?" he asked.

"Yeah. I can't sleep with all this turmoil."

I struggled to hold back my emotion. Going through with becoming a Min meant I would probably never touch Zawne again, never taste his lips, never smell his musk. *Will he let me slip back into his life?* I wondered if it was how Lordin had felt, if she had felt anything. I still wasn't totally convinced she was evil. I asked Zawne, "Did you hear the news about Emell?"

He nodded, twisted his face in a grimace. "It's hard to believe my dead fiancée's mother was arrested on suspicion of planned genocide. I hope it's not true. I only met the woman once at Lordin's funeral, but she seemed okay. I can't believe someone like Lordin, someone so divine, would have been raised by a murderer."

I suddenly felt bad for doubting Zawne, thinking he was somehow involved in the KS3 mess. His eyes were too sincere to be lying. I knew in that instant he had nothing to do with Emell's plotting. It gave me hope that Lordin was innocent too.

"It's not important now," I said. "I just wanted to say good night."

Or goodbye, I thought. *Goodbye forever, my sweet king. I must make this ultimate sacrifice for the good of our people. It's what Mama would have done.*

"Good night, Kaelyn," he said. Zawne blew me a kiss through the screen. I caught it, and tears spilled down my face.

"I'm going to miss you in my dreams," I said. It felt like my heart was being ripped in half. I could feel shards of glass tearing through my body, wrecking me until I quivered and lost my breath. Things had been so much easier three years ago, following Roki blindly through the pretend market. Why did Geniverd's salvation have to fall on me? Why couldn't I just have my happy ending?

"I'll miss you too," Zawne said, and he ended the call. No one had any idea what I had planned.

* * *

IT WAS difficult to keep my eyes closed for all the tears spilling out of them. I didn't think I had cried so much in my life, yet this decision was immense. I had said goodbye to my friends, to everyone I had ever loved, and when I awoke, I would face a terrible demise. I took a deep breath, hugged my blanket tight, and spelled Shiol over my heart.

"Welcome, Kaelyn," Riedel said as I materialized in the void. "We have been waiting for you. We've listened to your heart, and we understand you have made the decision."

"To become a Min," Hanchell said, visibly excited from the way her light pulsed.

"I have no choice," I told them. "If I don't find the cure for the virus right away, over two million people will die. I can't let that happen. I will gladly forsake my human life to save the lives of others."

"Which is why we made you queen," Riedel said. He seemed cheerful for once. I thought he had a soft spot for me and was glad to see me doing the right thing, the truly righteous thing.

"Do you suspect the cure is already made?" Hanchell asked.

"Yes." I nodded. "I'm sure Emell is waiting until the very last second to send it out. She probably had it made at the same time she engineered the virus. She must have it stored in a secret location. As a Min, I'll be able to read her thoughts and discover the location, thereby preventing millions of innocent deaths."

I thought Hanchell's electric light was smiling. "You are smart for a human," she said. "Now let me give you some prep before we do this. You will wake up to a horrible death. There is no way around it. Next, you will be a formless Min. You will experience an intense desire to occupy a human body, but be careful. There are two options for occupying bodies. You may either occupy the body for its entire life span, or just long enough to complete a task given to you by us. Upon completion of the task, you will exit the body, and they will have no idea you were ever there. The human thinks they are in control, but really, they're just on a very intense roller coaster. In the case of a long-term body possession, the human will take a kind of back seat in their own mind. It's like your friend Roki. His body's owner is dormant while Roki works missions for us and does whatever fun things Min do in Geniverd."

"You think you can handle that?" Riedel asked.

"Got it," I said. "What happens if I break the rules, like if I disobey a direct order or give away the Great Secret?"

"Death," Riedel said. "The Seeing Water will see to it personally."

"Who's the Seeing Wa—?"

"The universe does not deserve the mercy shown by the Seeing Water. We'll tell you more later," Hanchell said. "Time is of the essence. Go back to your bed. A Min will take possession of an undercover Gurnot working alongside you in the council. They will assassinate you upon waking."

"It's going to be brutal," Riedel said. "Prepare yourself. Pain is temporary. The sacrifice you're making is eternal."

* * *

IT HAPPENED FAST. I dissolved out of Shiol and opened my eyes to pitch-blackness. It must have been two in the morning. I figured I had twenty-six hours left to save the species. Realistically though, I only had another two hours before the death toll began to peak and spiral out of control. I briefly thought, *Wait, aren't I supposed to be murdered?*

I tried to get out of bed, and that was when I noticed Torio standing above me with a snarl. He wore all black and looked terrifyingly evil.

"Tori—oh!"

He had a rope around my neck and was strangling me. Torio had one foot on the edge of the bed for leverage, tugging the rope so its rough fibers chafed my skin. He was strangling me to death!

My instincts took over. I tried to pry the rope from around my throat, coughing and gagging as Torio shook me out of bed and threw me onto the floor. Then he stood over me as he screamed, "I've waited my whole life for this!" Torio was insane, bloodthirsty, and violent. "I want to look in your eyes as you die, Kaelyn!" He cackled, tightened the rope, and watched me squirm.

In that moment, I wished I could take it all back. I had never known such agony or fear. My eyes felt like balloons ready to pop, my teeth sank into my bloody tongue. And Torio, so crazed. His saliva dribbled onto my face as he strangled me.

"Not yet," he said. He got up, seemingly lost or confused. "No, not here. Not like this."

I managed to say, "Gur ... not."

"Yes," he said as he snatched me by the hair and dragged me toward the kitchen. I kicked and groaned but couldn't scream. My throat had been crushed, and I could hardly take a breath. How could someone hurt a person so brutishly?

"I have been a Gurnot my whole life," Torio said, dumping me on the floor by the stove. "I've been feeding my associates information ever since I became Head of Courtiers. I hate the establishment. And I hate you!"

There was a frying pan on the cooker. It was red hot. He picked it up, grabbed a hunk of my hair, and pressed the hot pan against the side of my face.

"Yeo-o-o-ow!"

It was like ice and fire all at once. It burned like nothing I had ever felt before, and I had to remember what the Crown of Crowns had said: *Pain is temporary.*

But it freaking hurt! Tears pooled in my eyes, the smell of singed flesh, burnt hair, and Torio's maniacal laughter. He tossed aside the pan and let me drop to the floor, where I writhed in agony, my throat muscles crushed, half my face melted off. "E—" I tried. "End it."

Torio laughed. "Gladly."

He pulled a pistol from his waistband and shot me in the head.

CHAPTER 15

I didn't want to hate Torio for what he had done, but it was hard not to hate someone who had just murdered me. I floated out of my body and lingered, ghostly, below the kitchen ceiling. There I lay, the back of my head busted open, with fragments of hair and brain splattered over the kitchen floor like broken eggs. And there was Torio, seething above my bloodied corpse.

Had he really wanted to kill me the whole time we had known each other? All the smiles, the good advice, the late-night talks of politics, and all the while, he had fantasized about murdering me. I was surprised when he put the gun to his temple and blew his brains out.

Torio's body slumped over mine. It was very much a murder-suicide.

It was then I realized I was floating. But I wasn't in a body. I didn't even really have eyes. It was difficult to comprehend. I appeared to be a shapeless cloud the color of fire, like a fist-sized ember. I looked like the auras of the spirits I'd once seen in Shiol. I felt hollow, weightless. I drifted listlessly, wondering how I hadn't realized Torio was a Gurnot. It seemed obvious now. Then some part of me, like a third, invisible arm, reached into Torio's fading brain to find the truth.

I didn't know how I did it, but I did. I had accessed a library of Torio's memories, and they were cascading in front of me: him as a child playing in the river, him as a teenager sulking through the halls of his high school, him in a vast complex I had never seen, surrounded by men I didn't know—Gurnots, perhaps—and his most recent memory, my own face seen through his eyes, ugly and frightened as he choked me.

"Bleak," I said, and rid myself of the images. I didn't want to watch my own death through the eyes of my murderer.

I figured memory snatching was my special gift. Roki had told me that every Min received one. I'd just seen Torio at different stages of his life too—his image, perceived character, height, and shape. That meant I might be able to witness some past events related to the memories I'd be viewing. *Pretty cool*, I thought. *It'll help me find the KS3 cure even faster.*

And that was when the urge shocked me. I felt an inexplicable desire to slip into a human shell. It was like an extreme thirst. I wanted to wriggle into my headless body, even into Torio's warm corpse, slither into it like it was a sleeping bag. I seriously considered it.

"It's dead," came a voice from behind me.

I whirled my fiery spirit cloud around and saw a thin woman standing, translucent, on the kitchen floor. She, too, had a small red cloud, only hers lived inside her chest. "What?" I asked her.

201

"I see you eyeing that dead body," she said. "Trust me, it's not nearly as fulfilling as a live human. Obviously, you're new. It's nice to see a baby Min!"

Oh no! It was my murderer! It was the Min sent to kill me. Yet ... she didn't strike me as evil. She seemed more aloof than anything. I asked her, "Why did you have to kill Torio too? He was innocent ... kind of."

"Oh," she said, "I didn't. I had already detached myself from him. The poor Gurnot shot himself out of guilt. I guess he didn't hate you as much as he thought."

"You could have stopped him!"

She laughed. "Silly baby Min. I don't have time for that. Don't worry, you'll shed your human feelings with time. Give it a few hundred years."

If I'd had eyes, I would have glowered at the wicked Min. She came across as mindless, like a dopey spirit floating casually through existence. It wasn't at all how Roki was, even though Roki was five hundred years old. I poked around in her memories, curious how long she had been alive. I found a barrage of images dating way back, machines and cities I didn't even recognize.

"Hey," she said, "I can feel you poking around in there." Then she laughed. "What a cool talent."

"Sorry." I was embarrassed. I hadn't thought she'd feel it.

"No worries," she said. "You were just testing your new power. It was like a tickle in my brain. I didn't even realize at first. But it's cool. Actually, I'm kind of jealous."

"Why? What's your power?"

She shrugged. "It's kind of lame. Basically, I can turn into a cat whenever I want. Sometimes I become a cat, and I just lounge around in the sun for weeks. I've become ... very catlike."

"Ah," I said. It explained her weird attitude. "Why can't I read your mind?" I asked. "I thought Min can read minds."

"Only the minds of humans," she told me. "Min are sheltered from being read by other Min. We can think all the naughty thoughts we want."

I willed my cloud into the shape of a thumbs-up and said, "Good to know." It meant Roki couldn't read my thoughts anymore.

And that was when it hit me for the first time. Roki and I were both Min. He was already five hundred years old, which meant we could theoretically be together for ... another five hundred years! That would be one heck of a relationship.

"Anyway," the Min said, "I've got to go."

"Wait!" I floated my burning cloud closer to her. "One more question. What am I? What is this cloud I am in?"

She giggled. "It's your Valer. Only Min have a Valer. It's how you'll be able to tell the difference between Min and humans."

"Wow," I said. "Thanks. That's incredible."

She waved and floated out of the room, and I called after her, "Thank you for killing me."

* * *

I SLIPPED through an open window and took to the skies. I moved faster than the fastest rocket known to man. Yet I couldn't concentrate. I had to stop in the middle of some fluffy white clouds and think about where I should go.

Emell's house felt like the safest bet. It was still the middle of the night, which was convenient, because I hoped to float over her body and suck out her memories while she slept, though I didn't understand how anyone could sleep while they deliberately killed thousands of people. I thought back to Lordin's funeral, remembering the exact location of the place. Then I was zipping across the bruised sky at lightning speed. I arrived at Emell's estate in less than a minute.

But now what? Could I float through the ceiling? Could I move through walls? I tried but it didn't work. I had to squeeze my fluffy cloud through a cracked window on the upper floor and then float slowly through the house. I followed the echo of voices to the ground floor, where I found Emell and Lordin—residing in Hagan's body—sitting in the study.

I knew it was Lordin, because I could see her red Valer suspended in Hagan's chest. Hagan even had a faint resemblance to Lordin—petite, cute, pale skin, and electric eyes. I flattened myself against the ceiling in the hallway and eavesdropped on their conversation.

"The death toll has reached three hundred thousand," Emell was saying. She looked very much like a supervillain in her smart black suit, her hands folded neatly on her mahogany desk. "Projections tell us it will have reached well over two million by the time we distribute the cure."

"It's a lot," Lordin said. She crinkled her eyebrows. "Is there nothing we can do to lessen the casualties? Wouldn't five hundred thousand, even six hundred thousand, be sufficient?"

Emell frowned at her. "You're sounding a lot like my daughter again. That's something Lordin would have said. She never did have the stomach for brutality. Lordin inherited too much of her father, his soft heart and his caring soul. Lordin did as she was told, but she did it with a corrupted conscience."

"Genocide is a serious business," Lordin said. "It would corrupt any person's conscience."

I didn't know if it was my newly heightened senses as a Min, but in that moment, I had a clear vision of the relationship between mother and daughter. I could sense Emell's untamed fury and Lordin's apprehensive nature. Lordin wasn't a heartless monster, but her mother sure was. I dreaded what I might find in either of their memory banks.

"It's not genocide, anyway," Emell said. "It's just a bit of culling. We're trimming the population, encouraging war, disrupting the seat of power, humiliating Kaelyn and Zawne. It's everything we've been working for."

Lordin nodded. She seemed unimpressed by the whole thing, as if it was beneath her. Then she said, "My informers have told me that Krug is considering siding with Nurlie against the islanders and the Surrvul rebels. If the fighting continues, Shondur will undoubtedly follow. They are still upset about the phosphorus situation. After Shondur, we can expect Lodden to send the elite Aska warriors into battle. The Gurnots will get involved. I predict a world war within two months. Every clan's secret ambitions will explode into the open. It will be all-out chaos."

"Excellent." Emell interlocked her fingers and leaned over the table, giving Lordin a death stare. "We just need to rid ourselves of the underwater weapons system. We must leave Gaard totally vulnerable while allowing them the illusion of power. When the world marches on the capital, I want VondRust to burn for what they've done to me."

Did she mean for what the King Emeritus had done to her? Was Emell really that petty? I had a hard time believing she would secretly organize global warfare over such a thing. However, she had been banished to the north of Gaard for over half her life. Perhaps her anger and disdain had evolved over time in that frozen place, mutated into something toxic.

Then I thought, *What if Emell poisoned Lordin with her toxicity? Maybe Lordin isn't inherently evil. Maybe she was just corrupted by her own mama!*

Lordin said, "My technicians are working alongside some undercover Gurnots to disarm the underwater weapons system. Surrvul has provided funding. With all the money we've made from these mergers, we can now hire engineers to build our own weapons system. Gaard doesn't stand a chance."

Yes, they do, I thought. *I'll tell Zawne about your plan, and he'll put an end to this madness!*

"Excellent." Emell reclined in her chair, looking pleased with herself. "What about the cure? Why won't you tell me where you've hidden it, Hagan?"

"It's better you don't know," Lordin said, her eyes darting around the room as if she thought someone might be listening.

She was smart. I had to give her that. Lordin must have known no Min could read her mind, so even if a Min intervened and tried to stop the rampant deaths, they'd never discover the secret location of the cure.

"I will make the cure available for mass production

the moment you give the word." Lordin hesitated, then said, "But the sooner the better."

"Hush!" Emell roared, face wrinkled in anger. Her eyes radiated hatred. "Stop it with your cowardice. You and Lordin would have been the best of pals. I've had to babysit you these past months like I had to babysit my daughter her whole life."

Lordin licked her lips and said nothing. Even I could see her anger mounting. It must have been hard to sit in front of her mama in a stranger's body and listen to such vile slander. How could Lordin stand it? What was her angle? I cringed when she bowed and said, "My apologies, Mistress Emell."

It was too wrenching to watch. Besides, I was wasting time. I needed to extract Lordin's memories and discover the location of the cure. It would be pointless to probe Emell. She knew nothing, only malice. Entering her head would be like plugging in to the mind of a murderous psychopath. I considered possessing her body. I could order Lordin to release the cure right away. But then I would be stuck in Emell's traitorous husk for the next forty or fifty years, and I didn't want that. I also didn't want VBione Corp to be labeled a hero for saving Geniverd from extinction. If anyone deserved to be labeled a hero, it was Raad or Zawne.

I let my new gift stretch away from me, like invisible tentacles, and reach into Lordin's memory bank. I was slightly worried Lordin would notice, but within seconds I was lost in a world of images and remembrances.

* * *

LORDIN WAS WRAPPED HEAVILY in furs. She was young, beautiful, just a girl. Her visage was as smooth as porcelain under her fur hood, squinting against the bright sun as she carried her suitcase across the snow-covered yard to the awaiting flyrarc.

"Wait!" Emell came running out of the house. "I must say goodbye, my daughter. This is a big opportunity for us. Through hard work and determination, you've been accepted to train under the Grucken. We won't see each other for a long time. Are you prepared?"

"Yes, Mama." Lordin nodded obediently. "I remember all your teachings. I will advance up the ranks until I've gained a reputation among the nobility of Geniverd."

"And you'll do this by publicizing your ascension through social media," Emell said. "Your story will rivet the masses. You'll be an inspiration to everyone who aspires to be more than a simple commoner. But above all ..."

"Keep my identity a secret," Lordin said. "I know, Mama. I can't let anyone know who I am. As far as the public is concerned, I am a nobody from Gaard. I am proficient in Decens-Lenitas, and through the Grucken's teachings, I will become revered."

"Exactly," Emell said. "We are not like the other upper-class dolts. Remember our hatred for the king and queen, for the rulers of Gaard. We work to destroy them. We must use Decens-Lenitas to our advantage, disguise our intent, and rise until we've taken over the throne. I am trusting you, daughter. I entrust you with my vengeance."

"I won't let you down," Lordin said. "I will mask my intent, cover the secret of my heart, and one day—"

"Topple the king and queen, and seize power!" Emell said, fist raised to the winter sky. She looked mad even then, bent on domination and ruin.

Lordin hugged her mama goodbye and boarded the flyrarc. She sat by the window and watched as they ascended above Gaard's northern Gilfoil Mountains, looking down at the rural estate Emell had been banished to all those years ago, a small outpost amid the frozen wilderness. Lordin looked down at Emell and smiled to herself.

And then she was gone, soaring over the rolling hills of snow to meet the Grucken.

* * *

LORDIN PEEKED through the stage curtain. It was a full house. The Grucken was onstage, giving his address to a batch of newly anointed Aska warriors. Jaken and Raad were among them, and in the front row of the crowd was Zawne.

"This is it," Emell said. She rubbed her hands together. There was no one except her and Lordin backstage during the Grucken's speech. "This is your chance to shine, daughter. All these years with the Grucken, and finally some face time in front of the nobility. And just at the right moment. I've begun acquiring small chemical companies and medicine manufacturers. I'm in negotiations with a lab technician and a gene specialist to begin preparation of the virus. No one has any clue what they're participating in. They think it's research."

"That's nice," Lordin said. "You've worked hard."

Emell scoffed, "Harder than you know, child. Anyway, who do you see out there in the crowd?"

"A lot of people," Lordin said. She was older than in the last memory, a beautiful young woman ripe in all the right places. "I see Prince Zawne, Heir Shirpo of Surrvul, Heir Raad of Gaard, Heir Zolo of Krug. There must be ten male heirs in the front row."

"And each for your taking," Emell said, still rubbing her palms deviously. "I suggest you focus on Zawne. He's ambitious, like his pigheaded papa. With Zawne, you might have a chance at the top. Even Jaken is a good choice, yet he is an Aska and strong willed. Zawne will be easier to control. The truth is, daughter, either of the king's children will do nicely. I want the former queen and the former king to feel pain beyond this world when we dispose of one of their sons. Then you will be on the throne with me by your side. They will grow sick from despair!"

"Yes, Mama."

Lordin still peeked through the curtain, her eyes on Zawne. Anyone could have seen his potential, his positive energy. No one would have suspected a hardened Aska warrior would grow out of him, then later a king.

* * *

LORDIN WAS AT LITHERN SHRINE, Zawne propelling himself down to her in his modified flyrarc like an action hero.

"You came," she said. "It's six in the morning. I wasn't sure you'd come this early."

"I couldn't resist," said Zawne, a fish-eating grin on his face.

"Now that you're here," Lordin said, "let's take a walk through the gardens and get to know each other."

The date sped by in blips and flashes, scenes of tea drinking and subtle flirting. Then they were in the hidden room at the back of Lithern Shrine, Lordin caressing the smooth varnish of the Grucken's piano. "Can you play?" she asked Zawne.

"Oh, yeah. Can you?"

"Yes." Lordin sat on the stool and lifted the lid of the keyboard. "Shall we compose a song together?"

Zawne beamed. "Yes, an original score that only the two of us will know." His excitement was palpable. By the glazed look in his eyes, the sparkling affection in Lordin's face, it was clear the two were already in love.

"I'll start." Lordin softly stroked the keys, beginning a gentle melody for Zawne to sing to.

"When I soar, we soar," he sang, the music trickling through the room.

Then Lordin came in. "I soar; we soar."

"I never yield; we never yield."

"We are forever one."

The music was reaching a crescendo, Lordin's tiny fingers flittering across the keys as Zawne sang, "I soar; we soar, my love. I never yield; we never yield, my love."

Lordin stopped playing, and the chamber fell silent. Zawne blinked at her. "Hey, what'd you do that for?"

"The lyrics," she said. "They're powerful. How did you think of them?"

"It's how I imagine we will be in the future," Zawne said. "Together we will soar above the masses as the rulers of Geniverd. We will never yield for any man or kingdom or army. We will reach the heavens with our power and our love."

Lordin's eyes grew wide. "Do you mean it?" She appeared dazzled by the idea, so excited she started to shake. "Do you really think we could rule the kingdom together?"

Zawne chuckled. "Of course," he said. "You are practically the new Grucken. The Crown of Crowns will surely pick you, no matter who your husband is. And I'm the son of the current rulers. My knowledge of politics and the six continents is greater than any of the other heirs'. We'd be unstoppable together."

Lordin wrapped her arms around Zawne, nearly choking him. "Then let us be together," she said, her facial muscles twitching as if two different emotions were battling for control. Her jaw trembled, lips quivered, and tears bubbled at the corners of her eyes. She looked elated and terrified all at once. "Let's be together," she repeated. "I want you, Zawne. I want to be your queen."

* * *

LORDIN'S MEMORIES fast-forwarded in a colorful blur, slowing and coming to a halt in Shiol, the axis of the universe.

Lordin was speaking with the light forms Hanchell and Riedel. The Crown of Crowns was telling her, "But you must make the decision soon. Either become queen alongside Zawne, or perish and become a Min."

Lordin looked more serious than in any of the other memories. She looked like a person who had just been told the universe was run by spirits. She asked them,

"And you say Min are free to roam Geniverd and do as they please, that Min can possess bodies?"

"Yes," Riedel said, "but this isn't an invitation to become all-powerful. This is a serious choice you must make. Rule Geniverd with Zawne, or live a thousand years as a Min."

Lordin's jaw had dropped. She licked her lips. "Let me think about it." But judging by the look on her face, she had already decided.

"I'll tell you honestly, I'm not sure if Zawne has the heart to be king. I might have to refuse your offer to protect him from his own failure. I don't want to become a Min, but I may have to. I mean, it would suck to give up my short human existence to become a spirit with superpowers and live for a thousand years with complete and total power over Geniverd." She shrugged and shook her head sadly. "But I might have to do it."

"The choice is yours," Hanchell said. "You've scored the best out of anyone we've seen in a long time. And not only in Geniverd. We rule multiple universes, dimensions, realms ... and you are one of the most virtuous and kindhearted creatures we have ever seen. In any case, you'd do well as a Min."

"And you mentioned something about an election," Lordin said. "Am I to believe there is a way to move up the universal ladder?"

"Yes," Hanchell said. She wasn't very intuitive for an omnipotent, universe-controlling spirit. Either that, or perhaps Lordin had used the Grucken's spiritual teachings to disguise the rotten part of her heart. Her intentions seemed pretty obvious. "Soon," Hanchell continued, "there will be a chance to become the next Crown of Crowns. It's only for Min with a partner."

Lordin nodded. "Okay, great. Good to know." She was nearly salivating at the thought of all that power, the chance to rule a limitless galaxy. "I'll give you my answer tomorrow," she said.

* * *

EVIL!

I paused the memory show and scowled at Lordin, hiding so shamelessly in Hagan's body. She had wanted power. She had killed herself to become a Min. I could see it now. I could see it so clearly. Lordin may have loved Zawne, but she loved power more. She had thirsted for it her whole life thanks to the influence of her wretched mama. And now she was tearing the world apart to help Emell exact her revenge. But why? What was her scheme? Surely Lordin wanted something of her own.

Then I heard Emell say, "And once you, Hagan, are savior of the world, we will blame the tragic loss of life on Kaelyn of Gaard. She'll be cast out like I was, leaving Zawne lonely and hurt. Zawne is weak. We'll pull some strings to get the Queen's Council disbanded, then maneuver you onto Zawne's new council using your well-earned title as Hero of Geniverd. It won't take much for you to seduce the heartbroken king once you're seeing him every day."

Emell laughed, spun her chair in a circle, and cried, "And then you will install me as your most loyal adviser!"

If I had been in possession of a body, I would have gasped. It all made sense. Emell had put the pieces together for me. Sure, Lordin had killed herself to become a powerful Min and chase after the Crown of Crowns' position. But in the meantime, she wanted to reclaim her place as Zawne's wife.

She really did love him, I supposed. She had fought her way from the frozen northlands to the capital, to Zawne's bedchamber, then died. Within two years of her death, Lordin had helped Emell organize a plan that would plunge the world into chaos, all so that she could find her way back to Zawne's bedchamber while at the same time securing her mama's approval. Her resolve was astounding. Lordin was diabolical!

I had to see more. I slipped back inside Lordin's memories ...

And was instantly viewing the night of her murder. Lordin's body lay cold on the walkway outside Vond-Rust Palace. Her Valer floated above the path, the murderer standing stunned below. He looked a lot like Torio had in the moments after he had murdered me: lost, confused, stricken by what he had done. A Min must have possessed Lordin's killer and then fled, leaving him vacant and afraid.

Something bizarre happened. Much as I had accidentally experimented with my new gift, so too did Lordin. She formed her Valer into a little flaming hand and reached for the killer. He shrieked, but she wasn't touching him. She merely pointed at him.

"Bees!" he screamed, gripping both sides of his head. "The bees are everywhere! The bees killed Lordin!"

The man ran off into the night, ranting about Ava-Surrvul Askas. I didn't get it. I had to seriously think for a minute before it came to me. *Oh*, I realized. *That's great. Lordin must have altered his reality, made him think bees had killed her, instead of letting him live with the awful truth of being a murderer.*

It was a nice gesture on her part to save the man the emotional anguish of being a killer. But how was I supposed to battle Lordin if she could distort reality? All I could do was view memories and some of their past!

I had been so distracted by my wandering thoughts that I hadn't noticed Lordin get up and move into the hallway, and now she was watching me. Lordin stood right under me, eyes fixed on my flaming Valer, cursing me silently with her wrathful stare.

CHAPTER 16

I flew away. I zipped down the hall, squeezed under the front door, and took to the skies. My mind was racing. It seemed like every hour I was bombarded with new and disturbing information. Now I had Lordin's elaborate history to dwell on, the innocent girl twisted into a power-hungry lunatic. Plus she was still in love with my Zawne! There was Lordin's ability to twist reality to consider. If that was the case ...

The photos!

I stopped midflight, hovering somewhere above the ocean. If Lordin could change reality, it meant she could have shown me falsified photos of Roki with other women. It meant I had lashed out at him for no reason, calling him a creepy Min when he was anything but. It made sense now that I knew the whole story. I had been the queen after all, and Zawne's wife. Lordin couldn't have allowed me to continue consorting with a Min. It could have ruined her plan.

Worst of all, I was nowhere nearer to finding the cure for the virus. Lordin must have disguised her memory of its location as a fail-safe against memory thieves. She really was prepared, much more than I was.

I decided to fly to Nurlie. It was the only move I had left. My plan was to find Roki, beg for his forgiveness, and ask him to help me save the world. I could only hope that he would forgive me.

* * *

ROKI WAS EASY TO FIND. I could sense the other Min and see their fiery Valers from a substantial distance. They were like little red beacons, pulsing more brightly the closer I got. But even without the Valers, I could smell Roki's toffee odor. I followed it to the scene of a great battle, Tomenistin, the port town that connected mainland Nurlie to the island.

P5 Protectors had made a wall of armor against the rebel forces, blockading the government building against the mob of angry, laser-toting Gurnots, Surrvul rebels, and island forces. It was hard to believe the agitators had crossed the water and reached the mainland, and that Tomenistin was now under siege. The whole place was on fire. I wondered if the supposed Gurnot Dragon from the news reports was among the attackers.

"Roki," I said, flying down to where he had pulled a family from a smoking apartment building.

He turned at the sound of my voice, then gasped when he saw my Valer. "Kaelyn, you're a Min!"

"And you're a hero," I said. "How many people have you saved today?"

He sighed and said, "Not nearly enough."

The family Roki had saved were scampering off down the sidewalk. They hadn't even thanked him. All they wanted was to escape the fighting, the laser beams, the desperate cries of the injured.

"If you want to stop millions more from dying," I said, feeling out of breath even though I had no lungs, "I suggest you help me. I know Lordin's got the cure, but I don't know where she's hidden it. Will you help me search?"

Roki didn't so much as blink. "Of course," he said. "Let's start looking. We can go right now."

I had a sensation of crying—again, even though I had no eyes. I rammed my little fire cloud against Roki's, which lived in his chest, and reveled in the sensation of our two spirit bodies rubbing together. It was like a hug, only euphoric and titillating. It was two balls of electricity warming each other with ethereal static. I wanted to stay like that forever.

And that was when I cried to him, "I'm so sorry!" I couldn't help it. I felt even more emotional as a Min. "I'm sorry that I didn't believe you. I thought you were bad." And even without a face, I felt wet with tears. "You were always the best thing that ever happened to me, Roki. Even after I was a total jerk, you still agreed to help me without another thought. You truly are amazing."

Roki laughed, which was weird to see, because his face was sooty and everywhere around us the world was burning. "I always thought you might return. I never lied to you, Kaelyn, but I can understand where your anger came from. I learned about Lordin's gift shortly after our little incident in Shiol, so I knew why you had freaked out. I just figured I would respect your wishes and wait it out." Then he squinted at me. "But how did you find out about her gift?"

"Oh," I said, "I forgot to mention, I can siphon memories from people and Min alike."

"Whoa!" Roki's eyebrows raised in an arc. "That's so cool! And pretty convenient, don't you think?"

"What do you mean?"

"Well, you became a Min just in time to find a secret cure that can stop millions of deaths. Your power is to steal memories, which will help us to find the cure. And me, because of my power to mask presences, we can fly around the world unseen and look at memories without anyone knowing."

"It's almost as if ..."

"The Crown of Crowns has known all along," he finished. "You and I are destined to be a team."

"But that would mean they knew what was going to happen years and years and years ago."

"Yes," Roki said with a smile. "Those guys ... I don't know if we give them enough credit. They may seem kind of blank and robotic, but they know what's going on."

"Incredible." I was at a loss. I had thought the Crown of Crowns was half at fault for this whole mess. Could it be that they had designed everything, that it was all part of some grand scheme?

"We should go," Roki said. "People are dying by the second. We must find the cure."

"And I need to find a body," I told him. "I feel itchy all over. I feel hungry, thirsty, and in great need of a human host."

"We can do it in Gaard," Roki said. "We'll find

someone who looks like you, the same age and everything."

"Okay, but I'd like to find someone who's about to die from the virus. That way, at least I'll be saving a life … kind of."

"Deal," Roki said with a nod.

"One more thing, Roki. I'm … I'm a little scared of Lordin. She caught me probing her mind. Do you think she'll come after me?"

"No," he said. "Lordin has fully occupied Hagan's body. It means if she uses her Valer to fly, people would be able to see a human soaring through the sky. It's too risky. I can move across space at huge speeds because of my ability to mask myself. I'm invisible when I choose it. But Lordin and the other Min occupying human bodies have to travel the same as ordinary humans. Flyrarcs, trains, buses, cars, boats. That is, unless they're certain that no human being can see them."

"Good to know," I said. I felt safer knowing Lordin couldn't easily show up unannounced and warp our realities.

"Now let's go get me a body!"

* * *

A YOUNG GIRL lay dying in her hospital bed. She was easy to find—the dead were everywhere. She was about twenty years old. She had a shade of skin like mine, kind of a warm beige. Roki and I hovered above her body, admiring her.

"What do you think?" he asked.

"It's sad," I said. "It's sad and horrific that these people are dying when a cure is being withheld. I hate that I have to do this, but I'd rather occupy a dying girl than a healthy one. Uh … how do I do it?"

"Ease into her," he said. "Lower your Valer into her chest, wrap around her heart, then spread throughout her body. It'll just take a second."

I lowered myself into the girl's chest cavity, immediately feeling her weakness and closeness to death. I caressed her heart, let my spirit flow into her veins, spread into her limbs, into her mind. Then I felt life bloom anew. Her sickness shed, and I opened the girl's eyes.

"Wow!" I sat upright, checked out my new hands, touched my new legs. I leaped out of bed and ran to the bathroom mirror. I felt alive, totally electric. It was like being in the best mood ever, a little drunk, and on the verge of a great pleasure. "This is amazing," I said, poking myself in the face. It was insane to see through someone else's eyes, yet I felt like myself. I felt powerful.

"Do you like it?" Roki asked.

"I absolutely love it!" I turned to face him, Roki grinning in the doorway. He had washed most of the soot from his face and looked handsome, rugged, like a lean street fighter.

"Good." Roki came and put his arm around me. The sensation was a thousand jolts, and I leaned into him, rubbing my face against his cheek like a cat just to feel the tingly warmth. For a second, I forgot all about our mission. I wanted to explore my new sensations and my newly mended friendship with Roki.

But then I remembered. I broke away from Roki and shouted, "Now let's go save the world!"

* * *

"LORDIN'S A DEAD END," I said as we hovered above the hospital. "She can distort reality, which probably includes her memories. Plus she's dangerous. We need another way. We need to figure out where she would have hidden the cure."

"We need a clue," Roki said.

"Exactly. We need a clue, but from where?"

"What about Zawne?" Roki asked. "Could Lordin have told Zawne of a secret place, a place so special she would feel safe hiding the cure there?"

"It's worth a shot," I said. "And you don't mind going to see him? I mean, he was the other man. Uh, maybe you were the other man. Either way ..."

Roki gently touched my shoulder. "I understand your love for Zawne. He was your husband, Kaelyn. Of course you will always have feelings for him. On the other hand, we have centuries to be together. I'm not jealous. Now come on, we have lives to save."

Roki led the way, the two of us streaking across the sky like comets. I kept thinking how lucky I was to have met Roki when I did. He was handsome, caring, unfazed by my craziness. He pulled people from burning buildings and fought to save lives. It was more than Zawne had ever done. Still, Zawne was my love too. Only, he was also Lordin's love. I was finding it a bit tricky to figure out who belonged to who.

I couldn't dwell on it. We arrived at VondRust and snuck in through the back door while Roki masked our presence. We found Zawne in his apartment. He was on a call with ... Raad!

"I understand your reasoning," Zawne said. His eyes

were red and puffy. Raad's were too. It was five o'clock in the morning, and they must have just discovered my body. "It's just, I think that, as queen, she should be buried in the royal crypt behind VondRust."

"She should be buried next to our mother at her home," Raad said into the screen. He was more imposing than Zawne. Both were Aska warriors, but my brother had been a warrior even before the training. He was stern and unflinching before the king. "Should you take my sister's corpse from us, there will be consequences, Zawne."

"You can't threaten me," Zawne said. "I am your king!"

Raad laughed. "Not if the Gurnots tear you limb from limb. If the fighting keeps up, you know damn well there will be war. If you spit on Kaelyn's memory now, Gaard will remember. Gaard never forgets."

Zawne sighed. He seemed stripped of life, empty, like he had been after Lordin's death. It must have been a crushing blow for him. Both his loves had perished. Zawne was the only human left to carry the secret of Shiol.

"I loved your sister," Zawne said. "I loved her with all my soul. You and I will work out her burial. I'm sorry to snap at you. It's just … it's just so devastating."

Raad softened. He looked to be holding back tears. "I understand," he said. "If it wasn't for my Aska training, I'd be in ruins. I'd be on the floor with a bottle of rum."

"Me too."

The two men lingered silently on each other's screens. The sorrow was full and sweaty, making them appear damp. Zawne surely knew I was a Min, that I wasn't gone for good. But Raad didn't. His heart was shattered to pieces.

"There's something you can do for her," Raad said to Zawne. "Emell, Lordin's mother, she murdered Mama. We need an investigation. We must check her alibi, do DNA samples, and review all P2 footage from that day and the previous week. We need proof for an arrest."

"I'll handle it," Zawne said with a sigh. He didn't seem shocked. I wondered why. Maybe Zawne was too defeated to care.

"I have to go," Raad said. "Papa is bleeping on the other line. This news will devastate him."

Oh no, I thought. *Not Papa. His heart can't take it! I feel like such a fool!*

Roki took hold of my arm. He had been right. Even without reading my mind, Roki knew my thoughts. "It'll be okay," he said. "We'll find a way to keep you in their lives."

"How?" I asked. Zawne had ended the call and was lying on his sofa, blinking at the ceiling like a zombie. "Tell me how, Roki. I can't leave them like this!"

"We'll have to figure it out later," he said. "I'm sorry, Kaelyn, but we have a mission to complete. You need to get inside Zawne's mind while I keep our presence masked. Rummage through his memories. Find the clue."

"All right," I said. But I was extremely distraught. Seeing Raad's teary eyes, hearing him talk about Papa, about my burial—it had jarred me.

I tried to relax. I took a deep breath, stretched out my gift, and drifted into Zawne's memories.

CHAPTER 17

A lifetime flashed by, the life of a royal boy grown into a man. I couldn't slow to watch Zawne's younger memories. It was as if my instincts had control over my power. They guided me to a dusky night on the beach, Zawne standing before his commander as his Aska training began.

"This is not a physical test," boomed the authoritative voice of Zawne's commander, a hulk of a man nearly seven feet tall. "This is not an athletic sprint to the finish line. This is not a day at the beach. This, men, is the greatest battle you will ever wage against your minds."

The commander, a man named Thun, paused to let the gravity of his words wash over the two dozen men gathered on the dusky shore. "Your mind will tell you to stop. The pain will be severe. The stress, the fatigue, the agony—they will destroy you. Your mind will beg for release. Your body will beg for reprieve. You will have none. The desert will burn you. The starkness of the ocean will swallow you. The traitorous brain in your skull will trick you. There is no way to overcome. Here, there is only suffering. There is only pain. Should you balk beneath it, you will die."

Thun paused, massive black waves breaking against the shore behind the nervous recruits. The air smelled of seaweed and driftwood. Zawne listened to Thun impassively. He already looked dead, unfearful of any pain, for there could be no pain greater than the loss of love.

"There will be no special treatment here," Thun said. He was looking at Zawne, at the spoiled prince. "Should you choose to wade into these waters, you will either die or overcome. There is no rescue. Your visins have been deactivated. There will be no calling for help, no food being delivered, no paths to guide you. All you have is your team and your pain. I suggest you embrace them both. Value your teammates, for without them you will die. Value your pain, for if you cannot embrace it, you will die."

Thun paused, puffed out his chest, and stared into each of the twenty-four recruits' scared faces. "Some of you are boys. You will probably die. Some of you are men. You, too, will probably die. The sharks will rip you to shreds. The leopards will chew on your bones. The hyenas will laugh at you in the night when you feel most hopeless. Should you give up, you will die of starvation and be stripped bare by the desert winds. Should you somehow make it to Lodden, the training will likely break you."

"I can't do it!" screamed one of the men. He dropped to his knees and shrieked, "Let me go home. I don't want to die here!"

Thun walked to the boy, glared down at him as he groveled in the sand. "Go," Thun said. "Go home, child. Congratulations, you've just cost your team a man."

The boy ran, scuttled through the sand and vanished into the night.

"Anyone else?" Thun asked. Again he was looking at Zawne. "If anyone wishes to leave, now is the time. Once you set foot in the water, you are beyond my help. You are forsaken to the wild and its untamed dangers. You are stripped bare, nothing but your rags and your packs to carry with you, nothing but your bones and loose teeth to be lost to the sands. As everyone knows, the route to Lodden is a no-go zone. Tech doesn't work. Drones don't fly. Flyrarcs are prohibited. Only over the next few months will you understand the meaning of loneliness."

No one said a word. Zawne was pensive. He doubted Thun's words. Zawne was thinking he could never be more alone than he was in that moment.

"These are your maps." Thun walked along the line of recruits and handed every fourth man a paper map. "This is your guide. You have no technology, nothing but this map to point you toward Lodden. You will first cross the Ganga Sea. All twenty-three of you will share the small raft over there." Thun pointed to a rickety platform of logs bound together by rope, a limp cloth sail on its shoddy mast. It didn't look big enough for a group of four, never mind twenty-three. There were six thin wooden panels affixed to rings on the edges.

"Some of you will die before this raft reaches Surrvul. Without working together, you will all die. The sun, the salt water, the harsh cold of the night, the elements to ravage your body. If you slip your toes into the water, you will likely be eaten by a shark. You have no fire. You have no water. It's one week of paddling to reach Surrvul's shore and the small cache of water placed ahead of your arrival. It will be your only mercy."

The men glanced at each other nervously, then glanced at the raft. No one said it, but they were clearly terrified. Half of them had probably never been in the ocean before.

"When you reach Surrvul," Thun said, coming to a stop and folding his massive arms, "you must trek through the wasteland to the other side. This means the entire western portion of the Surrvul continent. There are no people. It's a no-man's-land. There are small rodents, snakes, sand scorpions, and antelope. You may eat what you catch, if you can catch anything. Upon making it to the channel that separates Surrvul and Lodden, you must push your weary bodies across its shark-infested depths. In Lodden, you will begin the real training."

Everyone kept quiet.

"Bolster your thoughts," Thun said. "Steady your focus. Harden yourself. Brace for pain. When the pain comes, let it fill you. That's what being an Aska is about, accepting pain and using it as a tool. Should you cross this treacherous course and complete your training, you will be the most formidable of men, able to carry any burden and weather any storm. You will be greatly honored in our society and have far-reaching opportunities."

Thun nodded. "That's it. Your boat awaits. Upon reaching Surrvul, you'll split into groups of four and work together to survive. Good luck, men."

No one moved. Thun watched them with his arms folded. He had finished his pep talk and would offer no further assistance. It was only when the silence deepened into an inescapable dread that Zawne left the line, determination black in his eyes, and started for the boat.

The other men followed.

* * *

WITH MORNING CAME heat and dehydration. Six men rowed the crummy raft, Zawne included. He grunted and rowed with his mouth pinched. The current was strong in the ocean, and seventeen men lay in a pile in the center of the raft, half-naked, with their shirts tied around their heads as they chopped through the waves. They were sullen and grumpy, twisted into ugly contortions for the lack of available space. Mouths smooshed against shoulders, legs tangled in knots of limbs. And then someone screamed.

"Sharks!"

All around the raft were gray shark fins like arrowheads cutting through the water. Zawne kept rowing, his dull expression unchanged. But one of the other rowers lost his mind. "They're going to come onto the boat!" He took the paddle and tried to whack one of the passing sharks. The paddle smacked the water, and the man lost his balance and fell in.

There was a soft splash. A few bubbles rushed to the surface, then blood. Blood frothed around the exposed shark fins, and the man was gone.

Zawne shouted, "Someone take his spot! Keep rowing!"

* * *

FOUR DAYS later the twenty men left on board were very thirsty. There was no water. The sun beat down on them with unrelenting fury sixteen hours a day. The salt water had their lips cracked and dry, split and caked in blood. Zawne was deathly pale. So were the others. They were thirsty and lethargic and near death. They did what they had to in order to drink and stay alive. It was ugly.

* * *

THEY WASHED up on Surrvul's southern shore in the night, nineteen alive and one dead. Two of the recruits dragged the boy's corpse up the bank and into a patch of stark grass. "We should bury him," someone said.

Zawne shook his head. "There's no time. Anyway, we can't bury him deep enough without tools. The scavengers will get him."

The men looked unsure, glancing at each other with unease. They had survived the brutal week on the raft, and now they had to leave the dead boy on the beach to be eaten by vultures. In most Geniverd traditions, not burying the dead was bad luck.

"I'm with the prince," said a bald man. He was wiry and young, probably from Shondur, like Zawne. He stepped through the men and said, "We don't have time. Let's find the water cache left for us, rehydrate, then start walking. It's better to walk in the night and sleep in the heat of the day."

"What's your name?" Zawne asked him.

"Nkem," he said, "but it doesn't matter. We're all

231

nobodies here, food for sand fleas. Let's make our teams and get off this beach. I'll team up with the prince."

Another man came forward. "Me too. My name is Stingl, and I'd like to join the prince and Nkem. If the rest of you want to waste your time with burials, go ahead."

"This is rubbish!" a man shouted. He steamed out of the crowd and picked up the dead kid's body. "At least see him off to sea. I'll give him a worthy Nurlie burial, but I won't leave him in the sand."

He took the kid in his arms and waded waist-deep into the water. The others watched as he let the body drift away on the current. He gave a salute and uttered some half-forgotten hymn under his breath. Then he started shouting.

"Ow! Hey, get away from me. Ow! What the ...?"

He struggled to shore, no one daring to jump in the water and help. He started up the bank and collapsed, twitching with spasms in the sand. Zawne and the others ran to check on him, and in the light of the moon, they could see pink and purple sores where jellyfish had stung him. He foamed at the mouth, seized, mumbled something, and died. His body was pink, and his veins distended from the jellyfish poison.

"Anyone else want to paddle?" Zawne asked. He received only silence as an answer. "All right. Let's get into groups and find that water. The desert awaits."

* * *

"FIVE THOUSAND MILES," Nkem said. It was dawn, and they were still walking, Nkem, Stingl, and Zawne. The others were mirages in the distance behind them, like wavering shadows following through the awakening scrubland. "Coast to coast, I mean. Five thousand miles from here to the north coast. It'll take us maybe eight months."

Stingl laughed. "Yeah, only eight months."

"It is nothing compared to a lifetime of discipline," Zawne said. "I remember when my brother, Jaken, returned home from his Aska training. He was the same man, but different. His emotions had cooled. He was sharply aware of everything. He seemed like a stronger person, someone still capable of love yet capable of great horrors. I saw a secret truth in his eyes, and the possession of this truth strengthened him and gave him purpose. That's what I seek in this desert. I seek truth and purpose."

"Deep, man," Stingl said.

But Nkem wasn't convinced. "You'll get truth all right, Prince. You'll get truth in the way of pain and misery like you wouldn't believe. Let's talk again after you've been stuck inside your own head for two straight months. That's the real torment. You, your thoughts, your regrets, your secret truths. Your mind will haunt you until you've gone insane."

Then Nkem laughed, raised his hands to the great dust plain and said, "Welcome to your doom, Prince. Welcome to the infinite horrors of your psyche."

Zawne shrugged it off. His pace was fast, but Nkem and Stingl kept up well. All three were fit and lean, made for desert walking. "Nothing can compare to the recent horror I've faced," Zawne said, "my wife being decapitated by a crazy groundskeeper. Lordin had given the world so much. She had given me so much!

And some lunatic took it all away. The pain of this desert is nothing to me. The memory of Lordin will carry me through."

"Let's hope," Nkem said, "for all our sakes."

* * *

THEY SLEPT at high noon in the scanty shade of a cactus, and when they woke five hours later, the sun was a flare of death on the horizon. Nkem cut open the cactus, and they drank its milk. It was the only cactus they had seen thus far.

"I hope there's more of these," Stingl said. "I'm not sure what we're going to do for food."

"Or water," Nkem said.

That night, as they marched, the scuffling of many feet could be heard circling them as nighttime predators stalked them in the blackness. Zawne, Stingl, and Nkem walked clustered tightly to dissuade attack. If there was food to be had, it was too dark to find it. The same went for water or cacti.

As dawn's first light began to warm the desert sands, Zawne said, "We should walk in the day. We can find no food at night. We also risk attacks from animals."

So they walked through the day under the hot wrath of the sun and didn't sleep. They were far ahead of the other groups. The only sound was their harsh breathing and the call of the wind. As darkness fell, they used what few tools they had in their packs to set traps. Each man had an empty tin can. They dug three holes in the sand and placed an empty can in each one. "The dried juice on the bottom of the cans will lure scorpions," Nkem said. "We'll check them in the morning."

They caught one scorpion during the night and ate it raw in the morning, sharing the paltry bit of meat between them. The next night, they used the small tarp provided to make a solar still. They dug a wide hole and stretched the tarp taut over the hole, and through the night, the moisture dripped from the tarp into one of their tin cans. It was just enough for a sip, just enough to stay alive.

* * *

IT WAS six months and roughly four thousand miles later when Nkem was explaining to Zawne and Stingl about the primal history of the Ava-Surrvul.

"See, they used to farm salt out in these flatlands. It was maybe a thousand years ago, so the salt has mostly dried up. The Ava-Surrvul worked all day in the sun without water or food, chopping salt out of the ground in huge chunks. They shaved it, strapped it to their camels, and marched back to civilization to sell it. The tradition lasted until the unification of Geniverd, even after the advent of cars and machines. The Surrvul have always been a hardy people. They thrive in this wasteland."

"It's interesting," Zawne said. "But what I want to know is how you can still be so chatty after four thousand miles of stark nothingness. We've come across human bones, sucked water out of mud gullies, eaten lizards and venomous scorpions, had our skin flayed by the sun, and been forced to do disgusting things to stay hydrated ... and still you yap!"

Stingl chuckled. "It's Nkem's charm. Imagine how boring this would have been without him. Not to mention we haven't seen another person since the beach. I wonder if—"

"Better if you didn't," Zawne said. "I'm sure they're—"

Zawne stopped in his tracks. Up ahead was a shallow crevice in the desert, one of the many dried-up riverbeds that cut through the land. Climbing onto its rim were three leopards.

"We're in trouble," Zawne said. "Ready yourselves, men. It's another test!"

The leopards moved toward them with silent, stealthy resolve. They were nearly invisible against the sand, their yellowish coats the perfect camouflage in the scrublands.

Nkem was pulling his pocketknife from his ruck-sack, but Zawne stopped him. "No, brother. It will prove our worth as warriors if we can defeat our enemy without killing them. It will show our mercy."

Nkem nodded. "Got it." He dropped his knife in the sand, and the men readied themselves. They firmed their stances as the leopards began to charge.

The leopards worked as a pack. One dashed straight at Zawne, and the others flanked to attack Nkem and Stingl. Zawne's leopard leaped into the air and pounced onto his chest with its heavy paws, knocking him down and trying to bite out his throat. Zawne caught it by the muzzle and yelled in its face, "Not today, beast!" He flung it off him. At the same time, Nkem and Stingl were fighting desperately on the desert floor.

Zawne clambered to his feet and ran at the leopard, catching its paws in midair and headbutting it on the top of its skull. It gargled and landed on its feet. Its hair stood on end as it snarled, hissed at Zawne, and made its second attack.

But Zawne was fast. He kicked the oversize cat in the snout and knocked it sideways, then stood astride it. He punched its face—once, twice, three times between the eyes—until the leopard groaned and backed away snarling, then dissolved into the heat of the desert.

Zawne stood powerfully in the sand, his shirt ripped by the claws of the leopard. A primitive look had possessed him during the fight. It was as though the warrior spirit had entered his body, as though the memory of Lordin's tragic demise had turned him into a savage. He looked at the sky and roared in triumph.

Stingl was on the ground not far from Zawne, struggling beneath the ferocious attack of another leopard. Zawne ran to help. He drove the animal off Stingl, man and beast rolling through the scrub. They spiraled in a mess of fangs and claws, spritzes of blood flying as the leopard tore off chunks of Zawne's chest. It ended with Zawne on his back and the leopard in his grip. Zawne had his arm wrapped around its throat, choking the cat as it flailed and hissed. Then it was unconscious. Zawne pushed the leopard off him and into the dirt.

"Stingl!" Zawne stood up and dusted himself off. "Are you all right?"

"Fine," Stingl said. He was dabbing at the blood weeping from a gash in his arm. "It's just a flesh wound. But where's Nkem?"

Zawne looked around. There was no sign of Nkem. "They must have rolled into the riverbed," he said. "Come on, let's go!"

They found Nkem slumped against the wall of the

gully, blood leaking down his face. He was panting, hands limp in his lap. The leopard was gone.

"What happened?" Zawne asked. He skidded down the loose wall of the riverbed and knelt by Nkem.

"It ran off," Nkem said. "I shoved my arm down its throat, and it ran off gagging, but not before it clamped its fangs down on my head." He gestured to the tooth marks on his scalp, chuckling as he said, "That's probably going to a leave a mark."

"You bet," Zawne said, cracking a smile. He took off his shirt and ripped off a long strip. "Here, let me bandage your head. You don't want the wound to get infected before we reach the coast."

Whatever animalistic spirit had invaded Zawne during the fight had gone with the leopards. He was normal again, even cheerful, as he bandaged Nkem's head. He used the rest of his shirt to wrap Nkem's chest and Stingl's arm.

Afterward the three friends sat against the wall of the dried-up riverbed and talked about their victories. Stingl was a little upset because he had not defeated his own leopard, but Zawne comforted him.

"It's all right, Stingl. You faced a leopard and lived. We worked as a team to overcome wild beasts. That's what the Aska training is all about: perseverance, mastering the mind, the value of life, the value of others."

"Yeah," Nkem said. "There was no way Zawne or I could have defeated all three leopards alone. We needed to be a team. The same as we need to be a team for these next thousand miles. After that, a quick swim across a shark-infested channel. It should be a piece of cake."

* * *

IT WASN'T.

They stood on the shoreline, looking across the strait to Lodden. "It's right over there," Nkem said. "Maybe twenty-five miles."

"Twenty hours of swimming, I reckon, with breaks," Stingl said. "It's not bad."

Zawne was nodding to himself. He looked across the water to where the continent of Lodden lay shrouded in fog. "Not bad at all, Stingl. Our wounds have healed. Our minds have been fortified. We could walk another four thousand miles in our sleep, probably in half the time."

"I reckon you're right," Nkem said. "It feels like even though we have been eating bugs and dirt, I've gained muscle mass. I bet we make it across in fifteen hours."

Zawne flashed him a smile. "I'll bet we do it in twelve."

"You're on!" And with that, Nkem jumped into the water.

* * *

IT WAS EXACTLY fifteen hours later when the shoreline came into view. It was less than two hundred yards away. "I can see it!" Nkem shouted over the waves. Then he laughed. "I thought there were supposed to be sharks."

As if to spite him, a huge mass appeared beneath the water, rising quickly below Nkem's feet. Zawne screamed, "Look out!" but it happened too fast. The shark exploded out of the water and caught Nkem in its mouth. There was a quick image of Nkem's body being crunched by the shark's serrated teeth. Then the beast was back underwater, swimming away with its meal. Nkem was gone, only an inky trail of blood in the water to suggest he had ever been there at all.

* * *

THERE WAS a welcoming party waiting for Zawne and Stingl as they trudged out of the water and collapsed on the pebbly beach, exhausted. They sat on the rocks and panted while the waves broke against them.

Thun came over with a horde of P2 drones hovering over his head. "Well, well, I'll be damned. I didn't think you had the guts, Prince Zawne, yet here you are, the first two men to reach Lodden. You must feel so relieved."

"Huh." Zawne huffed. "I didn't think I had it in me. But now I know I can be supreme as a human being. I just had to look at life's challenges differently. I embraced my pain." Zawne glanced at Stingl. "And I embraced my teammates. Aside from them, I just remembered Lordin. I kept thinking of our first date, at Lithern Shrine, when we sang together and played the piano. I let her strength and love, my pain and guilt for her passing, and my teammates' support get me to the end. I would never have made it here without them. But there is one challenge I'm still working on."

"What's that?"

Zawne was weeping. Thun waited patiently, but the prince didn't speak. He just gazed out at the water, where his friend had just lost his life.

"Well, Prince Zawne," Thun said glumly. "It seems

you have learned the lesson of teamwork. You understand now the bitter truth of death, its inescapability.
Judging by your wounds, I'd say you looked death in the
face and overcame. You've defeated your mind's inter-
pretations of sloth, pain, fear, and infirmity. You've
learned that it's within your power to disable a foe's
supremacy while still preserving its life. Well done,
valiant comrade! I welcome you to your training in
Lodden. This will be your home for the next year and a
half. The physical and mental tasks we've prepared for
you are designed to solidify your learnings and to safe-
guard Geniverd, starting with the principles of Decens-
Lenitas."

* * *

I SHOOK free of Zawne's memories with a deep sense of
understanding. I had known the Aska trials were tough,
but I had never imagined that the hardships Zawne and
Raad had been forced to endure were so brutal. The
deaths seemed pointless to me. I couldn't understand
why anyone would subject themselves to such torture,
though I supposed in Zawne's case, he would have been
dead or at least hollow without his Aska training. The
loss of Lordin had torn his soul asunder, and the great
revelation of his training had mended it.

I took a second to marvel at Zawne's intense devo-
tion to Lordin. Her memory had literally turned him
superhuman, had him wrestling leopards and trudging
through the searing heat of the desert for months on
end. It made me doubt my own worth. Could I ever
have inspired Zawne in such a way? Asking myself the
question gave me the answer.

I loved Zawne and Zawne loved me, but he would always love Lordin more. She had been his first, his truest. If Zawne felt for Lordin what I had always, in the deepest chambers of my heart, felt for Roki, we would always be loved, yet loved in the back seat. Zawne and I were afterglows of other loves, ghosts of a feeling that could never be recreated.

CHAPTER 18

J had become introspective and hadn't noticed Roki staring at me. "Well," he asked, "did you figure it out? Did you get a clue?"

I snapped out of my daydream and looked down at Zawne, the poor man asleep on his couch, all alone in the world with his warrior's heart fractured into pieces. "Yes," I told Roki. "The clue is love, indefinable and incorruptible love."

Roki blinked at me. "The cure is in love? I don't understand, Kaelyn."

I smiled, still gazing at Zawne. I was happy Roki couldn't hear my thoughts. Zawne was such a good man. He deserved the best, and if I truly loved him, I would leave him alone. I couldn't put another hole in his heart with my confused feelings. I couldn't be with him and Roki. I had to choose.

"The cure is at Lithern Shrine," I said. "It was the location of Zawne and Lordin's first date. I think it is the only place of love that Lordin has ever known. If

CLARA LOVEMAN

she stored the cure to save humanity anywhere, it's going to be at Lithern Shrine."

I chuckled to myself. "It's funny, you know. For all Lordin's evil, she still loves Zawne. I can't help but think that whatever immoral path she is on now, she's still attached to her human feelings for him. I'm sure she's fumbling for purchase, trying to rise as a powerful Min while maintaining her relationship with Zawne. I can't help but wonder what she would have been like without Emell's corruption."

"We can wonder later," Roki said, taking me gently by the arm. "Right now we have a world to save. Let's get our butts to Lithern Shrine!"

* * *

SURE ENOUGH, Roki and I found the cure inside the piano's casing. It was a green substance in a small vial, wrapped neatly in cloth and tucked inside the guts of the piano.

"Got it," I said, holding up the vial.

Roki smiled. "Great. Now we just need to reproduce it and distribute it to the people."

I tucked the vial into my pocket, saying, "I have an idea. We'll go to my brother at NordHaven and introduce ourselves as defectors from VBione Corp. We'll say that the cure was already made, but Emell was withholding it. This pins the whole fiasco on her. They'll have no choice but to arrest her. Even if the investigation into Mama's death goes nowhere, at least Emell will be behind bars."

"I like your thinking," Roki said. "Let's get to it!"

We left Lithern Shrine feeling like the saviors of the

244

world, holding hands as we soared across the sky toward NordHaven. Once there, Roki unmasked us. The butler announced us to the household, and Tissa arrived after fifteen minutes, Rein and Forschi in tow. The canines barked with excitement.

"Hello. We're in mourning and meant to be in quarantine, so this had better be good. How can I help you?" Tissa asked. The dogs flopped down on the floor, their wee eyes watching me expectantly. Tissa looked like a whole new person. Had she always worn so much makeup? Her clothing seemed to be getting frillier and frillier each time I saw her.

Yes! I wanted to scream. *Yes, Tissa. You can give me a hug!*

But I had to keep my composure. I said, "My name is Cerna, and this is my associate Roki. We were the lead designers on the cure for the KS3 virus. We finished human trials yesterday, but the owner of the company, Emell, has refused to allow the cure to be released to the public. We think she's bent on world domination or something. So we reproduced the cure on our own and brought it straight here, hoping that Gaard-Ma and Gaard-Elder would help distribute it."

It was a lot. Tissa gaped at me, looking like I had just slapped her in the face. "You're serious?"

"We are," Roki said. "The queen herself tasked us with this before—"

"Then get in here right now! What are you doing dallying outside like a couple of salespeople?" Tissa gestured for us to enter, then shouted into her visin, "Raad, we have a cure. Forget the quarantine and get down here as soon as you can."

Tissa gave us a sad look. "Sorry, but as you know,

Gaard-Elder's sister—you know, the queen of Geniverd —was killed last night. He's obviously not in the best shape."

"We understand," I said. I was overwhelmed by the wish to reveal myself. It was hard not to.

Tissa turned to Roki. "Funny, the late queen had a friend called Roki."

Luckily, Raad joined us in the parlor at that moment, and Roki didn't have to reply. When we handed over the cure to him, I wanted to hug my brother and erase the sadness from his eyes. I wanted to celebrate our triumph with my family and friends, but I couldn't. I had to sit before them as a stranger and give him all the gritty details of Emell's operation.

"And you'll sign a testimony saying Emell designed KS3, unleashed it on the people of Geniverd, then refused to release the cure?" Raad asked.

"We will," I said.

Raad didn't answer. He was in go mode. He held up his finger for silence as he called someone on his visin and started talking. "I need a team to meet me at the VBione Corp main factory to reproduce the cure for the KS3 virus … Yes … Yes, the cure. I also need a team to arrest Emell again. This time we're not letting her go. I'll be at the factory in fifteen minutes."

Raad ended the call, leaned forward, and squinted at me. "You remind me of my sister," he said. "Not your body or your face, but your eyes. Yeah, you have the same eyes. It's like … I don't know how to explain it."

Raad shook his head, got up from the sofa, and said, "I'm sorry, Cerna, I'm grieving and acting weird. But I have to go now to deal with this cure situation. Thank you for bringing it to me. I'll have someone write a testimony for you to sign. Probably tomorrow. Emell will never see the light of day again for what she's done."

I was glad to hear it. Raad and Tissa left, the dogs following closely behind them. Roki and I lingered a moment in the empty parlor. "I'm happy we're finally getting justice for Mama," I said. "I'm also happy Raad will be the one to save the world, not Emell or Lordin."

"Me too," Roki said. "Can you imagine if they had gotten away with this? It would have been a travesty. Still ..." Roki sighed, clearly stressed out. "There is the war in Nurlie to deal with. Surrvul is throwing money around and operating from the shadows. We have a lot of loose ends about to catch fire. And speaking of fire, I need to see a friend of mine. I never did tell you I have a dragon for a friend. Anyway, I don't know what to do."

"Dragon ... Do you mean the one from the news reports, the one burning down noble mansions and clan retreats all over the world?"

"It doesn't matter," Roki said with a half smile. "We have too much to figure out. My fire-starting friend can wait."

"Okay," I said, and took Roki by the hand. "We will figure it out together. Now that I'm a Min, there's nothing in the world that can stop us."

He smiled, took my other hand, and drew me to him. Our eyes met, and it was like an explosion in my heart. Then I realized, *Roki and I are finally together. There are no secrets. I'm a Min. I have hundreds of years to be with Roki.*

We were standing with our noses almost touching, the heat between us undeniable. Then Roki said in a soft voice, "We have five centuries to explore these feelings. But I was thinking ..." He bit his lip, trying not to smirk. "I was thinking that when the selection comes around for the next Crown of Crowns, we should join as a team. It would mean ..."

"Being together for three thousand years." My breath had caught in my throat, and I thought I would cry. "I can't even fathom it."

"Me neither," he said. "Five hundred years has gone by so slowly. I've seen so much. To live six times the amount I already have is mind blowing! But if I'm going to do it, I'll only do it with you."

"Wow," I said, squealing like a piglet. "Imagine you and me, rulers for three thousand years. But ... it's a big deal. I need to think about that."

"Take your time. We should get a drink to celebrate," Roki said. "You know, like the first time we met."

"I'd love to."

But before we could go anywhere, a strange feeling enveloped me. Then two voices were in my head, saying, "This is Hanchell and Riedel. You must come to Shiol. We need you immediately."

I looked to Roki and he was nodding. "Yeah, I got the same message. They must be summoning all the Min. It sounds like an emergency."

"A Min emergency!" I cried. "That can't be good."

* * *

THE SHIOL ROKI and I arrived to was not the one I knew, the empty vacuum with its peaceful sky overhead. Rather, it was the bright and pulsing city Roki had shown me all that time ago. We were transported into a massive plaza, a place much like Coronation

Square in Geniverd's capital. Around us were other Min in human bodies, and also creatures I could hardly comprehend. There were lizard people, humanoid beings with pointy ears and short limbs, winged creatures without legs, orange-skinned people over nine feet tall, limbless blobs, and countless other life-forms. I could hardly keep from staring.

"This is the real Shiol," Roki whispered to me. "This is where the Min from other dimensions, other planets, other realities all live in harmony. It's why the city looks so strange. It's an amalgamation of a thousand different cultures. When we have time, I'd like to explore it with you. Even after five hundred years, I still haven't scratched the surface of Shiol."

"I'd like that very much," I said. But really, I was overwhelmed. Where did a newly minted Min begin exploring such a grand and infinite city?

"And those are Riedel's and Hanchell's true forms." Roki gestured to the Crown of Crowns, who had just revealed themselves above us on the podium. I balked at their true forms. They were three-headed monsters with scaly gray flesh, yellow eyes, and webbed feet.

"Incredible!" I said. "I can't believe I've been talking to monsters this whole time."

"Not monsters," Roki said. "They are from Dimension Z8. They were chosen as the best among us three thousand years ago."

"They've lived for almost four thousand years ... That's impressive."

I wanted to ask more questions, but the Crown of Crowns began to address the crowd.

"Hello," Hanchell said. Even as a three-headed monster, I thought she looked compassionate in her golden robes; there were twinkles of kindness in her six yellow eyes. "We have brought you here to announce that our tenure as Crown of Crowns is coming to an end. In approximately six months, the Seeing Water will pick our replacements. That means you clever Min have time to partner up and present your cases. Choose wisely. None of you will live long enough to have another shot at being orchestrators of our galaxy."

"The suitable candidates must not only be clever," Riedel said. "They must also be strong, wise, invested in the future of the universe, and willing to make the hard sacrifices to keep the balance."

I thought, *If trying to run Geniverd was stressful, what would running the freaking galaxy be like? If we were selected, how would Roki and I cope?*

"If you'd like to be considered for the position, please present yourselves to us sooner rather than later," Hanchell said, her gray tail wagging. "For now, we bid you farewell."

Hanchell and Riedel sparkled like static and then were gone. And that was when I looked through the crowd and saw Lordin glaring at me.

* * *

THE CROWD of aliens and interdimensional beings was gone. The square was empty. Lordin and I stood alone with the eerie strangeness of Shiol's megalopolis looming in the distance.

"You stole my cure," she said. Lordin made no attempt to attack me. She simply stood glaring at me in Hagan's body. It was creepy and intimidating.

"You were killing people," I said. "What did you think I would do?"

Lordin shrugged. "I'm just surprised you found it. It's not like I can blame you for trying to save the world. I wasn't comfortable with the death toll either, but I was powerless to my mama's commands. I needed to gain status in this body."

"So that you could schmooze your way back into Zawne's life?"

"Something like that."

"I don't get it," I said. "You both know the Great Secret. Why not just reveal yourself?"

Lordin laughed, folded her arms, and shook her head at me. "You guys were married, Kaelyn! Don't you think I tried? Zawne's a noble man. When I came to him in Shiol, I altered his reality so that he would see me in my original body. He told me he loved me even beyond death, but that he was a king and would not fold his commitment to his new wife, Kaelyn of Gaard, the daughter of my mama's enemy."

"Oh ..." I said. It was starting to make sense. Zawne had been honest with me the whole time. He'd had no intentions of cheating, so Lordin had needed to maneuver me off the throne somehow.

I said, "You used Emell's lifelong thirst for vengeance to try to dispose of me because Zawne rejected you. So you hatched an insane plot to spiral the world into chaos and get me banished for being a bad queen. Then you were going to insert yourself in Zawne's council and make him fall for you in Hagan's body!"

"Well," Lordin said, "it was Mama's insane plot. The virus would have been unleashed with or without me.

Yet by helping Mama, I kept my lifelong promise to get her revenge, while at the same time getting rid of you. There's only one thing you've got wrong, Kaelyn. There's one sticky detail you missed."

I crossed my arms and said nothing. I wished she couldn't alter reality. I wished everyone in the square could have heard Lordin's sick confession, though I had to remember she wasn't naturally sick. Emell had filled her with evil. Then Zawne had filled her with love, and the Crown of Crowns had fueled her desire for power. Lordin was trying to juggle all these personas, all these goals and aspirations. I had a feeling it was driving her to madness.

"I wasn't planning to become Zawne's queen," Lordin said. "Emell thought so, but she was wrong. See, I want to trick Zawne into sacrificing himself and becoming a Min. I need him to partner with me. I'm sure that together we can take over as the Crown of Crowns."

CHAPTER 19

"*N*ever," I shouted, suddenly angry at how Lordin planned to manipulate Zawne. "Not in a million years! I know you have a good heart somewhere inside you, but it's cracked and broken. You'll never get the universal throne, Lordin."

"Maybe not," she said, shrugging with cool indifference, "but maybe I will. All I need is Zawne."

"And to eliminate the competition," I said, suddenly understanding everything. "That's why you broke up Roki and me. You were scared of our power together. You were worried that Roki and I could ascend the throne instead of you. You're still scared of us and our bond!"

Lordin's face went dark. She started toward me. "I"—lips twisted in a snarl—"am"—balling her hands into little fists—"scared of no one!"

She raised her arm and I flinched, squeezing my eyes shut. Without warning, she flitted upward and, in a flash, was on top of me, hanging from my head, and we were skidding in all directions.

"Thief!" Lordin screeched as she made several attempts to grab my Valer. I used all my strength to unhitch myself from her, my Valer instinctively jittering around my body, its natural defense mechanism.

I panted. "I can't believe how foolish I was to believe in you!"

As I spun, my eyes hunted for her, knowing that she could see me. But then, in a shot, she was swinging at me again, and she tossed me into the air. I crashed heavily into the buoyant space. It felt like I'd hit the ground as my whole body cramped or spasmed.

I mustn't give in, I told myself, thinking about all the people who'd died because of her. I steadied my Valer, using it as bait, and fine-tuned my senses. Instantly I felt Lordin's presence just before she was upon me, and I lunged at her head, sending her hurtling several feet away.

I caught my breath, surprised at my superhuman strength, and looked up to see several amused Min staring at me. I didn't know if I'd struck something that had ended Lordin's spell or if someone had interrupted us.

Roki was there with a concerned look. "You all right?" he asked. "You kind of gaped out there for a second."

* * *

I EXPLAINED it all to Roki: Lordin's twisted motives, Zawne's loyalty to me, the whole bloated mess. We had left Shiol and were lying on the rooftop of the tallest building in Geniverd's capital city, watching the clouds go by as we tried to make sense of it all.

"It's wild," Roki said. "I hope Lordin doesn't turn into one of those perverse serial-killer Min."

"Me too," I said. "I hope she's all right. Her mama's in jail now in Gaard. So that's one good thing that came out of this. I just wonder how having her mama locked up will bend her mind."

Roki turned to me, looking offended. "Only one good thing came out of this? What about us? We're together again because of what happened."

"Of course," I assured him. "It's only you and me now, Roki. I've vowed to myself to let Zawne live his life. I won't lie to you, though. I still love him in my own way, and if I hadn't become a Min, I never would have left him. But things have changed. The world moves on. Raad taught me that. We must grow and face the future. You and I will face it together."

At that moment, I remembered that I still didn't know the identity of the Seeing Water. I asked Roki, "Can you tell me what the Seeing Water is?"

"I've only heard from secondhand sources," he said. Apparently, it's an amalgamation of the spirits of all the billions of babies and children unjustly killed in the universe since the beginning of time. It is 'seeing' because it can see through anything and everything in the universe. The 'water' represents the children's tears. Tears from having their lives cut short prematurely. Tears for saving us again and again despite what the universe did to them. The Seeing Water wields more power every time it gains a new spirit."

"Hanchell said that it is merciful. What is the Seeing Water saving us from?"

"From ourselves. The Seeing Water can end all our lives in an instant. It can destroy planets in the blink of an eye. Instead, it chooses to apportion power to the Crown of Crowns to help us look after our galaxy. It oversees all the Crowns of Crowns in all the galaxies in our universe."

"So we can ask the Seeing Water to help us? I mean, to stop Lordin?"

Roki shook his head. "You don't understand. It may be merciful, but its wrath is in proportion to the evil in the universe, the unrighteousness. Three great personal sacrifices of its choosing would be required to even approach its presence."

Just then I felt the presence of someone behind us. I craned my head to see an enormous man watching us. He had curly gray hair down to his shoulders, ashy-white skin, stern eyes. He was the hugest person I had ever seen. He just stood there watching us like a giant creep. "Who are you?" I asked, scrambling to my feet. "Why did you sneak up on us?"

"Sire," he said, ignoring me and looking at Roki, "we have a problem."

Roki didn't get up. He continued to watch the clouds flow by while he talked to the man. They seemed to be acquainted.

"What is it, Neuge? Give me the scoop."

Neuge's voice was like cannon fire. "King Zawne has managed to cool the fighting for now," he said. "A shaky truce has been reached between mainland Nurlie and the shadow government on Nurlie Island. As of now, there will be no referendum. The Ava-Surrvul reinforcements have scattered without their allies. The bloodshed in the streets has ceased. The medical Protectors are administering first aid and handing out antivirals for the KS3 virus. Things are looking up."

"Surrvul will be back," Roki said. "They were testing the will of the new king, poking the bear to see which clan leaders did what. Next time, they'll come stronger and faster and meaner. The other clans aren't dumb. I'm sure everyone is preparing for a dastardly conflict."

Roki got up, brushed himself off, and regarded Neuge. Roki looked more severe than I had ever seen him. "But that's all good news," Roki said. "So, what's the problem?"

Neuge hesitated. I saw then that he was a Min. Neuge was so wide that I hadn't noticed the Valer floating in his core. I thought it was strange that he avoided Roki's eyes, as if he feared to look straight at him. It was ridiculous, because Neuge could have crushed Roki with one meaty fist. Yet he appeared nervous.

"The problem, sire, is that you've been absent for several days since the conflict began. Our people must be given direction. There's talk of marching even without our allies. The people are restless. Many have lost loved ones because of the virus outbreak. They need an address from their leader. Some are calling for more fires, only this time with casualties by the thousands."

Leader, I thought. *Leader of what? Just who exactly is Neuge, and what the heck is going on? And who is the dragon starting the fires? Is Roki really friends with this dragon character?*

I shifted my eyes from Neuge to Roki. "Would you

care to explain this to me? I thought we were done with secrets."

Roki started laughing. "I'm so sorry," he said. "This is huge news for you. I totally forgot!" Then he said to Neuge, "Leave us. Gather the people, and I'll be there within the hour to give a speech."

Neuge bowed. Then he shot high into the clouds and flew away. I was left speechless and confused, glaring at Roki as he doubled over with laughter.

"It's not funny," I said. "Seriously, tell me what's going on. Are you the leader of a spiritual army?"

He took my hand and kissed it gently, his brilliant smile making me melt. "It's better if I show you. Come, Kaelyn. Should you choose to be with me for the next few centuries, you're going to need to know my secret job."

* * *

WE FLEW west across the ocean, farther and farther, until I could see Krug's coastline of sandy beaches.

Roki came to a dead stop fifty miles from land. He hadn't stopped grinning since the rooftop. "You're going to love this," he said. "Hold your breath."

"No, wait, what are we—?"

Roki took my arm and pulled me downward, laughing hysterically as we plummeted toward the water.

I screamed, "No! I don't want to get wet!"

But we didn't hit the water. We passed through it, plunging beneath the surface as if it were an illusion. Then we were hovering inside a hollow tube like a giant drainage pipe.

Roki explained, "I keep all the ports masked using my power. It's why I have a hard time keeping other things masked for long periods. I divert a ton of my energy to these secret ports. This one is my private entrance to the city. It's like a metal chimney sticking out of the water, but it's invisible to anyone who looks at it."

I had no idea what to say. *Secret tunnels? Hidden ports!*

"There are other entrances inland, on the beaches of other continents," he said, "other ports disguised as oil refineries, hatches, and pods that lead many miles below the surface of the ocean. Air locks and security systems. There are passenger trains in metro tunnels in major cities, all disguised by my power. It's quite high tech. Combined with my Min powers, it's superior to all else in Geniverd ..." He shrugged. "At least, all else that I know about."

"Where are you freaking taking me?" I blurted. It was hard to keep my panic in check. "Are you trying to say there is an underground tunnel system connecting all six continents to an underwater city?"

Roki's grin could have eaten the planet. "Yes," he said, teasing me with his eyes. "Come on, let's go see it."

We flew a significant distance underground, gliding through the hollow tunnel until we reached an air lock. Roki hit a button and the door opened. We stood inside a small room while machines groaned.

"It's for water," Roki said. "This tank is meant to purge any water before I go into the city. You know, in case my tunnel floods. This tunnel isn't made for humans. It's meant just for me. I haven't even brought another Min into the city this way."

"So, you're saying I'm special?" I asked. It was my turn to smirk and tease Roki.

"More than you know," he said.

The purge system finished. Then the door opened. We walked into a bare, sort of musty hallway and continued until we reached a red-varnished door. Roki stopped with his hand on the knob. "Home sweet home. Welcome to my house, Kaelyn."

We were in an antechamber. Roki took my hand and said, "This way. Come on." He led me through his mansion of a house, old picture frames on the walls and dozens of closed rooms. He was saying, "It's lavish, I know. I'll give you a tour another time, but right now we have to get to the city square."

I couldn't believe it when we exited Roki's house onto his porch and I was staring down at an enormous underground city. There were houses, tall buildings, streets, huge complexes. I even saw flyrarcs hovering beneath the domed ceiling. It must have been half the size of the capital!

"Are we beneath Krug?" I asked.

"About a hundred yards beneath Krug. We started building this place roughly a century ago. The more people we recruit, the larger the city gets. We have many Min on our side, so we use our combined power and influence to keep it secret and to expand. We also have the best architects and engineers in Geniverd working for us."

"Us? We? Our side?" I blinked at him, ready to explode if I didn't get some answers. "Roki ... who are you?"

Roki exhaled deeply, steadied himself, and looked in

my eyes. "I always wanted to tell you. It just never seemed like the right time. Kaelyn, I'm the leader of the so-called Gurnots. It's been my task to support them for the last hundred years, a direct order from the Crown of Crowns to keep the balance. Our proper name is Defiance. And now, as the leader of Defiance, I am serving my second year in office."

It felt like Roki had punched me in the gut. Leader of the Gurnots? The man I had fallen in love with was a freaking Gurnot! How could that be?

"I want to show you more. Let's walk to the center. I want you to see my people. We're not evil, Kaelyn. We're just tired of the upper class. I mean, why should anyone be born superior? We're willing to fight to free the kingdom from the tyrannical rule of the clans. Our views are directly in line with yours. We want to restore the balance between rich and poor."

I had no words. This was the ultimate shock. After so many twists and turns, betrayals and revelations, to find out Roki was the leader of the Gurnots—it turned my perception of the world inside out.

I couldn't believe the things I saw as Roki led me through the city. There were markets, people selling meats and fruits, artisanal crafts—only this time it was all real! And women with large round bellies waddling through the streets. They were pregnant! I had forgotten that the Gurnots favored natural births. I supposed it was also a way to keep their children out of the system. But I thought the most fascinating part was how the city smelled. I was so used to the controlled atmosphere I'd spent my life inside that I had never experienced such a bombardment of different smells.

There was the scent of fresh bread, of engine exhaust, of tangy human sweat. It was overwhelming.

"There are about six hundred thousand living in the city," Roki was saying as we went past a couple of kids playing with their dogs.

Dogs! I thought. *They're probably not even replicas!*

"But in the entire world, I'd say about a quarter are associated with Defiance. That means a billion people. When the time to rise above the clans is at hand, it will be an even fight. Yet we must pick our time to rebel carefully. It was unfortunate how much life was lost during the Nurlie Islanders' revolution, but it was a good test of our abilities. It may be the catalyst that will ignite global change."

"Where do I fit into all this?" I asked. We had reached the center of the city, a big stage and a huge throng of people waiting for Roki to speak. He must have had us masked, because we walked straight through them unimpeded.

"By my side," he said with a wink. "Only if you're happy. These people revered Lordin, and they can never know her truth, or they would be broken by it. As for you ..." He licked his lips, giving me an "uh-oh" look. "Well, many will hate you because of the pandemic—the decisions made through your council's process. They won't know the truth. But you're a Min now, and you're in a new body. No one knows who you are."

"Neuge did," I said, remembering how he had ignored me. Now that I thought about it, he had seemed perturbed to see Roki with me on the rooftop.

"Neuge is clever," Roki said as we climbed onto the stage. "You're new, and Kaelyn of Gaard is dead. I'm

262

sure he put the pieces together. But Neuge is loyal and won't say anything. Even if the other Min find out, they can't defy me as the leader, nor can they reveal your identity to the people. Trust me, Kaelyn, you're safe with me, and I'll protect your loved ones."

I did trust Roki. I trusted him more than seemed appropriate. I couldn't help it. He had been my dream man from day one, and now I was standing by his side as he was about to address thousands of Gurnots in a secret underground city. I wasn't queen of Geniverd anymore, yet I felt more like a queen beside Roki than I ever had sitting in my council chamber. As a Min, I had energy and power beyond mortal grasp. I had forfeited my original body and found confidence in the skin of my host. I felt complete, smart, aware of who I was. More than anything, I felt valued. I felt ready to face the next trial.

"My people," Roki said, his voice echoing over the attentive crowd, "thank you for joining the battle in Nurlie. Thank you for fighting for our freedom and sacrificing your lives for the good of the world. It was not the first fight, and it won't be the last. We have hardships ahead of us, foes the world over, and seemingly impossible odds. Yet we will prevail!"

The crowd cheered. I crossed my arms humbly and looked them over.

"We have battled the system for many years," Roki continued, "and I say to you now, friends, we are almost home. The moment of reckoning is upon us, upon the world. For too long has the upper class pushed our faces in the muck, humiliated us, and stood righteously atop their precious Decens-Lenitas. Well, I say, no more! Our numbers have grown in pace with our strength. The time is right to strike the heads of the hydra. Nurlie was only a taste. Prepare yourselves, my friends, for the ultimate battle lies just over the horizon."

Roki raised his fist. "The titans shall fall!"

And the crowd roared, "The titans shall fall! The titans shall fall! The titans shall fall!"

I didn't know what I was doing. I had raised my fist and was echoing with the others, "The titans shall fall! The titans shall fall!"

The audience whooped with delight, and the wave of praise continued for the longest time. When the applause died down, someone shouted Lordin's name. And just like that, a new wave of cheers began, interspersed with a chant of "Lordin! Lordin! Lordin!"

And I thought that of course they loved her. I was once like them. I'd only just died, yet they still grieved for Lordin. I wanted to forgive them, because they didn't know her as I did now. And as I watched, filled with sadness, the livestream briefly caught someone who stood out because he wasn't clapping. Roki must have seen it too, on his display, because he interrupted the shouting and asked for the man to be given a microphone. Then the camera zoomed in on the person. I couldn't believe my eyes.

"Tell us your name and what's on your mind," Roki said most gently. "Why do you not cheer for Lordin?"

"My name is Nnati. I will never cheer for Lordin."

There were loud gasps, but Roki was unmoved.

Nnati continued boldly. "Can't you all see?" he said. "She bought into the system. She supported Decens-Lenitas. By the time she met her untimely death, she wasn't one of us. We don't know whether she would have treated us differently if she were queen. Yes, her murder was horrific, and I wouldn't wish that on anyone. But she did not die for our cause, yet many among us look on her as a beloved martyr. I tell you now, she died for nothing!"

There was disquiet and murmurs among the crowd.

I was still in such a shock that I didn't notice the tears streaming down my flushing hot face. I had always known Nnati was defiant. Now I knew just how defiant. The sight of him made me smile. Perhaps I could still salvage something of my old life. Perhaps I could be Nnati's friend.

"Thank you, Nnati, for speaking your truth," said Roki. "No one should deny him that. He is not our adversary. The upper class, on the other hand, have become too powerful, too rich, too mighty. But observe around you what we've built right under their noses, for the powerful have grown weak and complacent in the long years without conflict. Trust me when I say we are strong and have a firm resolve. Our fight has only just begun, and our enemy is within our reach. They are crippled and slow with their pockets stuffed with money and their bellies bloated on our food. They've pushed us so deep into the dirt that they do not fear retaliation. But I promise you, brothers and sisters, they will fear us!"

By the time Roki finished his speech, I felt drawn to his cause, to the magic of his words. Roki's passion invigorated me. He was mine and I was his, and we were in the fight together. For the first time in my life, I had a purpose. I felt on top of the world. It no longer mattered what tomorrow may bring.

Roki and I walked off the stage, and I threw myself

into his open arms, thinking it was crazy that I had to die to truly live. I was free and unassailable in that strange place and in Roki's arms. No one was going to take that away from me, nor would they punish me for being there, far from my home.

Because I was home.

Stay tuned! Godly Sins, the second book in the Crown of Crowns series, is coming soon!

Sign up to Clara's mailing list on ClaraLoveman.com and be the first to hear news about her books. You might even get FREE digital copies of prequels, epilogues and sideways stories from the worlds of Shiol and Geniverd.

ACKNOWLEDGEMENTS

I owe an enormous debt of gratitude to many people who've supported my writing or played a role in shaping this story—particularly to Nick, Julie T, Leonora B, Lauren, Christine, Phebe, Phyllis, Jacquee, Helen L, Judith, Steve, Kate, Carol, Peggy, Branden, Keysha, Sean, Naveed, Lisa, Eva, Bernard, Kelly, Zion, James, Sally, Norah, Aaron, Arwen, Gareth, Stefan, Monica, Szilvia, Ruth, Caroline, Rowena, Beth, Ruby, Boe, Lewis, Sophie, Ruth, Anna, Hetty and Liz.

A special thanks to Charlie and Chris who have put up with me at home, and a big thank you to my parents for giving me the best life possible.

I'm also sincerely grateful to my readers for joining me on this journey.

ABOUT THE AUTHOR

Clara Loveman graduated from Liverpool John Moores University and has an MPH from the University of Sheffield. She lives in Maidenhead, UK, a riverside town not far from Windsor.

She loves connecting with readers and can be found on Instagram (@lovemanauthor) and on Twitter (@claraloveman).

On her website ClaraLoveman.com, you'll find more information on her releases and current giveaways.

Please consider leaving a review online if you enjoyed this story, even if it's only one or two lines. It will be a huge help.

Lightning Source UK Ltd.
Milton Keynes UK
UKHW040705060820
367795UK00001B/1